Lies and Deceptions

Lies and Deceptions

Kenneth Harrison

Seventh Window Publications

Lies and Deceptions © 2002 Kenneth Harrison

Published in the United States of America by:
Seventh Window Publications
P.O. BOX 603165
Providence, RI 02906-0165

ISBN: 0-9717089-0-8

For Pete Cummings

Acknowledgments

I would like to thank Pete Cummings, Debra Eastham, Leo Mansi, Anne Pillsworth and Ted Strojny, all of whom took the time to read early drafts of this book and gave thoughtful comments. I would also like to thank everyone at Gayhappenings.com for answering all my computer questions.

Friday Night

Jay was psyched to finally have an apartment and live off campus, even if the walls needed a fresh coat of paint and the kitchen floor was gold speckled linoleum. Having his own apartment was also more costly, but it gave him privacy, and he didn't have to share a bathroom with an entire floor of students. Although his father was fine with the news when he'd told him about getting a place to share with Steve, his mother was a bit concerned. She was afraid they'd spend all their time having parties and not studying. If only she knew that he didn't want the apartment to party but to be able to date and not worry about where to go if they felt the urge to get naked. So far the only skin he'd seen was Steve's firm pecs and legs as he either shaved the dark stubble off his chest in front of the bathroom mirror, or walked from the bathroom to his bedroom with a towel wrapped around his waist and the outline of his big pecker waving beneath.

"I'll pay your rent as long as you get a part time job," Jay's father had said in his staunch, Connecticut businessman way. Free rent was fine with Jay, so he'd found a part time job at a video rental store on Elmgrove Avenue. Working at the video store gave him enough extra cash to buy food and go to an occasional movie at the Avon Cinema. As far as Jay was concerned that was as close to a free ride as he was going to get.

Jay's mother was also concerned about furniture, but he and Steve had been able to scrounge up some old cheap stuff at the Salvation Army, and had been lucky enough to have found a decent bookshelf on the side of the road, and a coffee table that was the same dark wood. Buying used upholstered furniture was a bit strange, not to mention scary. The guy at the Salvation Army had said that it should be fine, but Jay was still a bit apprehensive about taking home the blue and white striped overstuffed sofa. Steve wasn't all that keen on it either, even after sticking his finger in a small tear in the back right side of the sofa. "If anything bites me, we're out of here," Steve had said. Nothing had bitten him, so the sofa came home with them. Once home, they'd doused the sofa with flea powder, vacuumed it, then powdered it again.

They'd returned the next day to shove an old red Formica table with matching chairs in the back of Steve's friend's truck.

Tacked onto the wall above the sofa were two posters of Madonna. The one on the left was from her *Like a Virgin* days, the one on the right was from her latest CD, *Music*. Cheap and easy or seventies retro, Madonna always appeared seductive and sexy. Jay never felt seductive or sexy, just average. And if he wasn't careful he was going to gain more weight than he needed. As it was he had a hard time finding a date; if his stomach got any more flabby it would become next to impossible. Unbuttoning his dark blue short sleeve shirt, he looked down at his far from firm stomach. He didn't have a gut, but it was easy to see how he could develop one at any moment. He ran his right hand over his undefined pectorals, feeling his fingers brush over his hard nipples. He didn't have a single hair on his chest, which made Steve envious although Jay didn't know why. Jay liked men with hair, which, to him, was the epitome of masculinity. Chest hair was so inherently masculine and deeply sexy that he could not imagine anyone wanting to shave it off.

Jay dropped onto the sofa and spread his legs out under the coffee table. He was neither overly masculine nor hip. Guys did not fall for him the way they did for Steve. And on top of that lack of body hair was in, which made it difficult for him to meet anyone he would find sexually appealing. Why couldn't he have been twenty in the seventies, when such things were the norm and acceptable? He'd probably have been the biggest whore if he had grown up back then. It would have been him sucking and fucking non-stop and probably becoming an AIDS casualty. Maybe it was for the best that he hadn't grown up back then.

Jay had always thought that if Steve wasn't so into looking good they would make a decent couple. But Steve was a bit vain, always keeping his dark hair cut short, his body hairless and firm. Everything he did was in the hopes of getting cruised. Even though Steve had been dating Dale almost a year, he still needed to be desired. Lucky for Steve his boyfriend didn't seem to mind too much. Dale was so good to him, always cooking him dinner and planning quiet nights together. If Jay had a guy like Dale he would be content. He sometimes wondered if Steve knew how good he had it with Dale.

Jay rubbed his crotch and wondered what it would be like to have someone to wake up to. He would give anything for that. Steve liked to tell him that being single had its perks, but Jay wasn't sure exactly what those perks were, nor was he too eager to hear about them from Steve. He'd seen Steve single and didn't feel like juggling a small army of lovers just to have a good time.

It was Friday night, and Steve was off to spend the night with his boyfriend. Jay's only plans were to study, jerk off, then wake up for work Saturday morning. He'd go out to a movie, but was afraid of falling behind in his studies. The last thing he wanted to do was get bad grades and disappoint his father. A weekend alone, just Jay and his school books. Pulling on the fly of his jeans, he heard the buttons pop free. He dipped his long, slender fingers beneath the elastic waistband of his green boxer shorts and grabbed his stiffening shaft. Once he was done, he'd be able to concentrate more on his school work.

———

Steve wound his way through the small labyrinth of a room, around the corner, past one open door after another. He couldn't help thinking that his roommate, Jay, needed to loosen up a bit and try out the video booths at one of the downtown porn shops. Every night Steve heard Jay's bed creaking as the guy jerked himself off.

It was sad, but it was also Jay's own fault. A little exercise would do Jay a lot of good, Steve thought as he stepped past a few more open doorways on his right.

The guys standing in the open doorways were old and sleazy looking. The room was filled with freaks and weirdos just looking to suck dick or get fucked up the ass. Rolls of toilet paper hung from dowels stuck into the wall. Next to each door was an ad for the film inside, if anyone really cared about which movie he could watch once he inserted his money into the slot. Guys standing in booths looked at Steve's crotch, eyeing his ample basket. One thin nelly bitch leaned against the door and tried to make eye contact with him. Steve wasn't about to lock eyes with some low life queen eager to suck dick. What Steve wanted was someone at least somewhat butch, maybe even handsome.

"How's it hanging?" the queen said as he ran his long fingers through his dark, curly hair. His deep brown eyes ran up and down Steve's muscular torso. "It looks a little to the left to me." His lips spread out into a smile.

"And what's it to you?" Steve asked.

The queen stepped back into the small confines of the stall, his face and body muted by shadow. "Come in and find out."

This guy didn't care. All he wanted was to suck cock, nothing more. He probably didn't give a shit whose cock he sucked, just as long as he got the chance to get some meat stuffed down his hungry throat. Steve grabbed his crotch, then walked into the small cubicle. The guy was already on his knees, pawing at the fly of Steve's cargo pants and lugging out his dick. Leaning his back against the wall, Steve felt warmth engulf his shaft. This guy was a fucking pig, he thought as he looked down at the dark image of the guy's head moving back and forth. The little fuck was doing a real good job sucking his cock. It wasn't going to be much longer before he blew his load. He bit his lip, then watched the little cock sucker work his magic.

"I'm going to cum," Steve whispered, but the guy kept sucking. Well, he'd done all he could do. The little fuck was going to get a mouthful, that was for sure. Steve bit his lower lip.

—

Dale stirred the contents of the twelve inch frying pan, watching as bits of green and black olives, mushrooms, onion and tomato rose in the simmering red sauce. To the left of the stainless steel gas stove was a sparkling white counter top with two bottles of red wine, the open one was the Cuvée that he'd used for the Puntanesca sauce, the other a bottle of Merlot he'd planned on opening just before dinner. At least he knew better than to start the fish or boiling the pasta before Steve arrived. Ten minutes late was one thing, even fifteen minutes was okay, but half an hour was too much. Why he even bothered making sure his short brown hair was perfect, the front bangs flipped up just right was beyond him. He walked across the white tiled floor of the small kitchen and opened the drawer under the stainless steel sink and took out the corkscrew.

Dale grabbed the Merlot. "I don't know why I do anything for the little shit," he mumbled as he used the sharp end of the screw to remove the foil wrapping before uncorking the bottle. He opened the light oak cupboard door and took out one of the crystal wine glasses with the twisted stems and poured himself a glass of Merlot. Then he noticed that the CD he'd put on earlier had finished. He'd just bought it the other day and hadn't even bothered to listen to it. The only song off the CD he knew was the title song, which he'd heard on the radio. Steve had taken up so much of his thoughts that he hadn't even listened to Madonna. The wine would breathe as he walked into the living room. He grabbed the wine glass, gave the Puntanesca sauce another stir with the wood spoon, stepped into the dining room, then into the living room humming the hit song off the new Madonna CD, *Music*.

He took a sip of wine, savoring its dry sharpness. The remote was on the leather sofa across the room from the mahogany entertainment center that matched the coffee and end tables in their smooth simplicity. On the floor was the jade oriental rug, not an imitation, with its decorative floral design in deep blues and reds. The hardwood floor had been stripped and redone the previous week, and Dale couldn't help but take notice of it every time he walked into the room.

Who would have guessed a kid from a welfare family in North

Providence would some day be able to own such a beautiful condominium not only on the wealthy East Side of Providence, but right on Blackstone Boulevard? And do all of it while still in his twenties. Late twenties, actually. He took another sip of wine, then stepped over to the sofa and snatched up the remote control. After a smooth turn, he pointed the long, flat instrument at the Harman Kardon stereo system and hit play. The Madonna CD began, which made him smile. To Dale's left was a bay window with a set of matching leather chairs on either side. He wanted to relax, but just couldn't.

"Fine, let him be late," Dale mumbled as he walked back into the kitchen to turn off the burner under the sauce. The last thing he wanted was to have thick Puntanesca. There was only one thing he liked thick, and only if it also had length. After turning off the burner, he downed the glass of wine and poured himself another. If he wasn't careful the wine would go right to his head, and he did not want to be trashed when Steve arrived. If Steve arrived. Sometimes he wondered why he'd ever given that boy a key to his place.

"Honey, I'm home!" It was Steve's deep bravado.

"And you're only half an hour late." Dale waited for Steve to appear in the doorway.

"I was studying." Steve's voice sounded closer. He appeared in the doorway in a pair of cargo pants and a tight navy blue t-shirt that showed off his hard nipples and upper torso. He gave Dale his best smile, then wrapped his arm around Dale's waist and pulled him in for a kiss. After pulling his lips away from Dale's, he kept his arm tight around him. "You've been working out."

"Glutes today," Dale said. Steve had the most beautiful brown eyes. Even after nine months they held him captive.

Steve wrapped his arms around Dale's waist and softly rubbed his back. He gave Dale a gentle kiss. "It's working."

"Is anything else working?" Dale asked as he slipped his hand down Steve's back, over the round curve of his ass and gave it a squeeze. He was so horny that he'd even settle for lousy sex, just as long as he got the chance to suck Steve's cock and blow his load.

Steve began to sway to the music, his crotch rubbing up against Dale's. "Maybe later tonight."

"I'll hold you to that," Dale said. He knew chances were that Steve wouldn't hold up to his part of the bargain. Either that or Steve would just be a lame fuck and not even get off.

"How about we eat." Steve moved away from Dale, then took the lid off the sauce. "Smells wonderful."

"I still have to make the fish and boil the pasta."

"Oh good, then I didn't ruin dinner," Steve said. He gave Dale a peck on the lips. "I love how you take care of me."

Dale smoothed his hand over Steve's firm chest and tried not to smile. "Someone has to feed you."

"Can I do anything?"

Dale knew enough not to believe that Steve wanted to help out in the kitchen. At least he did dishes. "Pour yourself some wine and keep me company."

———

Long hair wasn't easy to keep up, but Iris didn't care. She kept the ends trimmed, and spent a small fortune on hair products, but it was all worth it. If only her natural red highlights hadn't already started to fade. Soon she would be left with simple chestnut hair with little flair. She felt her hair on her bare shoulder, spilling onto the soft linen sheets. Ian held her from behind, his strong body pressed against her. Ian's right hand was on her stomach, moving down her slender waist, past her firm stomach towards her pubic hair. His fingers pushed through her bush as his dick penetrated her. Iris let out a gasp, then moved her hips back, feeling his shaft open her ass. Then his fingers played with her little nub and she let out a sigh. Ian pushed his entire length inside her, then pressed his moist lips on the back of her neck.

"You're so beautiful," he whispered, his hot breath rushing past her ear. Slowly, he eased his prick in and out of her. His fingers slipped over her clit, delving between the soft folds of her sex. "I want to make you feel good."

Iris raised her smooth right leg over Ian's legs, feeling his hairy limbs beneath hers. It wasn't a text book romance, but he was inside her, feeling her, making her want him. What more could she want? The way his fingers played with her, knew how to run over her clitoris, spread open her sex, drove her wild. Not many men made sure their partners also got off. Ian did, even if it was just with his fingers.

He thrust his dick into her deeper as his fingers dove into her depths. Iris let out a gasp as the length of Ian's fingers slid over her clit. She was panting, feeling him please her as she did him.

"Tell me, baby, tell me when you're going to cum," Ian whispered.

Iris tilted her head back, then felt Ian's coarse stubble on her cheek. He kissed her neck. She let out a groan.

"You're driving me wild," Ian said, sliding his left hand under her, then wrapping his arm around her body, holding her. "I love fucking you this way."

It was the only way he'd ever had her, despite the many times Iris had asked to do it missionary. Ian bit her neck as he heightened his finger-play on her clitoris. She let out a soft moan. Ian's shaft swelled inside her as her own climax began to erupt.

"Ian, I'm going to cum." She felt the first wave overcome her body as Ian pulsed inside her. Ian's fingers continued to move against her nub, driving her wild until she was spent.

Slowly, Ian eased his shaft out of her. Iris turned, then felt Ian's lips gently push against hers.

"You're the best," Ian said.

"Am I?"

"You bet." He rubbed her stomach. "I'm going to take a quick shower. Want to join me?"

"I'm just going to relax for a bit," Iris said. She watched his round ass, and his perfect torso move as he padded away from the bed in the darkness. Light escaped from the bathroom as he entered, and she saw his front as he turned and smiled at her, his dark curly hair falling in front of his face, reaching down to his eyebrows. His penis was at half mast, pointing in her direction. The tuft of hair on his upper chest was damp with sweat. Then the door closed, and she was cast in shadow.

Iris turned, then pulled the soft top sheet over her. Was she the best? She wanted to be. Margot, her mother, had always told her she had to be the best. If nothing else Margot had driven her to be the best interior designer possible, which did help get her into the pages of Architectural Design magazine. Only three years out of college and Iris was succeeding in Providence, but still Margot wanted her to move to New York, where she could become prestigious. Iris didn't want prestige, at least not for Margot's benefit. Iris could imagine Margot telling all her friends about her successful daughter living in New York City. What was wrong with Providence, Rhode Island? Historic architecture mixed with modern buildings. Iris loved Benefit Street with its historical charm. Walking down Benefit Street on a foggy evening always felt mysterious and made her feel as if she was walking through history. The Providence River, which separated the small downtown area from College Hill and the East Side, had old fashioned bridges that had been erected over the river for both foot traffic and cars and served as a reminder that Providence was proud of its history and was willing to hold onto it. It was that hold on history that defined the small city and gave it its charm.

Iris's friends were in Providence, too. Friends she'd made while going to college at Rhode Island School of Design. People who had helped her become who she is. People who had always stood by her and believed in her. She didn't want to leave her friends, especially when she wasn't doing poorly for herself. There was no need for Iris to move out of Providence, especially if it would only be to make Margot happy. Iris needed to make herself happy. How often had she told herself that and not taken her own advice? This time would be different. She was with Ian because she wanted to be with him, not because she thought Margot would approve of him. She and Ian were both in their mid twenties, professional and made a nice couple. Iris told herself that she liked Ian and didn't care what Margot thought of him. It had nothing to do with Margot.

—

Ian opened the door that led to the hallway so the steam would escape. At least with Iris he could count on his dick coming out clean. Right now she was probably brooding about why he never sticks it in her twat. Why women care about that was a mystery, especially when he always made sure to get his partners off. He grabbed the plush deep purple towel off the rod, then walked across the forest green and white tiles to the sink, which was one piece of porcelain that tapered down to the floor, obviously hiding the pipe inside. Above the sink was a simple medicine cabinet set into the wall. When he'd met Iris a year and a half ago he'd assumed her place would be full of shit, her being an interior decorator and all. He'd been surprised to find it simple and uncluttered. If only her personality matched her surroundings.

The claw foot bathtub was to the left of the sink and had two shower curtains hanging onto it from a circular metal ring suspended from the ceiling. Ian assumed not replacing the ancient bathtub with a more modern shower and bath was Iris's way of being bohemian despite her income. Reaching into the tub, Ian turned the metal knobs and tested the water pouring out of the faucet before closing the clear plastic shower curtain and pulling the stick up for the shower to run. His fingers smelled of Iris, and he could still taste her on his lips from when he'd gone down on her. If Iris wasn't so damn good in the sack he would dump her. She wanted too much from him. Why was it that women wanted to get married so much? He didn't want to get married. Not yet anyway.

Ian entered the tub from the end opposite the shower nozzle. The soap and shampoo were in the holder set into the wall at the head of the bathtub. The thought of marriage seemed suffocating to him. It had almost happened once, back in his junior year of college. When he'd gotten Clarice knocked-up. It had taken him a week to get it through her head that he was not going to marry her, even if it was his kid. Clarice had bawled her eyes out in front of him, but he didn't care. He'd only known her for six months, and he hadn't even finished school. It had taken him another week to convince her to get an abortion, for which he'd had to pay. He'd tried to get her to split it with him, but she was being unreasonable. The worst part was that she'd intended to stay with him after the abortion. She'd been such a bitch about the whole thing that he hadn't even wanted to sleep with her again, never mind continue to have a relationship with her. It had been bad enough that he'd had to spend time consoling her after the abortion. He'd bought her flowers. He'd even taken her out to lunch.

Ian soaped his balls, feeling them move in the loose sack, his limp dick resting just above his thumb. It hadn't been until after Clarice that he'd decided the safest thing for him was to butt fuck. Condoms broke, which was how his old pal Nick got forced into marriage. There was no way that was going to happen to him. If any girl didn't want to comply with his needs, then screw her. He always had Iris.

—

Dale couldn't sleep. Sitting up, he watched as Steve slept peacefully with his back to him. Tomorrow he had to go into the salon and open up. Once more he considered hiring a manager for the place, but didn't want the added expense. After all, he did enjoy running the salon himself. If only he could be more like Steve and not let things get to him. Dropping his feet on the floor, he felt the thick carpet beneath them. Once more Steve hadn't gotten off, and once more he hadn't seemed to be into having sex with him. Dale had mentioned bringing a third party into bed with them, but Steve wasn't into the idea. He'd said that things like that only bring the end to relationships. Dale wasn't too sure of that. Kyle and Trent had been together for over ten years now and they had an occasional three-way.

Sex had been great in the beginning, when they'd just been seeing each other once a week. Steve would drop by and they would just go at it. Dale used to love sucking Steve's dick, looking up at him as he watched, looking intense. It had been the same look he'd given him the times Steve had fucked him. Now having sex with Steve was almost the same as jerking off while being watched. The only difference was that Steve would pretend to be interested.

Maybe Steve wanted to end the relationship? Dale had thought of asking before, but had chickened out when push came to shove. He stood up and walked across the dark room, to the narrow hall that led past the guest room and opened up into the kitchen. The half drunk bottle of Merlot was still on the counter. Dale uncorked the bottle then grabbed a wine glass from the cupboard. He didn't have any appointments tomorrow, but he still needed to open up and wanted to order some supplies. He thought about going into the living room and turning on the television to see if the United States had a new President yet, but decided not to bother. He never could understand why anyone would want to have such a crappy job anyhow. You couldn't even get a blow job from a trick without it being printed in every paper across the country. Then, of course, everyone had to act like it was such a big scandal. Poor Monica Lewinsky had just wanted to have a little fun, she was just a damn intern.

Dale wanted to have a little fun, too. He'd thought about cheating on Steve, but didn't like the idea of going behind his back. If Steve hadn't been so opposed to a three-way Dale wouldn't be apprehensive about asking if they should open up their relationship. Dale just hated the idea of sneaking around behind his boyfriend's back, or having to keep secrets. Truth be told, Dale just needed a good fuck.

After downing the rest of the glass of wine, Dale grabbed the bottle then marched into the living room. He plopped his ass down on the sofa, kicked up his feet and poured himself another glass. If he was going to be a lush at least it was with a good Merlot.

Saturday

The Dale Pagnali Salon was as fashionable inside as the looks it gave its clients. Each hairdresser had his or her assigned area against the right and left walls, complete with all the tools of the trade. Each area was separate, yet not enclosed. The effect had been created with Greek pillars strategically set to corner off each stall. A wall had been inserted diagonally in the far left corner, and sported another chair and mirror. In the center of the room was a round, bleached oak desk where clients paid the hairdressers, and sometimes purchased hair products. The receptionist's desk and waiting area were on a lower level in the front of the salon, and a wall had been constructed behind the receptionist's desk so waiting clients could not view the hairdressers at work. Instead of the usual fanfare of tacky pictures of men and women sporting fashionable styles, Dale had prints of runway fashion shows of such designers as Chanel, Calvin Klein and Yves St. Laurent framed in simple black metal hanging on forest green walls. For Dale the salon was not only his work, but a second home.

Stepping behind the receptionist's desk, he opened the day planner and glanced at the schedule. Kyle was booked, and so was Shayna. It was still early, neither of them would be in for another fifteen minutes. Tony, the new guy, didn't have an appointment until one o'clock. Dale wondered if it had been such a good idea to hire someone with no local client base. Granted he'd cut hair in New York City, but that hadn't been the draw that Dale had hoped. And it seemed that Tony wasn't too pleased with the dribs and drabs of clients he'd received since he'd started four months ago. If things didn't pick up Tony might leave for another salon and drag the few clients he'd gotten with him. There was little Dale could do but keep his fingers crossed and hope for the best.

The front door opened and Kyle walked in, looking as handsome as always. It appeared that Kyle had been shopping at the Gap again, not that it mattered, with his stunning looks and gym buffed physique. Kyle flashed his pearly whites. "Did lover boy shoot last night or was his gun empty once again?"

"I won't be robbing any banks with him," Dale said before stepping away from the receptionist's desk. "I don't know what to do next, nor do I feel like talking about it."

"And what would you like to discuss, Al Gore's dick? I heard he's hung like a horse."

Dale followed Kyle to the corner chair. "And how do you know?"

"Trent told me about it. He said Al did a shoot for the cover of Rolling Stone magazine and his meat was so prominent they had to air brush it out."

"And you believe him?"

"It's all speculation, but have you ever seen Tipper not smile?"

The bell on the front door chimed again. It was either Shayna or the receptionist, Anita. Dale turned, but saw nobody.

"Hello." It was a woman's voice, but it didn't sound like anyone he'd expected. "I thought perhaps we could get an early start."

"Mrs. Fletcher," Kyle said as he walked past Dale, towards the waiting area.

"Dolores, please, dear," Mrs. Fletcher said. "You make me feel so old when you call me that."

Dale stepped into the back room, not wanting to have to watch Dolores shamelessly flirt with Kyle. Too often Dale had held back peals of laughter while wondering if her husband knew Dolores, who looked to be in her early fifties after her second face lift, enjoyed the attention of boys young enough to be her children. "Tell Dale that interior decorator he mentioned to me is doing a delightful job on my new house," Dolores said.

—

She hates me, Iris thought as she dropped her head in her hands and stared at the white tabletop. The floor plans for the living room of the Colonial house were in front of her, but Iris didn't feel like opening her eyes and staring at it again. Something contemporary and tasteful was what the old bitch wanted, but she couldn't decide on a single color for the walls, nor did she like any of the sketches she'd done of the floor plans for the living room. If the old lady wanted something contemporary why hadn't she and her husband purchased a new home instead going from one old Colonial to another? Perhaps by the time they had the living room finished Iris would have a better idea of Dolores's taste, or so she hoped.

Iris rolled the chair away from the desk, then looked to her left, at the wall that displayed sketches of her finished jobs. One of the houses she'd decorated had been featured in the August '99 issue of Architectural Design magazine. Her mother had been proud of her and bought several issues to show off her daughter's success. Although Iris was thankful that her mother thought she was successful, she didn't feel as if she was attaining anything great. She was making a living doing something she loved, but she hadn't done anything that she'd thought was stupendous, or truly worthwhile.

Behind her, on a simple teak bookcase, were furniture catalogues with bindings streaked with creases. She was not going to show Dolores any furniture until they found a wall color.

—

The hamburger and fries Jay had eaten for lunch sat in his stomach as if refusing to be digested. He loved hamburgers and fries, but hated them once they were eaten. He knew he should have gotten something more healthy, like a tuna sandwich or a salad, but neither seemed to offer the satisfaction that only a greasy hamburger could fulfill. Now he was paying the price. He leaned over *The Naked Lunch* by William S. Borroughs and tried to forget the lunch that would not go away.

"You're not going to spend another weekend night studying are you?" Steve whispered as he leaned over Jay's books.

Even in the Rockefeller Library, Jay couldn't get away from his lack of a social life. He let out a sigh, then glared at Steve. "Some of us are serious about school. I need to get decent grades."

"You're a much sought after commodity, don't let it go to waste."

Jay rolled his eyes.

"You're young,"Steve said.

"And out of shape, now leave me alone."

"What are you doing tonight?"

"Working."

"After work."

"Sleeping."

"Alone?" Steve asked.

Jay slid his chair back, then crossed his arms. "Have you always been this annoying or am I just noticing it now? I told you, I am trying to study before work."

"Come out with me." Steve pulled his chair in closer to Jay.

"You're not seeing Dale tonight?"

"No." Steve looked at the floor, then back up at Jay. He let out a sigh. "Dale wants a night alone."

"When did he say this?"

"I dropped by the salon to see how he was doing, he asked me to have lunch, then he sprang it on me."

Jay had to try to keep his voice low. The last thing he needed was to be kicked out of the library for being disruptive. "It's only one night."

"That's not all he said." Steve scratched at the fake wood table. "He wants time to think. Whatever that means. I guess he needs time away from me."

Jay placed his hand on Steve's knee. He couldn't believe what he'd just heard. Steve and Dale had always seemed happy together. "I'll be home after work, if you need to talk."

"No, I don't feel like talking about it."

"It might help," Jay said.

"I need to forget it, at least for tonight." Steve sat on the table and slowly kicked his feet. "Come out with me."

"I don't know," Jay said. He didn't feel like going out and coming home smelling like smoke.

"I don't want to go out alone."

"You don't have to go out at all."

"I'm not going to sit home and mope around. It would do me some good to go out. I won't do anything stupid if you come along."

"Sure," Jay said, knowing that Steve would only continue to moan until he agreed anyhow. "Just let me get some studying done."

—

All Ian had to do was ask Michelle to lunch and she was his. That much he'd known when she'd accepted his spur of the moment lunch date. On the street she'd looked to be in her early twenties; it wasn't until he'd learned that she was a college student in her final year that he'd known for sure. He'd seen her in the College Hill Bookstore, standing in front of the fiction section looking for something to read. She'd picked up *The Unbearable Lightness of Being* by Milan Kundera and thumbed through it. Ian pretended to be interested in some book by Ishiguro, but was really checking out the gentle curve of her ass against the cotton skirt that fell just above her knees. Her legs were smooth and thin, with subtle calves. Long, wavy auburn hair hung past her shoulders, and stopped mid back. Beneath the soft pink blouse her small breasts were barely visible, giving the appearance of youth.

"That's a wonderful book," Ian said. "When I was in college it was my favorite."

"A friend told me about it. She's reading it for class."

"Are you an English major?"

A slight blush rose to her face as she smiled, then shook her head. "No, I'm studying economics, but I like to read."

"Economics," Ian said, pausing to find something to follow with. "Are you planning on going into business for yourself or helping out a big company?" He hoped he was on the right track and not looking like an idiot.

Michelle smiled. "You don't know how nice it is to have someone ask me that instead of what I'm going to do with my degree. I'm thinking of getting a job on Wall Street. The stock market's amazing. I've been watching it since my sophomore year of high school, which was when I joined the stock market club."

"Maybe you can give me a bit of advice some time," Ian said, then put out his hand. "Ian Campton. Call me Ian, though." He pretended to be embarrassed by giving his full name.

Her hand was warm and soft in his grasp. "Michelle," she said. "Are you really interested in stocks?"

Ian held her gaze as he nodded. "I own some small and mid caps, but I'm supposed to diversify my portfolio. My broker keeps telling me to purchase more small caps, but I really don't know what's out there."

"It takes time to track it all," Michelle said. "It's easy once you get into it, though."

Like so many things, Ian thought as he looked over Michelle's figure. Her breasts were small, but her narrow waist and womanly hips gave her body form. And he couldn't stop thinking of her ass. "I should have you look over my stocks some time."

"You're putting a lot of faith in someone you hardly know."

Ian winked. "I'm a risk taker."

Michelle looked down at her feet as color rose to her cheeks.

The time was right, so Ian rose to the occasion. "Would you like to come to lunch with me?"

"Oh, I don't know," Michelle said.

"I'm not fond of eating alone, but I understand if you don't have time."

Michelle grinned then glanced briefly behind her, towards the Mystery section.

"Andrea's is right down the street," Ian said.

Michelle replaced the book to the shelf. "I can come back for the book."

"Let's be off, then," Ian said as he slipped his hands in his pockets to hide his burgeoning erection.

—

"Oh dear, I don't have as much time today as I thought," Dolores said as she stepped into the middle of the empty room, her chunky charcoal shoes tapping against the dull hardwood floor. Her charcoal colored dress fit her well, although the low neckline made the dress appear to be for a younger woman and accented the small wrinkles that were beginning to appear in her cleavage.

"We really need to find a wall color soon," Iris said as she held a sample of a light blue up to the wall between two of the four floor to ceiling windows, the type she'd only seen in Merchant Ivory films. Beyond the windows was the back yard. "Enough light does come through these windows during the day, so we don't have to choose too light a color."

Dolores didn't bother looking at the color sample. "Did I mention that I want a chaise longue? I've always wanted one. They're so decadent, don't you think? It isn't unreasonable to have one in the living room, is it?"

"You can have one anywhere you want, as long as it fits the room," Iris said. "But first we need to find a wall color, then decide on furniture."

Dolores stared at the walnut fireplace mantle. Iris hoped she didn't like it, since it would probably have to go. It was too ornate for a modern room, which was what Dolores had said she'd wanted.

"I think this light blue would be perfect for a modern room," Iris said.

"Will it go with the window casings?"

"We'll have to change them," Iris said. "A lighter wood."

"Yes, modern," Dolores said as if to herself. "And the mantle. It reminds me of my childhood in some ways."

"We can move it," Iris said. "The bedroom, perhaps. You do have a fireplace in the bedroom. The mantle is similar, I believe. If you would rather have this one, then we can have it moved."

"Timothy likes the one in the bedroom." Dolores walked up to the window and looked out at the orange and red leaves scattered across the lawn. "I've always been a very modern woman. Not Timothy. Timothy likes old houses, which is why we didn't have one built for us this time around. He told me that I could do whatever I wanted to make this house look new before moving into it."

"People buy old houses and fix them up all the time," Iris said.

"Yes, I suppose they do."

"What about the wall color?"

Dolores rubbed Iris's arm. "I like the blue, dear."

Iris walked across the room to where she'd left her brown leather portfolio case. "I've made some sketches for you, just so you can have an idea of how the room could look. I have copies for you, with other color choices in case you change your mind." She opened the portfolio to the sketch of the room in light blue. "See how I've chosen a simple light wood mantle."

Dolores looked on and slowly nodded.

Balancing the portfolio on her left arm, Iris pointed to the right of the fireplace. "We can put the chaise longue over here."

Dolores's eyes brightened, and a smile spread over her face. She looked briefly at Iris, then down at the sketch. "Really? You're so smart."

—

It was the end of the day and Anita and Shayna had already left. Kyle was still on the floor cleaning up and Tony was on the phone making plans for dinner. Luckily Tony had a new booking this coming Tuesday, so he was in a good mood.

Finished with his call, Tony ran down the three steps to the waiting area in his big motorcycle boots. Under his t-shirt his thick, muscular torso pushed out and made it look as if the shirt would rip away from his body if he moved the wrong way. Tony looked like a bad boy, right down to his bald head and goatee. He had also made Dale's loins stir when he had come in to talk to him about working at the salon, which hadn't hurt his chances of Dale hiring him. It had also helped that Tony had a decent reputation in New York.

"A few more new clients and I can stop dancing at Mirabar," Tony said as he walked past Dale.

"It will happen," Dale said, waving goodbye as Tony stepped out the door.

Dale didn't know what he was going to do with himself to pass the night. Steve wasn't going to be around to hang out with. Maybe order some take-out from Taste of India down the street, grab a six pack of Harpoon Ale? Was there anything good on television? He didn't know. Maybe he should go out and rent a movie? Something that would make him laugh.

"Spill it," Kyle said as he leaned against the wall at the entrance to the cutting room floor. "You've been moping around here since after lunch."

"I have a night alone," Dale said.

"I guess your lunch date didn't go well."

Dale sat in the chair, then rolled it against the wall where the name of the salon was displayed in large, crisp type. "I asked him what was wrong, and he said nothing. Something is wrong, but he won't tell me. Getting anything from him is like pulling teeth. He said he's had this problem before, but doesn't understand why it happens. Once he gets to know someone his libido dies."

Kyle knitted his brow, then stepped up to the desk. "And that's why you're free tonight?"

"Well, no," Dale said. "I wouldn't let it go. I told him it would be nice to have sex with a willing partner every now and again, especially when said partner happens to be my boyfriend. And that's when he got defensive, telling me that I needed to be more understanding, that I nagged him about it all the time, made him feel inadequate. Bla bla bla."

"He didn't scream, did he?"

"No, some heads did turn, but I don't think anyone knew what we were talking about." Dale closed the date book, then grabbed a pen from the pen holder and tapped it against the desk. "We haven't broken up yet; we're just taking time away. Until Wednesday." Dale felt his eyes water, and wiped the tears away with the heel of his right hand. He couldn't look at Kyle, who he assumed was giving him some pathetic type stare. "I'll use the time to get the salon computerized. I've been wanting to do that for a while."

"Whose idea was it to take time away?" Kyle asked.

"Steve thought it would be for the best, just so we can have time to sort things out. He thinks maybe I only want him for his dick."

"It is a big part of him."

Dale let out a chuckle, then covered his mouth as tears began to wet his cheeks. "I really love him, you know."

"You wouldn't torture yourself over him for so long if you didn't," Kyle said. "How about coming to dinner with me and Trent tonight?"

"I don't want to ruin your night out with Trent."

"We go out to eat every Saturday night, at this point it's far from romantic." Kyle picked up the telephone. "All I have to do is change our reservation to three."

"What if Trent minds?"

"Since when does Trent not enjoy seeing you?"

—

Ian had gotten out of the shower and stood in front of the open double doors to his closet with a damp towel tossed over his left shoulder. His hair was still wet and in disarray from having been towel dried. The right half of the closet was filled with fall and winter suits, all of which were in dark grays with a couple blues for a change of pace. The left half was all shirts in dark blues, dark greens and white.

Stepping back, Ian dropped himself on the firm mattress of his king sized bed. The ebony posts rose up six feet in the shape of obelisks. He smiled as he recalled the first night he'd sunk himself into Iris, who had gripped the left post on the footboard and concentrated on breathing the way he'd told her. She'd followed his instruction well and had allowed him to take full control. Once he'd been inside he'd made sure to wrap his arms around her, feel her beautiful firm breasts and please her. That night had made her his, and now he had another conquest. Michelle was going to be just a brief affair, something to keep his mind and libido going. Michelle was smart and attractive, and had the most amazing ass. He'd have to handle her carefully, though. Fucking up was something he could not afford, especially if it meant losing Iris. Ian needed her, she was something constant in his life.

Ian sighed, then rolled onto his stomach, feeling his stiff dick against the navy blue feather comforter. Tonight he was taking Iris out for dinner, after that they were going to her friend Norman Rezza's house for cocktails. When she'd first brought up the idea of going to Norman's Ian had hoped to sway her away from the party to see a play, but all Trinity Repertory Theater was putting on was *A Christmas Carol*. It was too early for Ian to start thinking about Christmas, and he knew that Iris wouldn't want to be reminded of any holidays just yet. As it was, Thanksgiving was just around the corner. Now he was left with a night of talk about furniture and wall coverings with a bunch of queens and women. There were a few of them he could talk to about sports, but the Patriots were playing so badly that he'd stopped paying attention. After dumping Pete Caroll everyone had expected them to do better this season. Now it was obvious that the team just sucked, and Ian was loath to have to admit that.

On the wall opposite the bed, sitting on top of the high boy, was a clock under a bell jar that Iris had bought for him at one of those flea markets disguised as an antique shop. Under the round white-faced clock with black roman numerals was a set of three brass balls that constantly spun as a reminder that the thing was still running. It kept good time, so it did come in handy. At the moment it showed a few minutes before six thirty. He had to get his ass in gear, they had a reservation at Hemenway for seven.

—

Dale walked into Romanza and scanned the small, dimly lit room crowded with tables for four. A fire crackled and burned in the fireplace across from him, giving the room a cozy atmosphere. Kyle and Trent were sitting at the table to the left of the fireplace. Trent had his back to the door, and the small thinning area in the back of his head was visible. Trent kept his blond hair cut short and combed forward, which made it appear that he didn't care about the bald spot, but Dale knew better. He'd recently been asking about getting a hair transplant, of which Kyle was not in favor. Looking up from his menu, Kyle waved at Dale.

"What happened?" Kyle asked.

"I got stuck on the phone with my mother," Dale said. "She's already eager to talk about Thanksgiving. The last thing I want to do is think about the approaching holidays. Once Halloween is done, so am I."

"Thanksgiving is just around the corner," Trent said. "Kyle and I are going to my parents for it. My mother loves him."

The waitress came by with her little white pad and pencil. "Do you know what you want?" Kyle asked Dale.

"You two order, I'll just pick something from the menu.," Dale said. He already knew he wanted the Gorgonzola ravioli in the vodka sauce, but pretended to study the menu all the same. If only he could have with Steve what Kyle and Trent have. He'd told himself he wouldn't harp on his separation from Steve, but he couldn't help it. Although he enjoyed being with Kyle and Trent, they were a reminder of what he might not be able to attain. Lasting relationships between gay men seemed to be the hardest thing in the world to find. Everyone was looking, but so few men seem to find them.

"Do you know what you want?" the waitress asked.

Dale lowered the menu, then looked up at the waitress. "Yes, I do, but I'll have the Gorgonzola ravioli instead."

The waitress looked confused.

"Shall we order an appetizer?" Dale asked.

———

Iris was astounded by the brilliant, lush colors that Norman had used to decorate the living room. She would have never thought of burnt orange walls, and filling the room with the deep green leaves of Ficus trees. In the very center of the room was a lovely cranberry sofa and love seat combination. A narrow mahogany table four feet in length was against the wall to Iris's right, two foot tall white tapered candles set in simple brass holders were set on either end, and between them was a beautiful bouquet of wild flowers overflowing from within a clear blue glass vase. How Norman was able to find wild flowers in November was a mystery, not to mention how much he'd paid for them. She knew he'd never tell her how much they'd cost. The floor had been re-done in a light wood and had an oriental rug in the center. Each color in the elaborate design of the rug was somewhere in the room. The set of three windows against the far left wall were draped in thick, deep green curtains with sheer whites beneath. On the wall, in elaborate frames, were old family photographs. Iris didn't think Norman was related to any of the people in the pictures, although she wouldn't put it past him to dig up old family photographs and hang them. Iris had counted four young men in leather body harnesses and biker boots walking around the room with platters of wine and hors d'oeuvres.

Iris leaned in close to Ian, who was taking in the sights. "Isn't Norman amazing?"

"To say the least," Ian said. "It looks like the usual cast of characters."

"Why don't you get us some drinks," Iris said to Ian as she took a step into the room.

Tyler was across the room, standing next to the floral arrangement talking to Rachel. As usual Tyler looked as if he hadn't combed his hair, and his dark suit was slightly wrinkled. But Rachel looked wonderful in a soft blue dress with a squared neckline and long sleeves. The skirt of the dress stayed close to her legs and stopped just above her knees, which helped show off her delicate calves. Whenever Rachel went out she liked to put on something other than the Chanel or Yves St. Laurent suits she wore to the office.

Tyler would know exactly where to find a chaise longue. If it was an odd item she always went to Tyler, who had a knack for getting hold of anything hard to find. He was probably the one who found that dress Rachel was wearing, unless she'd had it made special for her. He did have better taste than Rachel, and the two of them were famous for shopping together.

"Here you are," Ian said, holding a glass of red wine in front of Iris. "It's a Syraz"

Iris thanked him as she took the glass. "Have you seen Norman?"

"I'm sure he'll turn up," Ian said. "It is his party."

Iris searched the room for Norman's bald head, finding him at the far end of the room. His black suit jacket was open, exposing a colorful paisley vest against a white shirt. His bow tie was the same black as the jacket and slacks. He had a martini glass with a large green olive drowned at the bottom. Norman was talking to the ever-dapper Martin, who was biting into what appeared to be a stuffed mushroom and nodding. She was curious if Martin was still in the bidding on any new work. He'd stolen her last account out from under her and had done well with the job. Granted, she would have designed the office differently, but the architectural firm seemed pleased with what he'd done.

"Let's go say hello to Norman," Iris said. "After that we can separate."

"You're the only person I have anything in common with," Ian whispered to Iris as the two of them moved across the floor.

"A little experience outside your realm won't kill you," Iris whispered back, then she turned towards Norman. "Are we interrupting?"

"Not at all," Norman said, then leaned in to give Iris a kiss on the cheek. He shook Ian's hand. "Ian, you look handsome as always."

Ian pulled his hand away. "No flirting now, you know Iris gets jealous."

"Oh these straight boys, you can never compliment them," Norman said. "So what do you think of the place, Iris?"

"When you told me the color of the walls, I wondered exactly what you were going to do," Iris said. "It's wonderful."

"And I was hoping for decadent," Norman said.

"Everything you do is decadent, Norman," Martin said.

Iris took a sip of wine, letting the rich, fruity flavor glide over her tongue. "And you, Martin, are you working on anything new and exciting?"

"Nothing, really," Martin said. "Only some rooms and a house in Newport. It's not quite big enough to be called a mansion, but it's stately all the same."

"How nice," Iris said.

"So, Iris, what are you doing for the approaching holiday?" Norman asked.

Iris reached over and placed her hand on Ian's upper arm. "I'm going to meet Ian's family."

"So it's serious," Norman said, raising his eyebrows.

"It is," Iris said, although she'd never sensed that Ian might actually be serious about her. "What about you, Norman?"

"As usual, mom and dad insist I go visit them. Every year I invite them to come here, but they'll have nothing to do with it. Personally, I think they're afraid ."

"Of you Norman," Martin said. "I can't imagine why?"

Norman's eyes grew wide. "I know, sweet innocent me." He turned towards Iris. "Oh, that reminds me! How I could forget is beyond me." He folded his left hand around Iris's shoulder. "Ian, I hope you don't mind me taking Iris away for a tête-a-tête."

"Not at all," Ian said as he looked over his shoulder.

Norman held onto Iris's hand. "Come with me. There is something I have to show you."

"What is it?" Iris asked as Norman escorted her through the room, smiling salutations and nodding as he passed various guests.

"You'll see," Norman said as the two of them stepped into the hallway that led to the rest of the house.

The walls were eggshell and barren. If they took a left they would step into either the kitchen or dining room, to the right was Norman's study, and at the end of the hall was a narrow set of stairs and bare eggshell walls that Norman referred to as the servants' staircase. The two of them walked up the stairs with Norman leading the way.

"So, when do you think I'll see a diamond on your finger?" Norman asked.

"I don't know," Iris said as they approached the second floor, where a deep purple carpet ran down the hall. On the walls hung replicas of famous paintings by Botticcelli and Caravaggio.

"Just wait until you see this," Norman said, then escorted her into the library, where the far left wall was lined with dark wood shelves full of books. Across from her, with bay windows behind it, was an oak table with a set of matching chairs. In the middle of the table was a banker's lamp, and to her right, in the center of the wall was a fireplace with an ornate, dark wood mantle. On either side of the hearth were carved pillars in the shape of young men with large, flaccid penises and low hanging balls. In the center of the room, facing her, was a deep brown leather sofa with an oak coffee table that had assorted crystal liquor decanters on it, each filled. A high back leather chair and matching ottoman were to the left of the sofa.

"It's here," Norman said, stepping to the right, behind Iris.

Iris turned, and there it was, set against the wall to the left of the doorway: a leopard print chaise longue. Iris walked up to it, turned to look at Norman, who was beaming. He took a sip of his martini. "Can I sit on it?" Iris asked.

"Please do."

Iris placed her wine glass on the hard wood floor, then kicked off her shoes and took a seat. She put her legs up, then stretched out along the length of the chaise. "This is amazing!"

"I just bought it today," Norman said. "It's going in front of the fireplace. Can you imagine relaxing in that with a Judith Krantz novel, a glass of champagne and eating the most delicious truffles, Godiva of course."

"How decadent! Where did you get it?"

"You can't breath a word of this to Tyler."

"I promise," Iris said, eager to get the scoop.

"Well, I was in Boston last week for Sunday night at Avalon. If we had all night I would tell you about it, but we don't so I'll make it short. I found this amazing boy, smooth and muscular. He looked like he lived in a gym. Well, he had a small apartment on the South End, where he invited me to spend the night. How anyone could live there was beyond me. But, the next day I took him out to breakfast, and the two of us decided to visit a few shops. As it turned out, the boy has taste. He took me to this little shop owned by this supposedly straight man, Harold something or other. Just call him Harold. He's not very handsome, but the store has everything one would want to decorate a brothel."

"Do you have his card?"

"Of course I do," Norman said. "I even picked one up for you."

—

Jay leaned on the banister and dangled the green Rolling Rock beer bottle over the edge. Down below was the dance floor lit by strobing lights in blues and reds. To Jay's right was the glass enclosed DJ booth, where a bald guy spun the music. Men brushed past Jay's ass, some of them taking the time to grab it. It felt as if every man in the place was out looking to get laid. Jay was horny, but not willing to go to bed with just anyone. Yet another Whitney Houston song came on, Heartbreak Hotel. The song sounded like a cross between soul and rap. Jay was not so drunk that he could enjoy an endless round of Whitney Houston. Down below, on the dance floor, nobody seemed to mind. It was a sea of bodies moving to the music, and in the tidal pool was Steve. He'd found a group of three guys, two of whom were shirtless, to dance with and enjoy himself. Steve looked to be having a blast, despite his recent problem with Dale. So much for heartbreak.

Letting out a soft groan, Jay turned around, towards the brick wall just a couple of feet away and looked over the heads of the two drunken guys talking. It was a drawing of a naked man turned to the side. Jay had been told by Dale that the pictures gracing the walls of the Mirabar were the same ones that hung at the old Mirabar, back when it as on Allens Avenue. Dale had never been to the old Mirabar, but had been told by Kyle, who used to go with a group of friends. How anyone could go out every weekend was a mystery to Jay. The smoke and booze and whatever else people were taking was all too much for him.

To the right a tall guy, at least six feet tall, with a dark tuft of hair on his upper chest walked towards him. A piece of something white waved like a flag behind his ass. Jay assumed it was a t-shirt tucked into the back pocket of his tight jeans. It looked as if the guy was walking towards Jay. Jay turned towards the railing and looked down at the crowd. What was he, high? There was no way that guy was going to talk to him. He looked for Steve in the crowd, but couldn't find him. In his pants his dick began to stir. Great, now he was going to have to walk around with a boner.

A big hand with long, thick fingers appeared on the banister to the left of Jay. The hand was attached to a thick, hairy arm. The arm went up to a muscular shoulder, then a thick neck, and a face with dark hair that had a touch of gray on the sides. The man had a Greek nose and thin lips that formed a grin. Jay looked into his dark eyes and felt his dick stiffen more. It had been so long since he'd gotten laid that he couldn't control himself. Jay wanted to burry his face in the dark hair that covered this guy's upper chest. "Are we not having fun?" the man asked, his deep voice matching every inch of his masculine form. Jay swallowed. His mouth was dry, so he took a swig of beer. "I'm out of my element is all," he said, wondering how stupid he sounded. "I'm never comfortable in these places."

"That's because you don't go out," the guy said. "It's nice to see a cute guy that isn't a twink here. Sometimes I wish they would make the place twenty-one or over again."

How could Jay tell him that he was under age and that he'd only gotten in without having to wear a white bracelet that showed his youth because Steve had once blown the guy at the door. He placed his beer bottle on the narrow shelf at the top of the railing. "Everyone needs someplace to go. Even twinks."

"Is that what you like?"

"What?"

"Twinks," the guy said.

Shit, Jay thought. He stood up straight and tried to appear casual. "You were young once, I'm sure."

"I have a preference, that's all" he said, then put out his hand and gave Jay a firm shake. "I'm Erik."

"Jay."

"Nice." Erik slowly nodded. "What do you do for fun?"

"Nothing special, really," Jay said, wondering how long it would take for Erik to lose interest. "Sometimes I go to the movies, or just hang out with friends. I'm in school, so I study a lot. College."

Erik gave Jay the once over, then turned and leaned his back against the banister. He grinned. "So, what else do you do?"

"You mean, like knitting?" He meant sexually. Jay couldn't believe he was getting hit on. He didn't want a one night stand, not even with Erik.

Erik moved away from the banister. "Ouch. I guess that's a no."

"No! It's just that I don't do that. I don't trick."

"Now there's a first," Erik said, his eyes falling on Jay's crotch. "So, that's not a gun?"

"No, but it does shoot." Jay couldn't believe he'd said it, but the comment had put a smile of Erik's handsome face.

"And you're not a virgin?"

"Oh no! No, not at all."

"That's good. Virgins rate right up there with twinks."

"You have nothing to worry about."

"Good," Erik said. "That's good. Why don't you give me your phone number and let me call you."

"That sounds good," Jay said, then followed Erik to the bar.

Sunday

Steve steered his VW Jetta through the back roads of the East Side, past one expensive house after another. He had the radio turned down low and didn't bother to listen to it. All he could think about was how Dale hadn't shown up at Mirabar the way Steve had hoped he would. It would have been interesting to see his reaction, especially if he saw Steve flirting with some other guy. If Dale had shown up Steve hadn't planned on ignoring him, just the opposite. He'd wanted to talk to him, see how badly Dale would like to see him with another guy. That would have made Dale want him even more. It might have even been enough to make Dale beg to get him back. It would have worked. It had worked before, back when he'd been at boarding school in Connecticut. Steve had had to find some way to entertain himself out in the woods. He'd been on the track team and had fooled around with Kevin, the team's best at the triple jump. Kevin had been taller than Steve by an inch, with pale skin, soft brown hair and eyes. Steve and Kevin had often run together to keep in shape, and had spent some time alone having lunch in a secluded section of the woods behind the school on weekends. It had been in the shade of trees that the two boys had taken hold of one another's cock for mutual masturbation.

It hadn't taken long for Steve and Kevin to form a physical and emotional attachment and for the other boys at the boarding school to become suspicious about them. Nor had it taken long for Steve to notice the odd looks his classmates had been giving him, and knew that his father wouldn't take it well if he found out about his relationship with Kevin. He'd had to find a way to clear his name, so he'd stopped talking to Kevin. It had taken very little time for Kevin to become jealous and begin to approach Steve, only to be shrugged off. After a few days of being ignored by Steve, Kevin had become more insistent about needing to talk to Steve. And so it had been Kevin's persistence that made Steve's stories about how Kevin had made sexual advances toward him believable. Everyone understood why Steve could no longer be friends with Kevin.

The situation between Steve and Kevin had gotten so bad that the dean had had to talk to Kevin's parents. The day after Kevin and his parents had met with the dean, Kevin was gone from the school.

Steve shook his head as he recalled what had happened between him and Kevin. He'd done the right thing, that much he knew. If his father had found out he would have been sent off for psychoanalysis, which was the last thing Steve needed to deal with. His father was a firm believer that homosexuality was a psychosis that can be overcome, but Steve didn't always agree with him. If he could stop his desires for men, he would do it, but he couldn't.

It was a bit surprising that Dale hadn't been at Mirabar, since that was where single gay men went. Like all fags, Dale only cared about sex. That was why Dale had mentioned bringing another guy into bed with them. That only proved that Dale wasn't able to control himself. Dale was just as promiscuous as any other gay man. He'd probably been cheating on Steve left and right, the same way that Steve had gone out and gotten his rocks off behind Dale's back. Steve should have known better than to even try getting into anything serious with a gay guy. They just couldn't be trusted.

Steve rolled his eyes and slowly shook his head. Dale didn't need the sleazy element to get off. Steve wished he could get off just by rubbing his cock against Dale's thigh, or his chest. It had never been easy for Steve to blow his load unless he didn't know the guy sucking his dick or he was in a sleazy joint with some scumbag on his knees. Dale could never understand that about himself.

The stupid thing was that Steve missed Dale. It was the first weekend since they'd met that Steve hadn't slept over his house, or Dale hadn't slept at his apartment. Steve loved how Dale would wake up, rolling over to wrap his warm arm around Steve's torso and hold him close. He also enjoyed the breakfasts Dale used to make. They'd been simple, but delicious all the same. Steve would never think of making hash browns or eggs for himself the way that Dale used to. And everyone liked him, especially Jay, despite the fact that Dale didn't know who Renoir was, or anything at all about art history. Jay had always said that Dale was a genuine person, true to himself. Steve had always thought the same about him, despite how they'd met. Despite how they'd had such wonderful sex before he'd come to know him. And that was the problem, he'd gotten to know him. Steve should have known better than to attempt to have a relationship. Anonymous sex was easier, more exciting and less trouble.

Steve gripped the steering wheel of his VW Jetta. There was no way he was going to think about Dale. As it was he couldn't have a relationship with a guy like him, even if Dale did come back to him and beg him to stay. Dale was so obviously gay that Steve had sometimes been embarrassed to be seen with him. The guy went to every fucking homo movie that played at the Avon Cinema, not to mention the fact that he's a hairdresser. If that wasn't a cliché Steve didn't know what was. Dale had even begun to mention wanting to meet his parents. Steve rolled his eyes. His father would have a head fit if he brought a guy like Dale into the house. It was bad enough that they didn't know Steve was gay, but to tell them, then have them meet Dale would be rubbing their faces in it. There was no way he was going to do that. His father would cut him off from any inheritance, not to mention stop paying for college. It would be the end for Steve. There was no way he was going to work his way through school the way Jay's parents were forcing him to work.

If Jay took better care of himself, Steve would consider dating him. At least Jay didn't look like queer bait. Steve's father had met him briefly and had never even suspected. But Jay didn't care about his clothes, or looking neat and trimmed. It was no wonder the guy never got laid. Steve took a right onto Blackstone Boulevard, glancing to his left to check out some of the guys running on the walking path. No matter what the weather there were always people running or walking down the grassy center of the boulevard. The only time Steve had seen the area void of chic people trying to stay in shape was late at night. To his right were more expensive houses. It reminded him of the neighborhood he'd grown up in. Everything overpriced, all the lawns kept to perfection, even in the fall when leaves turned colors and fell to the ground.

The condos where Dale lived were coming up on the right. Steve slowed, looking up at Dale's condo on the left side of the third floor. The building had been split in half, with three condos on each side. From outside each condo looked exactly the same. He peered into the parking lot, but couldn't see Dale's cashmere Lexus ES 300. Steve pushed harder on the accelerator, sped past the condos. Blackstone Boulevard was ending up ahead, narrowing into Butler Avenue. Steve hooked a left, then drove through the smart little back streets of the high-end neighborhood. River Road was a few blocks away. Up ahead he saw the house at the very end of River Road. The place looked like a mini castle with only one turret. It was a great place, and Steve had wondered what the owners thought about the goings on just down the street, at the small park on the water. Taking a right, he drove down the incline to where the Seekonk River ran its course. Across the river were old factories that looked deserted, although Steve wasn't sure if they were.

There weren't too many cars parked along the first section of the road. Steve drove further, past the small pond on the right, where more cars were parked. Past the pond was a long grassy patch that went back and was lined with trees. A hill rose up on the left edge of the patch, the top of which was also covered with trees and winding paths. Steve knew that men roamed those paths, waiting and hoping to get their dicks sucked. He slowed down as he continued to drive. The men waiting in their cars were older, which didn't please Steve. An empty park bench came up on his right. The place was dead. Then Steve spotted a police cruiser up ahead and two cops leaning against the vehicle talking. The road curved off to the right for those wanting to exit the park. Steve considered driving straight ahead and continuing to the end of River Road, but he knew there would be very few people looking to suck him off if he did. He veered off to the right, just in time to see a cop on horseback making his way towards the other two cops.

Steve considered his options: the porn shop downtown or the one near the highway. He didn't feel like going downtown and hunting for a parking space. Both had video booths and the one near the highway had its own parking, but it was too clean and less sleazy. All he wanted was to have some little fag suck his cock, and he didn't feel like going out of his way to get the job done. He'd go to the one with parking.

—

It was a day of rest for Iris, but that didn't mean she enjoyed relaxing in bed the whole day. It was unseasonably warm, but she didn't feel like doing anything outside. What she wanted to do was go shopping, so she headed to Providence Place Mall to do just that. She would have called Ian and asked if he wanted to do something, but he'd already told her that he was busy. Some project he had to get done for Monday. She was also busy Monday, meeting with Andrew Tyler of the Law Offices of Tyler, Westcott and Allen. She'd designed a beautiful office for them, simple yet classic. Lots of leather and dark wood. Andrew Tyler was as excited about her interior designs as she was. Iris had an early meeting with Andrew to check out the construction work. All she needed was something smart to wear. Andrew was always well dressed, which meant he probably paid as much attention to the appearances of others as he did to his own. Plus he was very professional. Working all the time had ruined one marriage and kept him single. He'd even told her that himself. Iris assumed he'd married early, especially since he didn't look that much older than her. She guessed he was in his early to mid thirties.

Iris sorted through a few suits on the rack at Nordstrom, looking for a short skirt that would not make her ass look too wide. She found a light charcoal suit. Holding it up, she checked out the jacket. The lapels were narrow, cut into upward pointing angles. Once buttoned it would still be open enough for her to soften the look with some pearls or a simple gold chain. A pale pink or lavender blouse would look good with the suit. Her steps were muffled by carpet as she walked away from the suits, then clicked briefly on tiles, then became muffled again as she made her way towards the blouses.

There was a rack of blouses with three quarter length sleeves just off to the right. Iris wanted full length sleeves. She would also wear her hair up in a bun, which would make her look serious, but still keep her femininity intact. She would have to make an appointment with Dale. She made a note to call him at home. He would do it for her, she always tipped well.

—

It was the third time that Jay had jerked off that day. As much as he tried to concentrate on studying, he couldn't help but think of what Erik would look like naked. Grabbing the old, crusty towel from the floor, he wiped the jizz off his stomach, then tossed it back on the floor to his right. He was turning into the masturbation king of the year. Erik's phone number was on the old, worn bureau across the room from the foot of the bed. How could Jay help but think of Erik, who was handsome, built and, best of all, hairy. A gay man who didn't think he had to shave his chest to get a guy – now all he needed was brains and Jay would be his for life.

Then he remembered that Erik didn't like young guys. What was he going to say once Jay told him that he was an undergraduate? Chances were good that Erik would dump him flat. The guy had made it more than clear that he did not like young guys. Why the hell he had tried to pick Jay up was another question. Granted Jay didn't look young, but he did not look older than his twenty years. And if Erik did think he was older, that would be an insult. Would Jay be insulted enough not to sleep with him? He didn't think so. Jay was horny as all get out. There was no way he would turn anyone down, let alone a hot guy like

Erik.

Steve wasn't home, so he didn't bother putting anything on to cover himself. Not that Steve would mind, but Jay did have a small amount of modesty. After a quick shower he would go back to the books and not think about jerking off again. As it was he didn't think he had anything more to shoot. The kitchen floor wasn't cold. He was also happy for the unseasonably warm day since the cost of heating had skyrocketed. Thankfully he didn't have a car, so he didn't have to worry about the dreaded price at the pump, as they often called it on the news.

The telephone rang, so Jay stepped up to the kitchen table and picked it up. Erik's deep voice asked if Jay was home. Jay's dick began to come back to life. "Erik?"

"I usually play the phone game, you know, wait two days before calling," Erik said. "You're not like the other guys, so I didn't think it mattered when I called."

Jay smiled, then grabbed his stiff dick and twirled around on one foot. "I didn't know that game existed."

Erik let out a brief chuckle. "You really don't get out much, do you?"

"No, I don't. Hopefully that isn't a bad thing."

"It's refreshing" Erik said. "But that isn't what I called about. I called to see what your week is like."

"Classes end Wednesday at noon," Jay said.

"Are you going home for the holiday?"

"No, I'm having some friends over. A few of my friends aren't going home for the holiday either, so we're doing a pot luck. I'm making the bird, everyone else is bringing over the rest. We're doing the whole enchilada, from mashed potatoes to pumpkin pie. I'm taking Wednesday to prepare."

"Does that mean you're free Tuesday night?"

"Yes, I am," Jay said as he gently ran the tips of his fingers along the length of his shaft. "Do you have anything in mind?"

"If the weather was more dependable, I would say let's go to the park, but it isn't. We could go and get something to eat, unless you have a better idea. I'm not going to the movies on a date, though. I have to tell you now."

Erik scored points with his last comment, but Jay wished he'd been more imaginative than going out to eat. "Do you have a restaurant in mind?"

"What kind of food do you like? I don't do Italian. If I go out, I do not want to have anything I could make at home."

"Do you like Asian?"

"Asian," Erik said. "Four Seasons?"

"In Cranston," Jay said excitedly.

"You know it?"

"Yes, I do," Jay said. "What time?"

"Let's say I pick you up at six."

"That's great," Jay said, then started giving Erik directions to his place. After he hung up, he went into his bedroom and dropped onto the bed. He scratched at a spot of dried spunk on his stomach. What would Erik think if he knew Jay didn't have a car? Everyone Jay knew drove, so he'd never felt the need to get a car. Not to mention that his father would make him pay the insurance and gas, unlike most of his friends whose parents paid their way. It didn't matter so much to Jay, especially since his parents were well off, but not so much that they'd want the extra expense of paying for Jay. Plus his father was into Jay learning how to live in what he called the real world. He hoped his lack of a car didn't make him look younger than he was.

Jay rolled onto his side, grabbed his pillow and stuffed it between his legs. Maybe he should have slept with Erik the night they'd met. At least he would have gotten laid, which really was what he needed. After all, what would happen once Erik found out how young he was? What if Erik found out before Tuesday? He'd probably cancel out on their date, that's what would happen. No, they'd go out, then maybe Jay could win him over. Perhaps Erik would be less willing to stick by his rules if he liked Jay. Maybe he might want him around as a boyfriend. Now Jay was jumping the gun! Boyfriends? What next, images of the two of them in suits walking down the aisle?

"So it's come down to pillow fucking," Steve said.

Holding the pillow close to his crotch, Jay quickly rolled over and stared at Steve, who was leaning against the door frame.

"How long have you been there?"

"Long enough to wonder if that pillow is a consensual partner," Steve said, then walked up to Jay and sat down next to him. "I do believe there's a program for people like you. It's a twelve step program, PFA."

"Pillow Fuckers Anonymous, how very funny," Jay said.

Steve gave Jay's thigh a condescending pat. "Half the battle is admitting you have a problem."

"And the other half is knowing when to quit," Jay said.

"Fine, then," Steve said. "When do you think you'll hear from that stud you met last night?"

Jay grinned, then pressed the pillow closer to his crotch. "I already did. We made a date for Tuesday night."

"You might just get lucky for once," Steve said.

"And what about you? Did you talk to Dale?"

Steve stood, then took a few deliberate steps towards the wall. Without turning he said, "He was out. I'll try again tomorrow."

"Is that it?"

Steve turned, but still didn't meet Jay's eyes. "What if we talk about something else. Do you know what's playing at the Cable Car Cinema?"

"Why don't you check," Jay said. "If it's anything decent I'll go with you."

"Sure," Steve said before walking out of Jay's bedroom.

Reaching out, Jay dragged his hand hap-hazzardly across the floor until he found his discarded boxers. He slid them on. He felt bad for Steve, especially since it was obvious the guy was having a hard time with his break-up with Dale. Although he wasn't sure of the particulars to the break-up, he wasn't going to push it. He would be supportive of Steve, though. That is what friends did for each other.

—

If there was one day that could be ripped off the calendar, it was Sunday. The only stores open past six o'clock were grocery stores, which did Dale little good. Gripping the plastic handles of four Abercrombie and Fitch bags, he marched into his bedroom and dropped them on the bed. Granted he didn't need any more clothes, but it was fun shopping and looking at the wonderful boys working at the mall. None of the boys in Abercrombie and Fitch were even interested in him, not that he thought they would be. It was fun to fantasize, though. It did help take his mind off his present troubles.

Trent had said that Steve didn't seem to be worth all the headaches, but there was something about him that Dale liked. It was more than the way he'd always complimented him, or made him feel sexy. There was something about Steve that always seemed to be wanting warmth. Trent had half jokingly said it was Steve's heart, which had made Dale grin. At least he was still able to smile. Dale hadn't bothered trying to explain himself further, he knew Trent would only try to cheer him up if he did. But there was something about Steve that Dale couldn't let go of, something about him that Dale wanted to cook for and nurture. Something that, in an odd way, made Dale feel needed.

Dale began unpacking the bags, dropping the folded shirts in one pile, pants in another. Tomorrow he would start looking for a computer company that would get him up and running fast. Hopefully someone who could install the damn system and teach the staff how to use it. It would make keeping his books a lot easier, or so he hoped. How he hated doing everything by hand. Everyone said computers made life easier, even Trent. At the restaurant Trent had gone on about how much time his laptop saved him, not to mention the endless amounts of smut he'd been able to get off the Internet. Even though Dale had nothing against people downloading porn, he didn't want to bring it into his shop. Perhaps if he liked having the computers in the shop he would think of getting one for his condominium. After all, now that he was single he had a lot of time for doing other things.

Shoving his hands on his hips, Dale looked around and mumbled, "What would Madonna do?" *Like a Virgin*, Madonna's second album, always boosted his spirits. He'd bought it on compact disc years ago, it had to be somewhere.

Monday

For anyone else Dale would not have done it, or so he'd told Iris when she'd called Sunday night. Sitting back in the chair at the Dale Pagnali Salon, Iris closed her eyes and felt Dale run the comb through her wet hair. She couldn't help but think about Ian, and how he'd been over to relax and have a quiet evening with her. Their relationship had become somewhat of a routine for her, not that she minded. That was what happened when a relationship worked. And her relationship with Ian was working. And she did have feelings for him. Ian was handsome. He was the type of guy Margot wanted to see her with, and he didn't mind her career, even when it kept her from him. "How many men would understand," Iris's mother had once said, followed with, "When are we going to meet him?" Iris didn't know how much longer she could hold off having Margot meet Ian.

The idea that Margot might actually like one of the men she dated seemed surreal. Margot had never liked any of the men she'd dated, but Iris did think she would like Ian. Not only that, but her relationship with Ian was good. It was healthy, Iris kept telling herself. Some of it had become a little repetitive, but it was good. Perhaps if Ian wasn't such a nice guy Iris wouldn't be able to handle some of the dull routine, or how Ian never visited her without their having sex before he left. And when they did have sex it wasn't exactly the way she would like it, but that could change. Iris would be happy if he came by once and they did not have sex. Sex was not the end all of a relationship.

"You look so much sexier with it down," Dale said as he ran the comb through Iris's wet hair before taking a few strands between his fingers and cutting them.

"You don't know what it's like to do business with a man when you're a woman," Iris said, then smiled at Dale's reflection in the mirror in front of her. "You have to try to be the best of both worlds."

Dale shrugged. "Nothing worth it is ever easy." He clipped a few more ends, then ran his fingers through her hair.

"I guess so," Iris said as she inspected the salon by its reflection in the mirror. Dale did a good job keeping it clean and uncluttered. "How is the salon working for you? Do you still like the design?"

Dale's eyes widened. "I still get raves over it!" He grabbed the blow dryer and began to dry her hair.

Iris studied Dale's movements as he slipped his fingers under her hair and held it out. He seemed preoccupied, although she didn't know with what. She didn't think he'd lie about liking what she'd done with his salon. Would he? No, she didn't think he would. He cared too much about the salon, which was why she went to him. If she'd done something that didn't work he would tell her.

Dale turned off the blow dryer and put his hand on his hip while pointing the tip of the dryer at her reflection. "You're staring."

"You have something on your mind."

"Oh, Steve wants to take some time off," Dale said, then let out a sigh. "I'm taking the time to get this place up to date. Computers. I have enough space. I must. I'll let you know if I don't." He grabbed her long locks with his right hand, twisted it around his fist, then held his hand behind her head so her hair was pulled back tight. "All you need is a pair of thick rimmed glasses and you'll look like a real prude."

"Can we try for a sexy prude?" Iris said, playfully winking at

Dale.

"I prefer all or nothing, but we can give it a shot."

"Well then, let's try." Iris sat back and closed her eyes. Perhaps Andrew would recommend her to his friends if he liked her work? She had to make sure he was pleased, that much she knew. Luckily she trusted Dale to make her look as good as possible. Hopefully all the walls to the new office were up and not just a little more than half. She'd come across that a few times in the past, which never pleased her clients. She understood, but wished they wouldn't place a small amount of the blame on her.

"If you were more severe looking and had blonde hair, I would say you were trying to be Ivana Trump," Dale said.

"Thankfully I don't," Iris said as she looked into the mirror. Her natural highlights were almost gone.

Dale pushed a few bobbie pins into her hair, then pulled out some hairs on the side. "We can bring your highlights back, you know," Dale said.

"Without chemicals?"

"What, you think I'm God?"

"The next best thing," Iris said.

"A gay hairdresser," Dale said. "Where I come from we call that a cliché. And no, I would have to use chemicals."

"This will be fine then," Iris said as she fussed with the strands of hair falling on either side of her face. "I can't wait to go home and change."

"Is this a date or a client?" Dale asked.

"Oh please, a client," Iris said. "It's just that I bought this wonderful charcoal suit at Nordstrom and am dying to wear it."

Dale's eyes lit up. "Nordstrom. I love that store. What else did you buy?"

"A light pink blouse to soften the look up a bit. I don't want to look too harsh."

"A girl can't be too careful," Dale said with a wink.

"It's always good to have your wits about you," Iris said.

———

Ian wanted to throw the folder with the end of month reports across the room. One month PharmWeb did well, the next it seemed to be sinking in the mire of regulations and overspending. It was such a pisser to try to make money in healthcare these days, and everyone seemed to be so fucking concerned with the cost of prescriptions. He'd been on Brad, the CEO and founder of PharmWeb, to sell more everyday medical items the way physical drug stores did. Even a mail order outfit had to have front store items to help make up the difference of what it loses from paying pharmacists high wages to count tablets all day. He'd only been with PharmWeb a little more than a year and already his idea of obtaining a web presence had begun to pay off. The client base had increased slightly, which would mean more profit after three years if all went well. All they'd done for advertising was add the web site address to receipts and the current ads they ran for their services. The only cash that had been spent was for the upstart and maintenance of the web site.

Hopefully he'd be able to score with Michelle this week, which was why he'd told Iris he would be busy with work and wouldn't have time to see her. As Ian's father had always said, "Women are a lot of work and sometimes they just weren't worth it." But Ian's father had spent most of his life unhappily married. Ian only half agreed with his father. Women could be okay as long as you could find a way to hold them off enough to get what you want. All any of them want is to get married, hold men down and try to control them. Even though Ian's father had a wife who seemed to understand her place, he still got grief from her. Ian remembered how his mother had looked disapprovingly at his father that one time he hadn't gotten a promotion. Ian had been six at the time, but still remembered the look of shame on his father's face as his wife shook her head and said it was okay, that they would get by. How condescending his mother had been. Women didn't understand how hard it is to support a family. Very few women had real jobs, and the few that did turned into conniving bitches. His father had never liked women in business and neither did Ian.

The telephone rang, so he picked it up. "Mr. Campton, Gregg Tillinghast is on the line for you," Angela said in her sweet little voice.

"Take a message. If it's important I'll get back to him." Ian had hired Angela despite his father's advice of hiring only ugly women as secretaries. Angela was young, cute, knew her job and called him Mr. Campton from day one. If she'd been unattractive he would have told her to call him Ian. Now Ian had the upper hand, and Angela's formality was a constant reminder of what she was to him.

Ian had forty minutes before his meeting with Brad, so he decided to give Michelle a call. He got her machine. "Michelle, this is Ian. I've been thinking about you, and wondered if you would like to have dinner with me. It's been a long day and the last thing I want to do is eat alone. Give me a call and let me know if you're available around seven."

Ian leaned back in his chair and let out a sigh. Michelle would call back, he would ask her where she would like to eat. She would let him choose the restaurant, which he would do. During the meal Ian would feel her out and find a way to make her do what he wanted. If he was smooth about it she would comply. Like everything in life, it was about having the upper hand.

—

It was lunch time and most of the construction workers were sitting outside eating. The day was warm enough, probably one of the last nice days before winter rushed in and sent everyone indoors. Iris stood in the bare main room, where the receptionist's desk was being built in front of the elevators and the arch that would open into the hall of offices, all of which had walls erected but not a single door in place. Iris had arrived early, and took the time to inspect the work being done. She was pleased to see that for once everything was keeping to schedule. The receptionist's desk was set perfectly, the front curving inward on the sides to give the idea of enclosure. On the front of the desk would be the name of the law firm of Tyler, Wescott and Allen. Stepping past the desk, Iris looked about the spacious interior where an alcove furnished with a black leather sofa and chairs would serve as a waiting area. To the far left was the meeting room, directly across from her was what would be Andrew's office.

Footsteps echoed in the empty space. Iris paused as Andrew Tyler appeared in the doorway of his soon to be office. His dark blue suit made his white shirt appear even more pristine. "This is going to be wonderful," Andrew said as he walked towards her. "Even better than the drawings you made."

Iris made contact with Andrew's deep brown eyes and nearly blushed. "I'm just pleased that nothing has fallen behind schedule." She put her hand out, and Andrew gently wrapped his big fingers around it, then moved in closer. "How do you like your office?"

"I love it. Go inside," Andrew said, motioning for her to step inside.

Iris made her way across the plywood floor, Andrew not far behind. The room was spacious, the back wall practically all windows. Iris had wanted to put windows on the wall to the right, which was also an outside wall, but Andrew had wanted to save that space for pictures and another bookshelf. He'd also mentioned not wanting any direct distractions while he was working, and being able to see the outside world directly would be a distraction. As it was, he planned on positioning his desk so his back would be to the windows. The offices were high enough that blue sky and white clouds were visible. A shelf two feet deep had been constructed to make the windows appear less threatening to people with a fear of heights, the shelf forming a buffer between the room and the outer world. It would also give Andrew added storage.

"I hope I'm not wasting a lot of your time asking you to take a look at the space with me," Andrew said.

Iris turned, then leaned against the shelf. "Not at all. I usually check in myself to make sure everything's going as planned. I'm a little bit of a control freak that way."

"It's your project," Andrew said. "I can't blame you for wanting to make sure everything is running smoothly."

"Are you still happy with the plans?"

"Extremely."

Despite the coolness in the room, Iris felt a little warm. She walked towards the center of the room, a foot away from where Andrew stood. "It's not too late to change things, if you have any new ideas about what you would like."

"Well, I do have some ideas," Andrew said, meeting Iris's

gaze.

Iris thought she heard footsteps, but it could have been her heart beating. "About the office in general or something more specific?"

Andrew grinned. "Something more specific."

"Excuse me, but we would like to get some work done in here," the man in jeans, a t-shirt and a hard hat said from the doorway.

"Maybe we can discuss it over lunch?" Andrew asked.

Iris looked at her watch. She had to be in Boston to take a look at that chaise longue. She also wanted to look around the shop, maybe find out if the owner had a catalogue. "I wish I could, but I have an appointment."

"Sure," Andrew said, his smile fading.

Both Andrew and Iris walked to the elevator and took it to the first floor. They were both quiet on the elevator ride down, and Iris tried not to look at Andrew as the doors opened. She wondered if he knew how handsome he was.

"Do you need a lift anywhere?" Andrew asked.

"I got lucky and found a parking space right on the street," Iris said. "Call me and we'll set up an appointment." Iris had to try not to grin as she said that last bit, then walked out the glass double doors and onto the street.

Her Volvo was a few feet away from the building. She leaned back in the leather seat and turned the key in the ignition. She couldn't help but wonder how many women got turned on by Andrew. His ex-wife had to have been a real bitch to let him slip away from her. The guy had a job that he loved, what was the big deal about that? Iris was sure that he'd understand if his wife also wanted a career. Maybe his ex-wife was just lazy and had wanted him to be around all the time. After checking her mirror, Iris pulled out onto the street.

She couldn't help rubbing her legs together as she drove. Ian wasn't going to visit her, so she was on her own again. Not that it really mattered, since he never gave her exactly what she wanted. He was comforting, though. And handsome. And successful. He didn't mind her working either, and understood that she also had a career. And her mother would like him, that she could not forget. Iris rubbed her legs together again. She was horny. The on ramp to the highway was just up ahead, on the right.

After veering up the ramp, Iris merged onto 95 North. Slipping her left hand under her skirt, she felt between her legs. The moisture had begun to seep into her panties. She was going to have to buy new ones. She could always pick up a cheap pair at Apex, which was on the way.

—

E-mail, megahertz, gigs, DSL connection, 56k modems, hard drives, floppy drives, Zip drives; Dale was in a quandary over it all. He knew nothing about computers and had hoped someone would just tell him what he needed so he could buy it and get it all set up. Trent had given him the name of a small company that made computers, but they wanted to know what he needed, which was exactly what he didn't know. Now he was on his way up Route 146 North to some computer store where he would probably be asked the same questions. As if being thrust into the single life again wasn't bad enough, now he was going to have some nerdy computer geek bossing him around. Dale had images of glowing computer screens and thick rimmed eye glasses. If a single one of them had buck teeth he would walk out.

"It will keep your mind occupied," Dale told himself. The last two nights he'd spent alone, clutching a pillow and wishing it was Steve. The previous night he'd also kept hoping Steve would walk through the door and tell him how good he looked, then reach out and pull him in close for a kiss. Steve was a good kisser, if nothing else. A pillow wasn't firm, nor did it have any warmth.

The Mineral Spring Avenue exit was up ahead, so Dale went off into the right lane. The guy had said the store was just a few miles up the road in a strip mall on the left. Mineral Spring Avenue was filled with strip malls and fast food joints, so that little tidbit of information wasn't worth a damn. He kept his eyes open for Computer Concepts Limited. When he found it, he pulled into the parking lot. He'd written the name of the guy he'd spoken to on the paper above the number of the store. Bob. Why didn't he go by Robert? If Dale had been stuck with such a name he wouldn't use it. Dale went by his middle name, after all, John was just so dull. John Dale Pagnali, who wouldn't want to be called Dale?

Dale stepped into the store, the little bell hanging on the door chiming his arrival. There was a counter a few feet in front of him with shelves of boxes that had something to do with computers in a row behind it. Around the perimeter of the store were computers all lined up as if awaiting execution.

A burly man with dark brown hair, a white t-shirt and blue plaid shorts stepped out of the back room. Dale almost gasped when he saw him. No glasses. He was far from scrawny; probably in his early thirties.

"Hi, I'm Dale." He put out his hand and felt the man's big, thick hand grip his. Dale thought he was going to faint, but caught himself. "I called earlier."

"You spoke to me," the man said.

"You're Bob." Dale couldn't believe his eyes.

"Why don't you tell me what it is you need," Bob said.

Dale bit his tongue and tried to compose himself. None of the lines going through his head were appropriate for the situation. "That's why I'm here, I don't really know what I need. I don't know anything about computers."

"I see," Bob said, nodding. "Why don't you tell me what you want a computer for. What types of work are you going to do with it?"

"I mainly need it to keep track of appointments for each hairdresser, maybe even have it hold onto phone numbers, too. I own my own salon, did I tell you?"

"What about payroll?"

"Payroll? All I do is write out checks. It's no big deal."

"With the right software you can have the computer keep track of your inflows, outflows, payroll and inventory. It can even help you with taxes at the end of the year."

"And it's safe?"

"Just back-up at the end of every day and you'll be fine."

"Can I still do payroll at home?"

"Do you have a computer at home?"

Dale felt as if he was now over his head, but didn't want to stop talking to Bob. He shook his head, then forced a grin. "I don't know a damn thing about computers."

"Why don't I take you in back and show you your options," Bob said. "Maybe then you'll feel less stressed about the whole thing."

Dale followed Bob into the back room, where the innards of computers were exposed, and green boards with chips and metal strips littered the counters on both sides of the room. A few unattractive guys were busy tinkering with the beastly things, shoving things inside and pulling stuff out.

He followed Bob into a room small enough to be a walk-in closet. There was a cheap desk against the wall to the right, and a file cabinet on the opposite side. A computer screen sat on top of the desk, and to the left was a large black box that rose up a good two feet. If Bob closed the door Dale knew he would get a boner. Instead Bob pulled the chair out and asked Dale to take a seat.

"Let me explain a few things, " Bob said, then pointed to the big black box next to the desk. "See this. This is the main computer that is shared between the terminal you're sitting in front of and the one at the front desk. Both terminals have access to each other, which is usually fine for a small business. So all the files on this hard disk can be accessed from the other computer and vice versa."

Dale was already a bit confused. The computer was the black box on the floor and not the screen and keyboard in front of him? He smiled and nodded politely, hoping he wouldn't zone out on Bob as he continued to explain the mysteries of computers. All Dale wanted was to have him come into his salon, set the damn things up and show him how to use them. He could care less about how they worked, just as long as they did what he wanted, and all he wanted was something to keep track of appointments. The bit about also keeping track of his inventory and payroll sounded good, too.

"And this is what you could use to track inventory and do payroll," Bob said, reaching over from behind Dale and grabbing the oval plastic thing that seemed to be attached to the terminal.

With his big hands, Bob moved the plastic object across the maroon pad. Dale couldn't help but notice how thick Bob's fingers were. Bob's index finger clicked twice on a button on the object in his hand.

"What did you do?" Dale asked. "I'm already confused."

Bob put both hands on Dale's shoulders and gave them a squeeze. "Have you ever used a computer?"

"Not even a terminal," Dale said, hoping Bob wouldn't let go of his shoulders. "I just want to make things easier at the salon."

Bob walked to the side of Dale, folded his arms and smiled. "That thing I was holding is called a mouse. Put your hand on it."

Dale reached out and put his hand on the mouse, which was still warm from Bob's touch. He noticed two buttons under his fingers, then began to glide the mouse over the pad the way Bob had done.

"See the arrow on the screen move," Bob said.

Dale looked at the screen and saw the small arrow move over clouds, then over the small pictures that Bob told him were called icons. Bob had Dale double-click on various icons and gave brief explanations of how he could use one program for scheduling appointments and another to keeping track of payroll and inventory. After a while Dale began to think that computers weren't all that hard to use. All he needed to do was learn which pictures to click on to do what he wanted.

"Once these things are set up in the salon, will you show me how to use them?" Dale asked.

"I can get you started," Bob said. "If you feel the need to get more training, I can point you to someone who can teach you the rest. But I bet you'll catch on pretty fast. It's not that hard."

———

Z Bar was on the corner of Brooke and Wickenden Streets, not far from Michelle's apartment. Michelle had made a point of telling Ian that she would meet him there. Ian took it as yet another obstacle, and made a mental note to choose a restaurant outside of the city next time they got together. Unless, of course, he was able to get her in bed, which he thought was doubtful.

Ian had met Michelle outside Z Bar, then had taken her inside where they were seated in the far corner, where the lights were low and they were away from the front windows facing Wickenden Street. The street was just too busy and Ian didn't want to risk being seen by anyone. He'd told Michelle that the atmosphere was nicer without all the hullabaloo of traffic, which made her smile. Already he was scoring points.

"I've never been here," Michelle said as she opened the menu and looked inside.

"This is one of my favorite restaurants," Ian said. "Aside from Hemenway and Al Forno."

"I went to Hemenway once with my parents," Michelle said. "I love sea food."

"The fish here is wonderful," Ian said.

"I'll get fish then. Maybe the haddock or the cod."

"Do you like a Pinot Grigio?"

Michelle looked over the top of her menu. "I really don't know anything about wine."

"You'll like it," Ian said.

Michelle gazed down at the menu as the waiter came by and took their order. Ian ordered a bottle of Pinot Grigio, casually taking notice of Michelle's almost surprised expression. She'd probably never been on a date where the guy ordered a full bottle of wine before, let alone been out with someone who knew his wines. She was so easily impressed that she was almost not worth it. The thought made him smile. She might not be a virgin, but he bet her ass had never been used.

"So," Ian said, "tell me about your stocks. What do you like?"

Michelle's eyes lit up, then she began to speak and he knew he was in for it.

Tuesday

Steve slid the shoulder strap of his knapsack further onto his shoulder, then continued to make his way along the path that sectioned off the green. Around him were Georgian buildings in stone and brick. The wrought iron gates were to his left. It had been chilly that morning when he'd left for class, now it was warmer and he didn't feel the need to wear the jacket he'd slipped on before leaving the house. He walked towards the gates, then onto John Street.

In a couple of days Steve was going to have to drive home to Boston for the holiday. Sometimes he wished he'd decided to go to school out West, like maybe University of Southern California, and not some high brow school that his father had gone to. He was sick of having to go home for every stupid reason imaginable. At least he'd be able to get some laundry done without having to go to the laundr-o-mat and doing it himself. That was his only consolation. He'd wanted to tell his mother that he'd drive up Thursday morning and come back Thursday night, but she'd already informed him that he was to come up directly after classes Wednesday. He hadn't bothered telling her that he wasn't going to any classes the day before Thanksgiving. It would give him more time to get ready for the happiness that was his family. The mere thought made him want to retch. He didn't want to hear his father talk about how the world was coming to an end and how vices were taking over. Television and Hollywood were to blame for glamorizing drugs and lewd behavior. He'd heard countless versions of his father's tirade, each blaming a different vice, and he didn't need to hear yet another.

Dale had always wanted to meet Steve's family, like that would have ever happened. Steve's father would take one look at Dale and kick them both out. Perhaps if Dale was more butch Steve would be able to take him home and they could pretend to be just friends. But chances were that Dale wouldn't go for that, so there was little reason to even think about it. Plus they were no longer a couple, which was for the best. Steve had to admit that there had been times when he and Dale had been together where he'd been a little embarrassed, especially the few times Dale had tried holding his hand in public. Steve hadn't cared that it had been on Thayer Street, or even the East Side of Providence, where fags ran amok. It wasn't right, and if anyone gave them trouble it was only because they were asking for it. And if something had come of it, and there had been the kind of trouble that made the news, and his father had heard about it, there would have been real trouble. Steve would be cast out of his family; he wouldn't be able to afford to go to school; his life would be ruined. All because he liked to get his dick sucked by men. It was so perverted. His father was right about that. All fags seemed to care about was running around trying to get off.

"Steve!" It was Jay, the happy homo, flagging him down from half way down the block, near the arched entrance to the University campus.

Steve waved back, then walked up to him. "What's up?"

"Are you going to be home tonight?"

"I don't have any plans," Steve said, noting that Jay had had his hair cut short, with the front flipped up like all the fags were doing. "Do you need me for anything?"

Jay dropped his dark green book bag, then held up the navy blue plastic Gap bag. "I feel so stupid, but I have this date tonight and want to make sure I don't end up looking like a loser. You know how little fashion sense I have."

Steve didn't want to agree with him, but he was right. "Show me what you bought."

Jay pulled a green checked button down shirt from the bag. The material was thick, and it seemed well made. The color would look good on him, too. "Did you buy anything else?"

"It's all I had money for," Jay said.

Steve didn't think Jay had a pair of pants that didn't look old. He really did need something to go with the shirt. "Don't you have a credit card?"

"I don't like to use it," Jay said. "I really don't think it's that important."

Steve eyed Jay's waist. There was no way Jay would fit into any of his pants. "I should be home when you get there, we'll see what you have then."

"That's great," Jay said. "I'll see you then."

Steve watched as Jay walked onto the University green. Things would be much easier if Jay just gave in and started working out. He didn't see what the big deal was; after a while working out just became a part of your life. And once he saw the way a firm body attracted men, he would thank himself for changing his ways.

———

Harold had been eccentric if nothing else. The small store had been filled with brightly colored lamp shades, gold serpentine lamp posts, low dark wood end tables, and an endless supply of chaise longues in every type of upholstery imaginable. Iris had liked the zebra print, and some of the outrageous bright greens and oranges. Harold had said they glowed radiantly under black light, Iris could only imagine. Iris had thought she'd been the luckiest woman alive until Harold had told her that he'd only give her a thirty-five percent discount.

"But the normal discount for residential is forty percent," Iris had said, but he wouldn't budge. Iris knew better than to pester him further, especially after she'd tried and he'd squished up his little face and looked upset.

"These are very hard to find items, especially of this quality," he'd said.

Iris had had to agree that the quality on the chaise longues was good, although she hadn't bothered studying the other furnishings in the store. At least Gerald always gave her a forty-three percent discount, which was why she always went to him when she had a residential account. Gerald's discount would be enough to make up the difference in the price of the chaise longue.

Iris had taken back the photographs of Harold's collection of chaise longues to show to Dolores, and now she waited in the conservative living room of Dolores's present house. She stared at the fireplace, with the dark wood mantel and wondered how comfortable the winters must be while sitting in front of it with a quilt on her lap and a fire crackling in the hearth.

"Oh, there you are," Dolores said as she slowly made her way into the room. "I had a terrible headache earlier and had to take an Alprazolam to calm it down. They're brought on by stress, my headaches. I feel so much better now." Dolores threw up her arms and smiled. "Just like that song about everything being new again."

Iris didn't know the song she was referring to, nor did she want to see Dolores perform it. She nodded and smiled. "I'm glad to hear it."

Dolores sat next to Iris on the sofa, then softly patted her knee. "Now what is this we're looking at, furniture?"

"For the living room," Iris said, holding the folder on her lap. Slowly she opened the cover. "One piece in particular."

Dolores's eyes opened wide, the tips of her fake lashes almost touching her eye brows. "A chaise longue." She paused. "In zebra, how strange."

It was obvious Dolores didn't like it, which pleased Iris. Zebra would have been too extreme. "There are others."

"Oh, yes, well, is zebra in now?"

"It would be too much for what you want," Iris said.

Dolores slowly nodded. "Yes, it would."

Iris had been worried about nothing, Dolores was putting all her faith in her. All the same, Iris would make sure Dolores got exactly what she needed. Her friends would see the place and love it, then Dolores would gladly tell them who had designed it. Iris turned over the photo, showing the same chaise longue in a soft blue. Beneath that was one in a burnt orange, and beneath that, one in beige that she wasn't fond of, but would go with any interior.

"I like this," Dolores said as she softly stroked the photograph. Her eyes were slightly glazed. "When I was a little girl I used to imagine movie stars lounging out on these. One in particular, but I won't tell you who. It was a long time ago. A woman never gives away such things."

"It comes in other shades and fabrics," Iris said. "We can mold the entire room around it in a way that everybody will be in awe of it, but nobody will know that the chaise is what gives the room its unique flavor."

"We can?"

"Between subtle colors and those floor to ceiling windows nobody will be looking at any one thing. All we need to do is find one more uniquely subtle item." Iris placed her hand on Dolores's and gave it a gentle squeeze. "It will be our secret."

Dolores smiled. "Show me, dear, show me the other chaises."

—

Both Shayna and Kyle were finishing off their last two clients for the day while Tony swept some hair off the floor in his area. He'd already put his combs in disinfectant, and returned all his clippers to their rightful places.

"I cleared the top of my desk off for you to set up the computer," Anita said from the top of the steps leading to the cutting floor.

Dale looked up from the day's receipts and nodded. "I'll try to get you trained as soon as possible."

"I'm sure it won't be hard." Anita walked up to Dale and rubbed his head with her long, slender fingers. Her perfume, Red Door, drifted with her arm and lingered in the air. It was an old fragrance now, but Dale still liked it. "It's about time you did this."

"You're so good about things."

Anita's red lips thinned into a smile. "How's single life treating you?"

Dale didn't want to admit that he'd wept while hugging a pillow last night, or that cooking didn't hold the same enjoyment knowing it was only for one. Not to Anita at least, despite how much he liked her. Instead he nodded and said he was getting by.

"I can come in early tomorrow if you want," Anita said.

"That would be good," Dale said. "How about nine."

"I'll be here." Anita was on the stairs when the bell on the front door rang.

"Is Mr. Pagnali here?" It was Bob.

"Go right on in, he's waiting for you," Anita said.

Bob stepped up to the desk where Dale sat and gave his hand a firm shake. "I was able to leave the shop early," Bob said. "I left one of my boys in charge."

"Well then, why don't I show you where everything will go," Dale said as he stepped out from behind the desk and up to Bob. Shayna approached the desk with her freshly coifed client in tow and cruised Bob.

"Are these the two desks?" Bob asked, pointing towards the cutting floor and the receptionist desk.

"Will it be a problem?"

"Not at all," Bob said. "Can we prop open these doors to bring the boxes in?"

Dale was quick to say yes, then offer his assistance. He walked out to Bob's car, which was parked in front of the salon, and was disturbed to find he drove a Saturn station wagon. "Do you have children?" he asked.

Bob opened the hatch, then reached inside and dragged a box to the edge of the bed. "No, although we wanted one."

Dale noticed a pale ring of skin on the ring finger of Bob's left hand as he grabbed one of the two biggest boxes.

"I'll take the big boxes," Bob said.

"Let me take one, too," Dale said, reaching inside for the box that matched Bob's in size. It wasn't that heavy, but it was awkward. He helped Bob take in all the boxes, along with some cables.

By the time all the boxes were inside, Kyle and Shayna had left, leaving Dale alone with Bob. He watched as Bob opened them up and started to unpack. Bob started at the receptionist desk, placing the monitor on top, and a beige plastic box he called a mini tower on the floor to the left of the chair, where it was out of the way. What Dale wanted to know was why he didn't wear his wedding ring. Was he separated from his wife? Divorced? If so, why? Did he suck dick? Dale was sure he didn't, but it was fun to wonder all the same.

Bob grabbed some wires then ducked beneath the desk and began to connect wires to the back of the mini tower.

"Do you like Asian food?" Dale asked.

Bob looked up over the top of the desk. "Sure, why?"

"I'll pick some up for dinner, if you don't mind. The least I can do is feed you."

"You don't have to," Bob said, then ducked back under the desk. "I can pay for my own food."

"Oh please, at least I can say I did something constructive. Do you like Four Seasons?"

"In Cranston?"

"Yes."

"Get an order of Nime Chow," Bob said.

Dale went into the other room and placed their order, which the woman on the other end said would be ready in ten minutes. Dale wondered how much longer it would take for Bob to get everything set up. Watching Bob do all that work made him feel a bit useless, but it would all be worth it in the long run.

"I'm going to go get our food," Dale said.

"Good timing. I'm not sure you want to watch me snake wires under the floor," Bob said.

"Snake wires?"

"Either that or have you tripping over them."

"Do what needs to be done," Dale said, then went to his car. He didn't bother to lock up in case Bob needed to go to his car for something.

———

Steve drove past the Dale Pagnali Salon. Dale's car wasn't there, just a blue Saturn station wagon. He'd already driven past Dale's condo twice and hadn't seen his car in the parking lot. Was he already dating? The idea seemed absurd, especially since Dale spent most of his free time with his friends, watching stupid movies or gossiping about each other over dinner. He couldn't imagine Dale cooking for anyone other than him, although chances were that he would be doing that sooner or later. That was if he was out on a date. He might as well head home so he would be there before Jay. He hoped Jay had bought some new pants on his way home.

—

The laser printer sat on the desk and took up far too much space. Dale knew he'd have to buy a small table to put it on. For now it would just have to do. Dale stepped up to the cutting room floor, then saw Bob still fiddling with the computer at the desk. He held up the bag with their dinner. "Are you still fiddling with that thing?"

"No, I'm playing a game," Bob said. "FreeCell, I'm addicted to it."

"FreeCell? What is it?"

"It's a card game."

"There are worse things," Dale said. "We can eat in the back room, if you want. I have some paper plates and plastic forks in there."

Bob agreed, and the two men went into the back room and sat at the small table tucked amongst shelves of hair products. Dale spooned out white rice onto paper plates as Bob watched, then he pushed the small white box that contained Bob's dinner up to him. In a round plastic container was the sauce with chunks of peanut floating on top. Next he pulled out the thick, tubular Nime Chow. He placed one on Bob's plate, then the other on his. The Nime Chow had already been sliced into halves, and Dale picked up one half and brought it up to the peanut sauce, then scooped some sauce onto the roll. He couldn't help but look at the pale ring around Bob's finger.

"I'm divorced," Bob said. "I saw you looking."

"I'm sorry," Dale said as he lifted the roll to his mouth and held it there. "I hope it wasn't horrible for you."

"It's a long story," Bob said.

Dale slipped the end of the roll into his mouth, then bit down. Bob watched as Dale's lips surrounded the roll. Dale felt his face flush as he chewed, tasting the sweet sauce mix with mint, bean sprouts and shrimp.

"How is it?"

Dale liked anything tubular in his mouth, but didn't want to say that to Bob. He nodded instead, then swallowed. "Good as always."

"You look like you're enjoying it."

"It's been a long time."

"Same here," Bob said, then winked at Dale.

—

Jay had taken Steve's advice and bought himself a new pair of pants from the Gap. He hoped Erik wouldn't be too late, as it was it was five past six. Although Steve wanted to stay and see what Erik looked like, he'd gone out to help Jay feel more at ease. But if Steve were there Jay would have someone to talk to. He told himself not to look out the window again. It wasn't as if he knew what Erik drove anyhow. Jay dropped himself onto the sofa and tapped his feet on the floor. He didn't know what he was going to say to Erik, and hoped something would come up that they had in common. What if he never showed? Getting stood up would suck. That would be it. He would just not bother dating. It really wasn't worth all the aggravation. He covered the face of his watch. He was not going to look. Erik was probably just running late, or maybe he took a wrong turn.

A car door slammed shut outside, and Jay forced himself to stay seated and wait. There were footsteps coming up the stairs, then on the porch. It was him. Jay stayed put and waited until the doorbell rang. He counted to ten, then stood and took a deep breath. Act casual, he told himself as he walked out into the hall. Erik's face shone through the oval window of the front door. He opened the door, then said hello and asked Erik inside.

"Sorry I'm a little late," Erik said.

"I didn't notice," Jay said as he closed the front door. "I just have to get my coat."

"No kiss?"

It would be a simple kiss, Jay thought as he turned and walked up to Erik. Erik kept his hands by his sides as Jay gently pressed his lips against his. Erik pulled away, then softly stroked Jay's lips with his tongue. Then Jay felt Erik's arms around his waist, and he opened his mouth to Erik's tongue. Already Jay's dick was responding to the deep kiss as he slid his hands around Erik's waist, feeling his tight body beneath the gray thermal shirt. Their lips parted, then they gave each other small, soft kisses.

"You don't know how bad I wanted to do that," Erik said, holding Jay close enough that he could feel Erik's erection against his thigh.

Jay tried to calm his breathing. "And I thought it would just be a simple kiss."

"That wasn't a simple kiss?"

Jay stepped back. "I should get my coat." He turned to walk into the other room to get his coat off the kitchen chair, then felt Erik grab his waist and pull him closer. "Not just yet," Erik said as he pressed himself against Jay's back and kissed his neck.

"Not yet," Jay said, his voice quavering. Erik's hard shaft was rubbing against Jay's ass as his big hand slid around Jay's waist and started rubbing the outline of his dick. Slowly, Jay turned to face Erik, then kissed him once more. As far as he was concerned dinner could wait.

—

Bob looked back and winked at Dale before stepping around to the driver's side of his car. It took everything Dale had not to swoon or to chase the hunk down and try to get him into bed. Flirtatious straight men were nothing but trouble, although they were awful good for the ego. Dale closed the door, then looked around the salon. The computer wasn't that difficult to learn, at least he'd caught on to scheduling and would show Anita tomorrow. He would show it to the others as they scheduled new appointments. At the end of the day he would keep them around and explain some of the more difficult tasks. Hopefully the notes he'd taken would help him to remember everything. The program they were using was capable of doing a lot more, but for now all Bob wanted Dale to concentrate on was scheduling. Later in the week Bob said he would set Dale up with a notebook computer and show him how to do payroll and the rest of the tasks he would need to know.

Walking up to the receptionist's desk, Dale looked over the notes he'd made on scheduling appointments. Anita already had computer experience and probably already knew how to do everything, so he wasn't all too concerned about teaching her. It was the others, although they would probably catch on fast. It really wasn't hard, which was what amazed Dale. It made him wonder why he'd waited so long to get the salon up to date. But then he wouldn't have met Bob. Not that he thought he would get anywhere with Bob, his being straight and all. Or at least having been married. Dale wondered what it must be like to be married to someone like Bob. Bob was so butch and virile. What would it be like to crawl into bed with a man like that and have him naked and ready at his side? Would he take you by force, or just pull you in close and wrap his big arms around you? Dale sighed. He would never find out.

Lucky for him Bob was such a nice guy. Dale still couldn't believe he'd come by and spent all that time making sure Dale knew what he was doing. It was probably the norm for computer companies, especially if they had a client who knew nothing. Bob had shown him everything, from how to make the mouse do what you wanted, to using the Tab key to move from field to field. The best was how Bob had Dale sit down and actually do all the tasks. "The best way to learn is to do," Bob had said, placing his warm hand on Dale's shoulder and giving it a squeeze. Dale had had a woody the entire time Bob stood behind him. If Bob had noticed Dale's raging hardon when he'd stood he hadn't let on. His dick was still hard, yet another reminder that he didn't have anyone in his life.

It was getting late. Going home to nothing didn't appeal to Dale. The last thing he needed was to sulk around his apartment for another night. Maybe he would go to the movies to kill some time. He grabbed his stiff dick, then wandered into the cutting room. He sat in the chair kitty corner, unbuttoned his shirt and ran his left hand over his firm chest. What if Bob's hand had slid into his shirt and felt up his chest; dipped into his pants, feeling the tip of Dale's dick? Dale unfastened his belt buckle, then the top of his pants. He unzipped his fly then pulled down his Calvin Klein boxer briefs. Grabbing his hard shaft, he watched himself in the mirror. What if it was Bob grabbing his dick? Placing his fingers just below the swollen head of his shaft, Dale rubbed in a circular motion. He closed his eyes, then relaxed and enjoyed the feeling. What if Bob did this to him?

"Oh Bob," Dale whispered.

—

Jay and Erik got a booth to the right of the large, open room with round tables in the middle that sat parties of ten or more. Four Seasons wasn't a fancy restaurant, but the food was so good that nobody cared. At first Jay had been afraid that having already had sex with Erik would make things between them seem odd, but he was pleased that that wasn't the case. He was also pleased that Erik had been a good partner. Their bodies had moved together from one position to the next, the contact between them never broken. It had seemed so perfect to Jay, but that could be only because it had been so long since he'd had sex with anyone.

Erik looked at Jay from across the table as he slipped his fork beneath white rice covered with Kon Po Chicken. "So, you have no idea what you're going to do after college?"

"Maybe teach," Jay said. "There's only so much you can do with an English major."

"You can do anything you want," Erik said. "Look at me, I majored in Math. My family thought I was nuts, but I have a job going around teaching people how to use their systems. I travel a lot, which helps. If you don't mind having the company ship you all over the place, they'll take you."

"I don't know." Jay played with the shrimp covered in black bean sauce. He pushed the shrimp into the bed of rice, then pulled it out. "I might go back to school after this."

"To get your doctorate?"

"Maybe," Jay said, suddenly realizing that he'd taken the conversation into dangerous territory. "What do you have?"

"A BS." Erik wrapped his legs around Jay's calves. "If you

want to teach, it might as well be college."

"You think?"

"I think you're adorable."

Jay shoved a shrimp into his mouth and bit down. Already his dick was beginning to stir in his pants, and he hoped Erik would come inside when he dropped him off. "You're just saying that," Jay said, hoping the heat he felt on his face wasn't a noticeable blush. He pushed his fork through the rice.

"No, I'm not," Erik said.

When dinner was over, the two men went back to Erik's black Nissan Altima. On the drive home Erik kept his hand firmly placed on Jay's thigh, squeezing from time to time. They sat in front of Jay's apartment with the engine idle, making small talk about movies, books, Madonna.

"Want to come in?" Jay asked.

"I don't think I could keep my hands to myself," Erik said, then leaned in close to Jay for a kiss. When their lips parted he said, "I don't want you to think I'm only after you for sex."

"Does that mean I'll see you again?"

"You bet."

Wednesday

"**Y**es, Mom, I'm excited about it," Iris said, clutching the phone to her ear as she waited for the light to turn green. "I just wish I could be with you and Dad."

"It's not like we're going to be alone," Margot said. "You're not my only child. And we'll see you *and* Ian at Christmas."

The light changed, and Iris put her foot down on the accelerator and took a left. "I think it's nerves. What if they don't like me?" She veered to the right of the V shaped tip of the Turk's Head Building, which split the road in half.

"I can't imagine that," Margot said. "You are my daughter after all."

"I hope that's enough." The pillars of the opening of the Arcade were on her left. To her right was the sleek, modern Fleet Building.

"Listen to you, after all you've done. Sometimes I think I believe in you more than you believe in yourself."

"I have not done that much." Iris slowed down for the red light. "Sometimes it feels as if I've done nothing at all."

"Iris! How many women make the pages of top architecture magazines? You're so wrapped up in your life that you don't have a clue as to how much you've done. How many women your age own a successful business that gets top publicity?"

"I lucked into that, mom."

"Oh, Iris, give yourself some credit."

"Mom, I have to go."

"Okay." There was that pause that let Iris know Margot wasn't happy with her. "Good luck with your meeting, and with Ian's family."

Iris dropped the telephone on the passenger seat, then took a left when the light turned green. She didn't have a meeting to go to, but she didn't want to spend too long talking to her mother. She loved her, it was just that Margot had high ideas about how well off she was. Iris knew Margot talked her up to her friends, so who knew what they thought she was. It wasn't as if she was designing interiors in New York or Boston. Iris sighed. At least she was pleased with her for something, although Margot had always been impressed with her work. Iris had learned at an early age that the only way to please her mother was to work hard and get good grades. That same strategy carried over to her career. It had always been her boyfriends that she'd never liked. Except for Ian. Or rather, she liked that Ian wanted Iris to be successful, and was successful himself.

It was after five the day before Thanksgiving and for once on street parking was easy to come by. After parking, Iris went straight into the building and up to the future law offices of Tyler, Westcott and Allen.

The office was dark, and Iris flicked the switch, filling the room with the overhead glare of a dangling light bulb in a yellow cage. The wiring had just been installed. Soon the walls would be painted, carpet laid down and the lighting fixtures in place. Everything would come together. Methodically, Iris walked across the room, looking around as she approached Andrew's office. She'd been thinking about her last meeting with him, and had even had a few masturbatory fantasies about him. She didn't want to ruin her future with Ian, who had always been good to her, and hoped her brief infatuation would quickly pass. She was about to meet Ian's parents, that was a big step.

Already she was beginning to feel excited. She walked up to the window and looked out at the darkening sky. Below was the street, and a few drivers making their way home to their families. Was Andrew one of those people, or was he already home? Maybe he was taking a shower, dipping his head back into the hot spray, water cascading down his chest.

There was a ding, then the sound of the elevator doors opening. It was probably just the guard making his rounds. There was nothing to worry about. But still the image of headlines about an interior designer having been brutally raped and murdered flashed through her mind. Female paranoia.

"Iris?" Andrew called out.

Iris held her breath. What was he doing there? What was she doing there, and how would she explain it? She took a tentative step into the main room.

"I thought that was your car," Andrew said, walking towards her in his dark suit. "Checking things out again?"

"I can't help myself," Iris said, desperately trying to not look into his dark eyes as he approached her. He was so close to her now, and she couldn't look away. "When I get something in my head I can't let it go."

"I know the feeling," Andrew said.

Iris felt her knees buckle, so she leaned against the wall for support. That was when Andrew moved in close to her and gently brushed his lips against hers. Iris wanted to tell him that she couldn't kiss him, but the words wouldn't form. She was breathless as he pulled away from her, then met her gaze. And when he kissed her briefly again, she kissed him back. Soon the kisses were long and deep, and Andrew's big hands were on her thighs, hiking up her short skirt. His right hand slid over her nylons, then dipped inside them, past her panties, his fingers brushing against her swollen clit, rubbing it before dipping down further.

"You're so wet," he whispered as he used both hands to slide down her panties and nylons. Then he went on his knees and she felt his tongue on her, caressing the folds of her sex.

Iris breathed long and deep as she stepped out of her pumps, then felt her nylons being pulled off completely. She bit her finger to keep from moaning. Then Andrew moved back and looked up at her. Their eyes met with unsated desire.

"Fuck me," Iris whispered.

Andrew stood, then kissed her full on the mouth. She could taste herself on his lips and on his tongue. Her scent seemed to fill the room as she unzipped his slacks, then felt his stiffness, which seemed to be more than she could handle. "Go slow," she said.

Andrew pressed his face against Iris's shoulder, then she felt him move into her, his thick rod parting her tender lips. How long had it been since a man had wanted her this way? Andrew's cock felt so good sliding inside her that she thought she would cry. She wrapped her arms around him, then lifted her left leg and brought it around his ass.

"Fuck me, Andrew," she whispered. "Please, fuck me."

Slowly, Andrew slid his hips back until the rounded tip of his dick was at her entrance, then gently slipped it back inside. Andrew reached down and cupped Iris's ass in his hands, holding her steady as he continued to move. His hot breath was in her ear. "You feel so good."

Iris gripped him as she felt the slow pleasure of his movements, a pleasure she had not felt in a year and a half. This was what she'd wanted for so long. A moan escaped her lips, and she tilted her head back.

—

Steve maneuvered his car through the narrow space between the back of the brownstones, which looked like an alley littered with expensive cars. As promised there was a parking space saved for him next to his mother's Volvo. His father kept his Mercedes garaged, so there was no telling if he would be home. Steve wished he wasn't, the last thing he wanted now was to have to talk to him. After flipping the switch on the floor to open the trunk, Steve got out of the car then pulled out the laundry bag stuffed full with dirty clothes. He'd have to come back for the green laundry basket that held yet more clothes to be washed. As usual the basement was cluttered with boxes and old furniture his parents refused to throw away or give to The Salvation Army. There was a soft blue overstuffed sofa covered with clear plastic against the far wall. Steve knew that under the center seat cushion was a juice stain from one of the many times he'd sat there watching television when he was a kid. Dismantled and propped up in the corner to his right was his first big-boy bed. They'd even saved the box spring and mattress, which was leaning against the wall next to the dark wood frame. His sister's white bedroom set was also down there, pushed in close to his old bed. The bulky white bureau took up most of one wall, and the two end tables stood in front of the mattress and box springs as if holding them at bay. Steve knew that in one of the many boxes piled one on top of the other was the wood bi-plane that had dangled from the ceiling over his bed, and the lamp with the clown at its base. He'd once had a poster of Neil Armstrong walking on the moon, but had taken it down the summer before he'd begun high school.

Once he'd begun high school he'd also become more sexual. He'd begun to look at his male friends differently, and had also had sexual dreams involving them. That had been how he'd gotten involved with Kevin. Once Kevin had been forced to leave the school, Steve had taken down the posters of his favorite bands. He'd found himself becoming aroused by the images of the male band members of such groups. The walls of the dorm room he'd shared with Sam had become vacant where his bed was, Sam still kept the posters of bands he liked up on the walls. Although Steve had wanted to ask Sam to take down his posters, he'd known that if he had, he'd have to explain himself. For Steve the dorm room had become a place where he slept and hoped his dreams and fantasies would no longer involve naked men.

It hadn't been until the summer before his senior year that he'd fully given in to his perverse desires and had begun to find outlets for his sexual needs. He'd scoped out adult bookstores in the seediest neighborhoods of Boston and had gotten his dick sucked in video booths. After, he'd go home and crash on his bed and tell himself that he wouldn't do it again.

After leaving his laundry next to the washer and dryer, he trudged across the room to the narrow staircase that led to the kitchen. Dread sat in the pit of his stomach and threatened to come up like a night of sickness as he made his way up the stairs. Thankfully the kitchen was empty. He looked to his left, down the hall, then into the dining room entrance to the right. Empty. The God Bless this House magnet, with the picture of the happy country house they did not own was still on the refrigerator. He slowly walked down the hall to keep his work boots from making any sound. He peered through the doorway, into the living room to see his mother sitting in the high back Victorian chair, the light coming from the Tiffany lamp was cast on the book in her hands. It looked like The Bible, which was typical. She'd always been prone to re-reading the Bible around the holidays. Her dark hair was streaked with gray and tied up in a bun the way she'd always worn it. Around her neck, on a delicate gold chain was the small cross she'd always worn. Things never changed. Steve stood with his back against the wall and composed himself before taking another step.

"Steve, is that you?" his mother said.

"I'm home," he said, walking into the living room.

"Oh, thank God." His mother placed the book down on the side table and rose to hug her son. She'd always seemed so frail and about to break when he hugged her, and this time was no different. "I had no idea when you would be here."

"I didn't know either. It's been crazy trying to get things done."

"I know you need to study, but I do hope you're making time for friends." She smoothed her hand over Steve's shirt. "You've never had a lot of friends. A social life is important, too."

"I have friends, Mom." Steve reminded himself not to roll his eyes. How many times had he heard this from her before. It was obvious what she was getting at, but he wasn't about to bring it up. How long could he dance around the lack of women in his life? His father didn't seem to mind having an overly studious son, just as long as Steve took time to settle down once he was done with college.

"Did you bring anything with you?"

"I still have stuff in the car," Steve said. "I brought laundry with me, too."

Steve's mother looked concerned. "Nancy left not too long ago."

"That's okay, I can do it."

"No, don't. It's the holiday. I'll do it. Your father will be home soon, I'm sure you want to spend time with him."

Steve held himself back from rolling his eyes. "Sure, that would be great. Why don't I get my bag from the car."

———

Iris was still against the wall as Andrew slipped his dick out of her, then he gave her a gentle kiss. She lowered her skirt, then bent down and picked up her discarded panties and nylons. When she stood, Andrew slipped his arm around her waist, but still kept some distance from her. "Can I take you out to dinner?" he asked.

"I don't have time," Iris said. "I shouldn't have even been here."

"Another time, perhaps?"

Iris tried not to look into his deep brown eyes, but was captivated by them. She didn't want him to think she was a slut, or that she was looking to have an affair. And what would he think of her once he knew about Ian?

"Does that pause mean no?"

"I can't," Iris said, then took a slow breath. "I have a boyfriend. Someone I've been seeing for a year now." She slipped out of Andrew's embrace, then walked to the middle of the room. "We shouldn't have done that, but we did."

"I don't regret it."

Iris crossed her arms and looked down at the floor covered in saw dust and dirt. "It isn't fair to Ian. I don't know what I'm going to do."

"Do you love him?"

Did she love him? Iris wasn't sure. When she spoke, her voice was soft. "Yes. He's a good match."

"A good match?"

"Don't make me explain myself."

Andrew walked up to her. "You don't have to."

Iris looked up, straight at Andrew. He seemed so gentle and kind. "I appreciate that." If she'd met Andrew before Ian, she knew she would be with him instead. But she hadn't, therefore she couldn't have anything more than a business relationship with him.

"You're an amazing and beautiful woman, Iris," Andrew said. "I hope he treats you well."

"He does," Iris said, although she didn't fully believe it.

"Then I won't bother you any more." Andrew took a step back, then extended his hand. His fingers wrapped around Iris's delicate hand as they shook, then he turned and walked towards the elevators. She watched as he waited, then turned to wink at her as he entered. The doors closed, and Iris felt a pang of regret. He'd felt so good inside her, fucking her the way Ian never did. Now he was gone. She'd told him about Ian and he'd left. As awful as it felt, she knew it wasn't worth jeopardizing what she had with Ian by mentioning it. It wouldn't happen again. It shouldn't have happened in the first place. Andrew was business, nothing more.

After bunching her panties and nylons into a ball, Iris took the elevator down to the first floor then went to her car. She drove home feeling guilty for what she'd done, and convincing herself that it was nothing. She parked in front of her house, then got out of the car. A white oblong box with a red satin ribbon and bow was propped up against the deep green door of her Georgian house. She picked up the box and slipped off the ribbon. Inside were a dozen red roses. They were beautiful. How had Andrew known where she lived? There was a small card inside the box, under the soft green tissue paper. She opened the card and read:

Looking forward to seeing you tonight.

Ian

Oh, how thoughtful of him, Iris thought as she fished through her purse for her keys. She would have to put the flowers in water.

———

Jay couldn't believe what a mess he'd gotten himself into as he shoved the plastic wrapped frozen turkey into the refrigerator and closed the door. How he would get a turkey cooked and ready for a houseful of people was beyond him. Twenty minutes per pound couldn't be that difficult, even for someone who had never cooked a turkey before. Jay only hoped there weren't any secrets he didn't know about. He wondered about basting and oven bags. Also, how did one make a stuffing? What actually were giblets? He'd thought about getting Dale's number and asking him over, but with Steve having problems with his relationship that didn't seem to be an option. Dale would probably know all about cooking and stuffing and such things, though. He thought that Erik might also, but didn't want to risk calling and scaring him away. Thankfully all he had to worry about was the turkey, everyone else was bringing the rest.

This was his first night alone in a while and he'd decided he was going to enjoy the peace and quiet. Despite the fact that he'd gotten laid the previous night, he was all horned out. Steve had always said the more sex you have the more you seem to crave it. It seemed as if he was right. All he could think about was how nice it was rubbing against Erik, the scent of his chest as he nibbled on his tight nipples. Erik's balls had fit so well in his hand. It was warm beneath his nuts, too. He didn't know what it was that Erik liked about him, but he was glad for whatever it was. That meant that he'd get the chance to feel Erik's shaft in his mouth, and run his tongue along the thin cord of flesh under his balls.

Jay grabbed his bulging crotch and let out a huff. Why was he thinking about sex so much? It was driving him crazy. But never before, in his limited sexual experiences, had he felt so fulfilled without penetration. "Let's just rub," Erik had said as Jay lay on top of him, feeling Erik's hands gently caressing his back.

"Where I come from they call it dry humping," Jay had said. They had already been in every conceivable position, and although Jay had been ready to blow his load he'd wanted to see Erik's dick spurt. Sitting up, Jay had leaned over the side of the bed and grabbed the tube of KY lubricant from the floor and squirted some in his palm. After lubing both their pricks, Jay had rubbed them together, watching the two fleshy tubes glide one against the other as he'd held them both in his fist and rocked his hips. It hadn't been long before both he and Erik had shot their loads.

The memory was enough to make Jay cream in his pants. Perhaps if he hadn't been grabbing his crotch he'd have been able to control himself. Shaking his head, Jay stomped into his bedroom to change.

—

Steve sat on the bed in his old bedroom with the cordless phone in one hand while he used the other hand to flip the pages in his small black phone book, hoping to find somebody he knew in Boston who had come home early for the holiday. Steve's Boston friends weren't always around, nor could they be counted on to have the same telephone numbers as the last time Steve had been in town. They were guy's he'd met at bars and on the street while spending time at home during school breaks. Most of them had been tricks he'd ran into at a bar and remembered, most of them college students or guys with disposable jobs. He dialed a telephone number and waited. The annoying operator came on after two rings and told him the line was no longer in service. Someone had to be home. The last thing he wanted to do was listen to his father carry on about his college days and how good they had been. It was bad enough that the first comment his father had made was about how the Democrats were making a mockery of the electoral college.

His father believed that Florida belonged to the Republicans, and that Bush was obviously the victor. The popular vote meant nothing, he didn't know why it was even mentioned on the news. If Pat Buchanan had had a chance he would have voted for him. At least Bush had moral fortitude and honest values, just like his father. It was enough to make Steve want to put a knife to his throat. Steve had spent his youth listening to his father condemn anyone who didn't agree with his values, he didn't need to listen to any more of it now that he was out of the house.

Name after name, not a single one of them was home. The only answers he got were changed numbers and answering machines. He called each and every number until he reached the last page, then collapsed on the bed and stared at the ceiling. Perhaps if he'd kept contact with some of his friends during the school year someone would have thought to call him. But he hadn't. Steve let out a groan then looked around at the empty walls. He had only once choice to save his sanity, and that was to lie. He would tell his father he was going out to meet some friends and go for a coffee somewhere, or even a drink. He could always stop at Moonshine and see what was going on there. It's not like his father would ever suspect him of going to a gay bar, nor did he know anyone who would go to such a place. Maybe the night would turn out okay after all.

Thanksgiving

Dale parked his cashmere beige metallic Lexus ES 300 on a patch of dirt in front of the small ranch, grabbed the brown bag with the two bottles of wine, then got out and looked at the peeling steel blue paint on the house and the half dead lawn. His older sister's beat up Chevette was parked in the driveway, and Dale wondered if her husband was going to be there. On the way up he'd listened to Madonna's first album on compact disc. That album had been his introduction to Madonna, and the start of a love affair that he didn't see ending any time soon. But despite the upbeat tempo and all around fun songs, it had not been enough to make him smile for the holiday with his family. Not even after listening to "Lucky Star" twice. Dale pulled open the screen door, then let it rest on his side as he opened the front door and walked inside. The place was an orgy of beige and brown. Couldn't his mother splurge once and get the place redone?

The faint scent of a cigarette drifted towards Dale from the living room, where his sister sat with one hand on her pregnant belly and the other clutching a cigarette. Her deep brown hair, once soft with a healthy shine, was dry and limp as it hung past her shoulders. As if a pregnant woman wearing an oversized t-shirt wasn't bad enough, she had to wear one that had the words Under Construction over the belly in faded blue. She took a drag off the cigarette, exhaled a stream of smoke, then said, "I would get up but I finally got comfortable."

"Don't worry about it, Sarah," Dale said. "Happy Thanksgiving."

"Same to you."

Dale took a left into the dining room, taking notice that his mother had put the extra leaf in the kitchen table. She'd also bought two new chairs at some low end store. It wouldn't have been so bad except the new chairs were a lighter brown than the original set. Thankfully they were of the same design. He continued on to the kitchen, where his mother stood over the beat up counter with a hand-crank can opener and a can of corn. Dale looked so much like his mother and always worried that he would develop the same tired, worn out expression she always seemed to have since his father had passed on from a heart attack four years ago. Bending slightly, he gave his mother a hug and a kiss on the cheek.

"I think Sarah and Frank are fighting," his mother said, then rolled her eyes. "She says he's working, but I don't know."

"Where are the kids?"

"In the backyard. Ed's running around and Laura's moping. She's got the curse, or so it seems. You can never tell with teenagers. Fifteen was a hard age for me, too." She attached the can of corn to the opener and began to crank.

"Mom, let me do that."

"No," she said, moving away from Dale. "Go say hello to Ed and Laura, they've been asking for you."

Dale pulled the bottle of Sauvignon Blanc from the bag and opened the refrigerator. He tucked the bottle between two plastic storage containers. On the top shelf there was a bowl of yellow Jello with fruit suspended inside that made him want to retch.

"When is Sarah due?" Dale asked.

"Next month. I don't want her drinking."

"I think she knows better."

Mrs. Pagnali turned and gave Dale the cold, angry stare that let him know she knew better than to believe him. Knowing that look very well, Dale went out the kitchen door that led to the backyard.

Swinging on the old metal swings was Ed, eight years old, playfully kicking his little legs out as he swung up, then tucking them under as he pulled back. His short blond hair was a reminder that he was not a Pagnali, but a McDougle instead. "Uncle Dale!" Ed yelled as he swung up, then jumped off the swing and landed with a thump on the ground. After getting up and dusting off the knees of his dirty jeans, Ed ran up to Dale and gave his legs a hug.

Dale pulled the boy off him and took a good look at his dirty face, which looked more like his father's with every passing year. Was that chocolate around his mouth? Dale fought the urge to drag Ed into the bathroom and wash his hands and face. He knew Sarah hadn't bothered to bring the boy a change of clothes, so he would have to eat dinner in the dirty rags he had on. "What in the world have you been doing?"

"Playing," Ed said, his face aglow. "Did you like my jump?"

"Amazing!" Dale saw Laura sitting in a green plastic chair against the back of the house. "Why don't you go and swing while I talk to your sister."

"Will you swing with me?"

"Maybe later," Dale said, then watched the boy run to the swings and jump on the same one he'd been on before. Dale waved and watched as he started to swing. He walked up to Laura and pulled the empty matching chair closer to her before taking a seat. Laura's dark hair was tied back in a pony tail, a style that complimented her high cheek bones. She looked up at him and smiled. She was pretty, even with the three small blemishes on her chin.

"Hi, Uncle Dale," she said, then gave him a kiss on the cheek.

"What's up?" Dale asked.

"Nothing."

Dale looked out at the yard and recalled a time when the grass had been greener. "I used to chase your mother around here when we were kids," Dale said, almost able to hear Sarah's youthful screams and giggles as he looked around. "She laughed a lot back then."

Laura turned towards Dale and raised her eyebrows. "She laughed?"

"She still has it in her, somewhere."

"I always thought she had that part of her killed off."

Dale grinned, then slowly nodded. "What about you?"

"What about me?"

"What's with the sour look?"

"Let's not get into it, Uncle Dale." Laura leaned back in her chair and let out a huff.

"Sure," Dale said, "we don't have to talk about it." But that didn't mean he couldn't change her mood. If he had to grin so did Laura. Dale leaned back and started humming "Like a Virgin."

Laura sat up and stared at him as if he was crazy. "'Like a Virgin?' Is that supposed to mean something?"

"I like Madonna."

"I know that."

Dale continued to hum, bobbing his head with the rhythm. "I refuse to be in a bad mood on Thanksgiving."

"Are you stoned?"

"No, close your eyes and give in to it."

"What?"

"Close them."

Laura did, then Dale leaned in close and started to do wop the tune in her ear. Soon Laura had a grin and her head started moving with the tune. Dale stood up and started to do a little dance as he sang the first line of the song and motioned for Laura to join him.

Laura giggled, then shook her head as Dale went back to do wopping the rest of the lyrics. He did a little shimmy in front of her.

"Hey, wait for me!" Ed ran up to Dale and began mimicking his movements, then started humming along. Throwing up his arms, he began to sing along.

Laura burst out laughing as Dale and Ed continued dancing and singing. Dale put out his hands and motioned for Laura to join them.

"Come on," Ed pleaded. "It's fun!"

Laura stood up and danced next to Ed as the three of them continued to sing the rest of the song.

—

Ian and Iris had arrived at his parents' house before anyone else, which Ian felt gave them the option to duck out first. The last thing Ian wanted to do was spend all day there. He'd known his father would not like Iris, although he wouldn't make his feelings known to her. All day Ian had been dreading having to listen to his father say how a man's role was to take care of the house and keep his wife in control. Ian had been in college the last time he'd brought a girl home. Her name was Cynthia. Ian hadn't intended to bring her with him, but Cynthia had caught him as he was about to drive off and had invited herself along. While talking to Ian's father, Cynthia had made a big thing about how she was majoring in Political Science and hoped to make it to Washington. Ian had gotten quite the talk from his father once the two of them had been alone. There was no way Ian could explain to his father that Cynthia was a little slut who was game for anything when it came to sex and that had been why he'd dated her. His father hadn't been pleased with Cynthia, so Ian had dumped her the following day.

Now he was in the backyard with his father, taking in the fresh air. Outside was warm for fall. Brown leaves littered the backyard, waiting to be raked up once his father had a chance to get to it. Iris was in the kitchen talking to his mother, who wanted to show off her kitchen and the best way to cook a turkey, since Iris had confessed to not being the best cook. His father hadn't seemed pleased to hear it either. Ian figured he could use his parents' dissatisfaction with her as an excuse when the time came to dump her. Once Michelle came through.

"I suppose you take her out to eat a lot," Ian's father said, slowly shaking his head. "I don't trust a girl who can't cook. Never did."

"I'm not planning on marrying her, Dad," Ian said.

"Really?" Ian's father gave him a sideways glare. "Then why the hell did you bring her?"

"She wanted to meet my parents," Ian said.

"She nagged and you gave in. Big mistake," his father said. "A career girl, if you can call choosing furniture a career. She's too self assured."

Ian looked back and saw Iris in profile in the kitchen window. She was saying something to his mother, who wasn't visible. "I'm not going to marry her."

"But you gave in to this, so she'll expect you to give in if she nags you enough about marriage."

"It won't happen."

"I just hope she doesn't start talking to your sister. All I need is for her head to get full of that feminist crap. It's bad enough she's not married yet. Thankfully she has a boyfriend, so we know the dykes at that fancy school she insists on going to didn't get to her."

—

"It smells nice in here," Gabrielle said as she tossed off her jacket and threw it on the bed in Jay's room. She'd recently cut her red hair short and started wearing more slacks and pull over tops. Jay still couldn't get used to seeing her new look, but if she wanted to butch it up to get a date it was her choice. So far it wasn't working for her.

Tom was in the kitchen, unpacking the box of liquor he'd brought along and lining up the bottles on the kitchen counter next to the sink. "Gabrielle, what are you drinking today?" He grabbed a bottle of Kettle One vodka and moved his long, slender arm away from him so the bottle was visible to all. "Only the best."

"I'm an Absolut girl myself, but if you have orange juice I won't complain," Gabrielle said.

"If you're going to drink, then please eat a little something," Jay said as he pulled the oven door open and peered inside. The stupid little spike hadn't popped yet and he was hoping the bird wouldn't burn.

The sound of the toilet flushing came from the bathroom, then the bathroom door opened. Out walked Vera in her sexy leather pants and spiked shoes, both of which matched the black sheen of her hair. Her tight purple top showed off her big tits and didn't hide the fact that her nipples were hard. "Have we met?" Vera said in her thick German accent. She held her hand out to Gabrielle and introduced herself before turning to Tom. "Do you have Tanqueray or Bombay Sapphire?"

"For gin, only Tanqueray," Tom said. "If only someone had martini glasses."

"Put it with tonic," Vera said.

Jay playfully glared at Tom. "Nor do I have green olives."

"Heathen," Tom hissed. "And if you could please bend your knees when you check on the dead bird it would be appreciated. I'm sick of looking at your ass."

"And I was hoping you would kiss it," Jay said.

"I don't rim," Tom said, then held out the highball glass he'd filled. "Gin and tonic."

Vera wrapped her fingers around the glass then took a sip. "Wonderful."

The doorbell rang and Jay made a mad dash to answer it. It was Allan and Mark holding out metal pans. "The bird is still cooking," Jay said.

Mark walked in first and gave Jay a kiss on the cheek. "That's okay." Allan stepped inside and gave Jay a light peck on the lips.

"And what did we bring," Tom asked from the kitchen as Allan and Mark stepped inside, followed by Jay.

"Squash and yams," Mark said. "Jay, where do we put our coats?"

"The bedroom," Gabrielle said.

The oven door creaked as Jay opened it again and gawked inside. The little plastic thing still hadn't popped. He hoped it wasn't broken. There wasn't any noticeable defect, not that he would even know what to look for.

"What are you studying?" Vera asked.

"Boys, would you like a cocktail?" Tom asked.

"What do you have?" Allan asked.

Jay hoped the bird wasn't going to dry out.

"Geology? How interesting," Vera said.

"I can make anything," Tom said.

"Really?"

The doorbell rang again. Making his way to the door, Jay hoped it was someone from the Butterball help line ready to give him a clue about cooking a turkey. Instead it was Alma's round, latina face, her lips and nails a deep red as she held out a cherry cheesecake. "It's the only cherry I'll ever find," she said in a thick French accent that had thrown Jay for a loop when he'd first met her, then he learned that she'd grown up in Paris.

"Come in," Jay said.

Everyone in the kitchen was laughing, or so it seemed

"Why, Jay, you look stressed out," Alma said. "And I thought you had a date last night."

"I'll be better once we eat," Jay said.

"Darling, it's only Thanksgiving," Alma said. The heels of her black pumps clicked against the floor as she made her way inside.

"Alma!" Vera said, then reached out and gave her a hug.

"Jay, when should we start heating up the vegetables?" Allan asked.

"Once the bird is ready," Jay said, wondering if the damn bird would ever be ready.

"What, no ice?" Alma said.

"No glasses," Tom said.

Jay went back to the stove and looked in on the bird.

"Then use a highball glass, I don't have to be chic around you people," Alma said.

The plastic stick wasn't up. The bird was browning, though. Jay closed the door and took in a breath. Tom would have everyone trashed by the time the bird was done. The pans Allan and Mark brought, along with a pecan pie, a pumpkin pie and a cherry cheese cake were all on the kitchen table. If only the turkey would finish cooking. Was there a turkey recall he didn't know about?

"Darling, please, I left my Valium at home," Alma said as she rubbed Jay's back. "Perhaps a drink will help."

"I don't need a drink," Jay said.

"Then come into the other room and tell Alma what's wrong."

"It won't pop up," Jay said.

Tom gasped.

Alma's eyes darted from Jay's crotch to his frantic gaze. "*Mon Dieu.*"

"The bird!" Jay said.

"But of course." Alma slowly pulled Jay close to her and gave him a hug. "It is only a bird, darling."

As comforting as the hug was, Jay still couldn't help feeling like he was going to ruin everything. If he'd begun cooking earlier Tom wouldn't have had time to get everyone plastered before dinner.

Vera went over to the stove and pulled the door open. "I know I'm just a dyke, but it looks like a boner to me."

Both Jay and Alma looked inside. The yellow stick had popped up! Jay had acted like a fool for nothing, perhaps he did need a drink. He turned towards Tom.

"Name your poison," Tom said.

———

Iris sat next to Ian at the dinner table, and across from Ian's sister, Donna. Donna would look so much better with a little make-up and softer colors, Iris thought. That deep purple blouse only made her look pale and did nothing for her eyes. Her long hair looked as if it had seen one too many cheap perms. Appearances meant so much, which only made Iris feel more guilty for what she'd done with Andrew. Ian squeezed her knee then smiled as his father carved the turkey. This was not like Thanksgiving at her parents' house, which had always been a reason to invite everyone in the family who cared to join them.

"Everything looks so delicious," Iris said, trying not to look around too much. All the furniture was too big for the room, especially the cheaply done imitation Victorian hutch across from her, which seemed to eat up the wall and was dangerously close to the back of Donna's chair. One forceful glide back and the chair and hutch would collide.

"Wait until you settle down and have a family of your own," Ian's mother said.

Iris smiled. She wasn't sure she wanted a family, at least not yet. She wanted to concentrate on her career first, but she knew that would be the wrong thing to say. Ian's father sat there, looking as if he was just waiting for her to say the wrong thing to pounce on her. Lately she'd been thinking about Andrew, despite how much she tried not to.

"I can't wait for my little girl to grow up and have some

babies," Ian's father said. Donna looked as if she was ready to kill him but chose to grin instead.

"Could you lift your plate a little, Iris," Ian's father said.

"Ian says you have your own business," Donna said to Iris. "You're an interior designer."

"Until you get married, of course," Ian's father said.

"My mother would kill me if I gave up my career," Iris said. It was the first time Donna had genuinely smiled.

"I wouldn't call choosing wall color a career," his father said.

Ian's mother held out a dish of corn. "Have some vegetables."

"I see it as more of a hobby," Ian's father said.

Try as she might, Iris couldn't hold herself back. "My work was mentioned in Architectural Design magazine a few months ago. That one article helped me land a contract with a major law firm in Providence."

"Which firm?" Donna asked, her eyes wide with excitement.

"Tyler, Westcott and Allen," Iris said.

"I've never heard of them," Ian's father said.

Donna glared at her father. "I think that's because we don't live in Providence."

"It's a small, local firm," Ian said as he gave Iris's knee a squeeze.

It was the first time Ian hadn't been supportive, and Iris was a bit surprised that he would let his father influence his judgment. "It's actually a pretty large firm," she said. "Probably the largest in Providence."

Ian's father let out a chuckle. "It's not like Providence is some big city, like New York."

"Donna, could you hand me your plate," Ian's mother said. "The stuffing is a new recipe I got from *Food and Wine* magazine. It sounded so good I couldn't resist trying it."

Ian patted Iris's knee. Across from her Donna seemed eager for an all out fight between her father and Iris.

"Sometimes I don't know what I would do without *Food and Wine* magazine," Ian's mother continued. "Iris, you really should get a subscription."

Iris smiled politely. A subscription to *Food and Wine* for a woman who didn't cook made little sense.

—

The turkey had come out a little dry, although nobody seemed to care. Tom had gotten everyone pretty toasted on wine during the meal, and now all anyone wanted to do was tell stories about dates past and present. Alma's story about how she'd fucked a brother and sister in one night, but not at the same time, was by far the best. She'd been in high school and had slept over her girlfriend's house – the parents knew nothing about their daughter's lesbian tendencies, nor did the brother — and was caught sneaking to the bathroom to take a piss. The brother, as it turned out, was waiting for her to exit the bathroom to make his move. Alma had told the story with such fervor that by the time she'd finished everyone had felt slightly inadequate.

Alma slipped the last of the pecan pie on her plate into her mouth as Jay told them the final scene of his date with Erik. "I can't believe you didn't ask him in. Darling, what were you thinking."

"I didn't want him to think I'm easy," Jay said.

"Honey, you are the least easy gay man on this planet," Tom said.

"At least he's had sex within the last seven days," Gabrielle said as she slipped her arm along the back of Vera's chair.

Tom sat up straight and raised his head high. "Didn't anyone notice my freshly fucked look?"

"I thought you had hemorrhoids," Mark said.

"Either that or a butt plug," Alan said.

"Tom, darling, can you make me a martini. I am so over this wine," Alma said, waving her fingers over the half drunk glass in front of her.

Tom stood and began mixing Alma a drink. "It isn't anything like Alma's delightful story, but he's hot. I've never had an older man before."

"How much older," Vera asked.

"Fifty-two."

Allan looked as if his eyes were going to pop out of his head. "Fifty-two!"

"Do you call him daddy?" Mark asked.

Tom stirred Alma's drink before draining it into a high ball glass. "And he spanks me when I'm naughty."

"Please don't tell me you wear adult diapers, too," Mark said.

"No, you heathen," Tom said as he handed Alma her drink. "I've never been anyone's little boy before. I kind of like it."

The doorbell rang, and everyone stopped talking. Jay wasn't expecting anyone else. Steve wouldn't be home yet, nor would he ring the doorbell. He got up and answered it to find Erik standing there with a bouquet of wild flowers. Holding them out, Erik said, "I bought them yesterday, hopefully they're not too wilted."

"I don't believe you," Jay said as he took the flowers and gave Erik a gentle kiss on the lips. "Come in and meet everyone."

Jay made introductions all around as he went to the cupboard and found the vase Steve had used when Dale had bought him flowers. He filled the vase with water and dropped the flowers inside. Behind him the room was abuzz with questions for Erik. Jay was pleased that his friends had taken to keeping Erik busy while he arranged the flowers, taking in the vibrant yellow and purple petals with lush green leaves rising up here and there for added color. Nobody had ever bought him flowers before. He couldn't wait to tell his mother, who feared he would remain alone for rest of his life. Holding out the bouquet, Jay turned and placed it in the middle of the table.

"Oh darling, they're beautiful."

"Why didn't you come by earlier," Vera said.

Mark winked at Jay as Allan raised his eyebrows and grinned.

"The only flower I ever got was a corsage on prom night," Gabrielle said. "Sad to say, but the corsage was the best thing that night."

"Gabrielle, that makes me so teary," Tom said, then turned to Erik. "Would you like a drink?"

———

The car was silent as Dale took the long way home, driving along Allens Avenue, past apartment houses that landlords didn't keep up and shady store fronts. The setting sun didn't help cheer him up any. He considered driving through downtown, but chose not to bother. Seeing the vacant city streets would be more depressing than going home with nothing to look forward to. He stopped at a red light and rubbed his thumbs against the steering wheel. The mall was probably closed, along with every store he would want to visit. Maybe there was a convenience store on the way? He could pick up some egg nog or orange juice or something. He wasn't in the mood for anything sweet, but maybe his mood would change.

—

Steve was almost in Providence as the sun began to set. He'd escaped his parents' place early with the excuse that he had to study, which seemed to worry his mother a little. His father had been pleased to hear that Steve was taking school so seriously. He grabbed his cell phone and dialed Dale's number again. Still no answer, only the stupid machine. How much time was Dale going to spend with his family? In the past he'd never stayed any longer than needed. He tossed the phone on the passenger seat, watching it bounce from the corner of his eye. In front of him highway stretched out, with cars speeding past. He was doing seventy miles per hour, so he pressed his foot on the accelerator and sped up to eighty. Dale had to be home by the time he got there.

—

"They're from a different generation," Ian said as he steered the car down the expanse of highway. "He didn't mean anything by it."

Iris looked out her window, watching the driver of the VW Jetta next to them toss his cell phone into the passenger seat and mumble to himself. Maybe Ian was right? She could just be overreacting. But why hadn't Ian at least tried to stick up to his father for her? It had almost been like a small part of the Ian she knew and loved had melted away. Donna had seemed more ready to stick up for her than Ian. She watched as the VW Jetta sped up and disappeared on the highway.

"Come on, baby," Ian said as he rubbed her shoulder. "Don't take it to heart. I know you're successful."

"It isn't that, Ian."

Ian sighed, but kept his voice calm. "He's my father, what can

I say?"

"How about all the stuff you tell me," Iris said. "That I can keep my career if we get married, and that more women should be independent."

"Is this really worth getting into an argument over?" Ian said. "You know how I feel. My father wouldn't understand. What, are you suddenly on some type of big crusade?"

"Ian, this is about you not sticking up for me."

Ian turned towards her. "Is it?"

"Yes," she said, although she was beginning to wonder if perhaps she wanted to be angry with him to hide her guilt about having had sex with Andrew. The Providence Place Mall was on the left, looming above the highway. Soon they would be taking the exit for Route 195.

"You're moping," Ian said.

"Let's not talk about this anymore," she said, leaning back in the seat. If Ian had stuck up for her, they wouldn't be having this argument. She had to admit that Ian's father wasn't the easiest man to deal with, and that perhaps Ian was right about not making too much out of it. Ian wasn't a bad guy, even if he couldn't stand up to his father. She had to allow him that one fault, he was only human after all. At least he never cheated on her, like she had done to him.

"If you want I can just stay at my place tonight," Ian said. "It will give you time to cool off."

"No, stay with me tonight," Iris said. "It'll be fine."

—

There weren't any cop cars visible on Blackstone Boulevard, but still Dale drove at a steady twenty-five miles per hour. People were jogging along the grassy path in the middle of the boulevard as if it was just any other day. Didn't these people ever take a day off? The plastic bag from the convenience store was on the passenger seat. Buying egg nog and orange juice didn't have the same effect as finding the perfect shirt to go with some slacks, then having to go elsewhere for shoes. Plus the guy behind the counter of the convenience store was not as hot as the boys at Abercrombie and Fitch.

There was a blue Saturn station wagon parked in front of the condominiums. Wasn't that what Bob drove? Someone was standing out front. It looked like Bob. Dale let out a playful giggle then sped up a little, turned the corner, then drove into the parking lot behind the building. For once he was not going to go in from the back. He was going to greet Bob out front. In his haste to get out of the car he almost forgot his groceries. Don't run, he told himself. Don't even skip. But he couldn't help walking a little faster than normal, at least until he reached the front of the building. He acted surprised to see Bob. "I didn't know you were here."

"I didn't tell you I was coming," Bob said. "It was a spur of the moment kind of thing."

"Sometimes those are the best," Dale said. "Come inside."

The two men walked into the hall, then up the stairs to the second floor landing to where Dale's condominium was. "How was your holiday?" Dale asked as he unlocked the door.

"Good, I saw my family. My ex-wife dropped in to visit my parents, and see how I was doing." Bob followed Dale inside and looked around. "Nice place."

"It's simple, but it's home," Dale said, turning to give Bob a friendly, coy grin. He put out his hand. "Can I take your coat?"

Bob took off his coat, which looked like something straight men wear to go hunting. If he was to guess he would say Bob had bought it at Macy's. The rest of his wardrobe was pure Gap, simple and classic.

"Feel free to put on some music while I hang our coats. I have the new Madonna if you haven't heard it yet." Dale made his way to the hall.

"I didn't know she had a new album," Bob said.

Dale stopped in his tracks and turned towards Bob. "Do you live in a cave?"

"I work a lot," Bob said.

"I guess so. Why don't you just go over to the stereo and put it on. Go on!" And with that he resumed his pace down the hall to the coat closet on the left. Every radio station in the world was playing Madonna's new song and Bob didn't know she had a new

CD out. He had to be straight. But if he was straight then what exactly was he doing visiting him? Was his life that dull? The CD started playing and Dale couldn't help but tap his foot to the joyous music. He closed the closet door then walked in time with the joyous sound. When he was in arms length to Bob, he asked, "How do you like it?"

Bob nodded, smiling as he watched Dale slowly move his hips to the music. "It's good."

"Do you dance?" Dale sang along with the CD.

"Not really," Bob said. "I haven't been out since the divorce."

"Just move a little," Dale said, then felt Bob's big hands on his sides, the left one sliding around to the small of his back, where his ass began to curve out. Dale stopped moving and his eyes locked with Bob's. There were two options open to Dale now, faint or kiss him. Dale chose the kiss, fainting was just too dramatic. Bob met Dale's kiss with equal force. Their lips parted, then Dale felt Bob's tongue push into his mouth, sliding over his own tongue. Bob's right hand slid up and held the back of Dale's neck. Their lips parted.

"Are you okay?" Bob asked.

Dale smiled. "I couldn't be better."

———

Steve drove past Dale's condominium just in time to see Dale walking inside with another guy. He slowed down and studied the two of them, then pulled over to the side of the road. As the car idled, he waited for the lights to come on in Dale's condominium. He watched the two silhouettes as one handed the other, whom he assumed to be Dale, his coat. That guy had to be some new friend of Dale's, not a trick or anything else. Dale couldn't have replaced Steve yet. Not this soon. Dale never went out, so how could he have found anyone who would want to be around him, especially since he was such a queen. Once again there were two people in the window, one of them doing some silly dance. That one had to be Dale. Dale was moving closer to the guy. The other guy put his arms around Dale.

Steve hit his steering wheel. How could Dale replace him so fast like that? Then he noticed the blue Saturn wagon parked out front. Wasn't that the same car that had been parked in front of the salon? He revved the engine, then sped down the street, not paying attention to where he was going. He could not believe Dale had replaced him with that asshole. He hit the steering wheel again. How could he have let this happen? Who did Dale think he was, some great lover? Sure, what a joke. The light up ahead turned yellow, if he sped up he could make it. The engine revved, and he booked through the intersection.

"Fuck you," he mumbled. Dale, that little queen. He would see soon enough that he'd made a mistake. Fags didn't fall in love the way Dale thought. If they did they wouldn't spend so much time looking for meaningless fucks. They wouldn't lie and cheat on each other if they were in love. Dale didn't know how good he'd had it with Steve. Wait until everything around him came down, then Dale would know what a good guy Steve was. Hadn't Steve told him before what a good guy he was? Like that homo Dale had with him was better than Steve. He would probably do nothing but fuck every cheap little faggot on the East Side, if not the entire state. Dale would realize his big mistake and come running back to him. Maybe Steve would take him back, maybe not. It would all depend on his mood.

Dale's salon was up ahead. He drove past it, then parked around the block and got out. There was a rock on the sidewalk and he picked it up. He would give Dale something to think about. There was an alley between Dale's salon and a row of shops next to it. Steve knew it led to the rear of the store, where there was a window that led to the room where all the faggy hairdressers washed the customers' hair. He gripped the rock. This would give Dale something to think about.

—

Jay was happy to finally have time alone with Erik. He played with Erik's hairy balls as he rested his head on his chest. It felt so good to have Erik's warm body close to his. "I'm so glad you dropped in," he said.

Erik gave Jay a little squeeze. "So am I."

"Want to spend the night?"

"I was hoping you would ask."

The front door opened, then there were footsteps. "Steve?" Jay called out as he pulled the sheets over their naked bodies.

"I'm home," Steve said. He peered into Jay's bedroom. "Didn't know you had company."

"This is Erik," Jay said.

Steve waved. "How did it go?"

"We had a great time," Jay said. "Did you see the flowers on the table?"

Steve nodded, then pushed his hands into his pants pockets. "They're beautiful."

Steve seemed to have a slight edge to him, like something had gone wrong. "How was your Thanksgiving?" Jay asked.

Steve rolled his eyes. "Tiring. The same thing year after year. I should have stayed here." He turned on the balls of his feet and walked to the doorway where he paused and shook his head. He turned and looked at Jay and Erik, then walked out and closed the door.

Jay thought there was something sad about the way Steve was acting, and wondered if he'd talked to Dale. He wished there was something he could do, but knew better than to meddle in other people's business. It was too bad, but Steve would get over it. He was resilient.

Erik kissed the top of Jay's head. "Everything okay?"

"I was just thinking about Steve," Jay said. "He just got dumped by his boyfriend."

"That sucks."

"I know," Jay said. "And Steve's such a nice guy. I don't understand it, and I doubt Steve does either."

"He must know why the guy broke up with him," Erik said. "It would be rude to hold back that type of information at a time like that. Actually, it's not right to hold back anything from someone you're dating."

Jay turned, then wrapped his right arm around Erik's chest. He let out a sigh. What would Erik do if he found out the truth about Jay? He had to tell him how old he really was and that he was only going for his BA. Not now, though. The timing was wrong, and it would look like he was holding back information. But how long could he wait? "Let's talk about something else. I feel like we're gossiping."

Erik gently rubbed his open palm over Jay's upper back. "Who said we have to talk?"

"What do you have in mind?"

"Give me a kiss and find out."

Jay turned to look into Erik's eyes. It was as if Jay was the luckiest man in the world, but only as long as he was able to keep his age a secret.

"Stop thinking about Steve. He'll find someone," Erik said as he firmly held onto Jay's torso, then slowly tossed Jay onto his back.

"Hey, what are you doing?" Jay called out, half laughing.

Erik knelt on the bed, puffed out his chest and flexed his biceps. "You are my man, and I'm going to kiss you!" Then he lunged at Jay and gently kissed him.

—

Dale was on his knees sucking Bob's cock in the living room when the telephone rang. It couldn't be that important, he would let the machine pick up. Grabbing the base of Bob's shaft, he continued to suck. Then the machine picked up and he heard the rugged voice of the Providence police officer telling him that something had happened at the salon. That was when Dale stopped what he was doing and lunged for the telephone.

Friday

Iris's heels tapped amongst the sound of splintering wood as she walked through Dolores's house. The workmen had already begun removing the frames from the windows in the living room. The fireplace mantle was next to go, then the walls would get painted and the new frames and mantle would go up. As she had hoped, once Dolores got started she was easy to please, and the rest of the house seemed to come together. Now the real magic was happening. The dining room wasn't going to be touched, except for new window casings and the walls were going to be painted. In the kitchen the counters were being torn off to be replaced with slabs of marble. The island was also being rebuilt with a stove and grill in the center.

The crew hardly noticed Iris as she walked through the house; they'd seen her through a few projects before and she trusted this one contractor and used him often. She'd even recognized a few of the men. She'd make sure to get them something for the upcoming holiday since they'd more than likely be winding down just before Christmas.

Stepping out of the kitchen, Iris found herself back in the main entrance hall, standing in front of the door flanked by long, narrow windows. The wide staircase gently curved up to the second floor where the den, master bedroom, and two guestrooms waited to be torn apart and reborn. As she was halfway up the stairs, her cell phone chimed. It was Dolores asking her to come to a party that Saturday.

"I know this is such short notice, but there isn't a single thing of interest going on this weekend. Plus it's only a simple thing, so nobody should feel put out," Dolores said. "Cocktails and hors d'oeuvres. Casual, but not too casual. It's been so long since I've put anything like this together that it's exciting. My chef thinks I'm nuts. He's scrambling about, putting a menu together. It feels like it did when Timothy and I were first married. Oh Iris, working with you on the new house has made me festive again." Dolores sounded almost giddy, which made Iris wonder which prescriptions she'd taken before her call.

She and Ian didn't have any plans for Saturday, at least none that she was aware of, so she agreed. It would be just the right way to shake off the horrible time she'd had at Ian's parents' house.

—

Everything was going so well, then some stupid vandal had to go and throw a rock at the salon and break a window. It was probably some drugged up kid looking for something to do. The cops who had met Dale at the salon were nice, but nothing like the cops in porn movies. For once Dale would like to get stopped by some hunk of a man in uniform. Dale leaned forward and thumbed through the magazines fanned out on the coffee table in the waiting area of the salon. Hopefully the guys putting in the new window wouldn't make a mess. He'd be concerned about his stock but it was more than evident that those two straight guys didn't care about shampoo or any other kind of hair products. Nor did they care about looking good. Dale wondered if their beige uniforms had been soiled before they'd put them on or if they'd put them on then rolled around in dirt.

Bob had been so nice helping him board up the window. Dale wouldn't have known the least thing to do if it hadn't been for him. He wasn't sure if Steve would have been so nice. But then again, would Steve have had a piece of plywood available and known how to board up the window? Dale had to be fair, Steve wasn't a bad guy. He'd never treated Dale poorly, or been outright mean to him. In fact, he would have been happy if it had worked out. If only Steve had been able to get off. Dale couldn't imagine how horrible it must be not to have an orgasm. The very thought of it was horrifying. At least Bob didn't have any problems getting off, that was for sure. If anything he was the opposite sort, which was a delight after dating someone whose gun was never ready to shoot.

Dale thought about asking Bob to go with him to Dolores's party. At first he wasn't going to go, but Kyle and Trent had pleaded with him to go so he'd given in. It was short notice, hopefully Bob didn't already have plans. Dolores had said dress was casual, which in her circle must mean tie no jacket. Dale hated wearing ties, they were always so restricting, like a dog collar. Since it wasn't going to be catered he wondered what the food would be like. Hopefully she had decent cooks. She was rich enough to afford a good staff, or so Dale assumed.

"We're all set," one of the two window installers said, thrusting a paper and pen in front of him. Dale studied the guy's dirty fingers and bit his tongue. Offering a manicure to a man who didn't even bother cleaning under his nails would be useless. Instead he took the sheet, which listed the window and installation prices.

"We just need you to sign," one of the men said.

Dale took the pen in hand and scribbled his name on the line. "Can you send me a bill?" Dale asked.

"No problem," the guy said, then his friend joined him and the two left as Steve peeked inside and said hello.

"Come on in," Dale said, looking Steve over. He was still hot as ever. "What's up?"

Steve looked around. "I thought you would be closed today."

"We are," Dale said. "Some kids broke a window last night, so here I am. It's fixed now."

"You look good." Steve reached out and rubbed the tips of his fingers against Dale's stomach. "Still working out."

It was the same as before, which brought a smile to Dale's face. "It hasn't been that long since you dumped me."

Steve stepped back, folded his arms, bounced a little on the balls of his feet. "New computer, nice. When did you decide to get that?"

"Last week," Dale said, curious about Steve's reason for being there. He told himself not to get bitchy, despite the fact that he was entitled to it. He was the one who had been dumped.

"Do you have time for a coffee?" Steve asked.

"Is that why you came here?" Dale asked, taking a good look at Steve and noticing that slightly frantic look in his eyes.

"I saw your car parked out front, so I came in." Steve stepped up to Dale and gently rubbed his upper arm. "I miss you."

That was all Dale needed to hear. He missed him, how nice. Stepping back, Dale crossed his arms. "I don't have time for coffee."

"You don't miss me?"

"I don't want to be played, Steve."

"Dale, this is me. I've never played you." Steve's eyes grew wide and needy. "Why are you saying that? Don't you miss me?"

It couldn't be true, Dale thought. There had to be something more going on. "Are you asking me to get back with you?"

"I miss you, Dale."

Drama was the last thing Dale needed after having to replace a window. He believed Steve missed him, and that he wanted him back. But what would that mean, a relationship that was dead in the sack? Sex wasn't everything, but it was necessary. Hadn't Steve been right when he'd said that they weren't meant for each other? He did care about Steve. At one point he would have even said he loved him. He did love him.

"You don't even want to try?" Steve asked.

"We can't talk about this right now," Dale said.

"I don't believe this."

Dale tried to compose himself. He needed a clear head before going to the mall to find just the right tie to wear to Dolores's party. He did not need to think about Steve, who had dumped him. It wasn't the other way around. Madonna would never deal with this type of drama before shopping. Madonna would put her foot down and let her needs be known. Nobody fucked with Madonna or played with her emotions.

"Come on, Dale."

Dale looked directly into Steve's deep brown eyes. "You have to go."

"Dale, you don't mean that."

"Please leave."

Steve slowly walked to the door, opened it, then took a step outside before turning towards Dale. "I love you," he said before closing the door.

Dale stood there looking at the closed door. If Steve had said that earlier he would have gladly taken him back. Not now. Not after Bob had made it clear that he could meet someone nice who could please him both ways. Granted, he'd only just met Bob, but he'd been so nice to him. There was a small part of Dale that still wanted to cook for Steve. Take care of him just a little. Hold him and be held. But it couldn't be. Dale's eyes became moist with tears and he wiped them away. Madonna wouldn't cry. He wasn't going to cry either, or so he told himself before sitting down on the steps and sobbing.

—

The front door was thrown open, then slammed shut as Jay sat at the kitchen table reading a copy of *Vile Bodies*, which he'd saved for when he had a few days free. The book would also take his mind away from thoughts of telling Erik the truth about his age. It was obvious that the longer he waited the worse it would sound when he did tell him the truth. Would Erik make an exception on his "no twinks" rule? Hopefully he would, but Jay didn't think so.

Jay opened the book, turned to the first page as the front door slammed open. Then someone was stomping through the living room, into the kitchen. It was Steve, who turned to look at Jay briefly before disappearing into his bedroom. Jay hoped something hadn't happened between him and Dale. Didn't Dale know how much Steve cared about him? Wasn't it obvious?

After putting the book down on the table, Jay went over to Steve's bedroom door and knocked gently. "Is everything okay?"

"I'm fine," Steve said, his voice strong and raw. "Come on in if you want."

Jay opened the door and moved into the deeply shadowed

room to find Steve lying on the bed with a pillow covering his eyes and the bridge of his nose. Poor Steve. He was feeling so bad and there was nothing Jay could do to help him out except be there. Perhaps if Steve lifted the shade some natural light would stream into the room and make him feel better. But Jay didn't want to tell Steve what to do, he didn't want to nag him or become bossy. Steve would do things as the time came. This was only a minor setback, he would come back and be his joyful self again. "Do you feel like talking?"

Steve let out a huff then wrapped his arms over the pillow that covered his eyes. "Dale wants nothing to do with me, what more can I say."

"I'm sorry," Jay said. If only he knew what was going through Dale's head. Couldn't Dale see what a great guy Steve was? Didn't he know that Steve would do anything for him?

Steve let out a sigh. "It was his decision."

"He's making a big mistake."

"I know," Steve said, his voice cold and harsh. Jay assumed Steve was trying to be strong and gave it to him. If that's what Steve needed to do, then so be it. He must have been hurt. Jay couldn't imagine how horrible it must be to fall in love with a guy only to have him throw it away at the drop of a hat. He would be bitter if that happened to him. "So, what are you going to do with your day?"

"Wallow in misery, then go out and try to forget," Steve said.

"I'll leave you be," Jay said as he made his way to the door. "I just wanted to check in on you."

———

"I told him Dolores is odd and he still said yes," Dale said to Kyle as the two of them poured through the rack of ties at Nordstrom. He couldn't believe the mall wasn't outrageously busy the day after Thanksgiving. The stores were full, but not mobbed like usual. "I can't believe you talked me into going."

"It's not that bad," Kyle said. "Anyway, you'll be hanging out with some of the wealthiest people in Providence."

Dale held up a tie with abstract sprays of deep red and green. "That should really make me look good to Bob." He decided he didn't like the tie then put it back.

Kyle shook his head as he sorted through the rack. "What's his dick like?"

"What he lacks in length he gains in width."

"Small?"

"Average. Six inches hard."

"At least you won't gag." Kyle held up a tie with small triangles in muted blue, yellow and green that formed lines on a muted cranberry background. "What do you think?"

Dale reached out and felt the quality of the silk against his thumb. "Did I mention that he has big balls."

"Really?"

"Huge." Dale did like the tie. He took it from Kyle and held it under his chin.

"I bet he's a gusher," Kyle said. "Those colors look great on you."

"And quick to blow," Dale said, looking around the store. "I need a mirror."

"Over here," Kyle said, motioning around the corner of the counter.

Dale studied the tie against his skin. He did like those colors. Maybe a new shirt was in order? Something blue. Green would look too much like Christmas. "Do you think a cock ring will help him hold back?"

"I doubt it. They're only good for making your basket stand out as far as I'm concerned. You just need to teach that boy a little self control."

"He said he's always been that way." Dale started walking towards the racks of shirts a few feet away. "I need something else."

"I didn't think you were only going to buy one thing."

"I have to look good for my stud," Dale said.

"Is that all he is to you?"

"Right now, that's all I need," Dale said, although he also thought Bob was sweet and kind. Kyle didn't need to know that, though. His only wanting Bob for sex sounded much more exciting.

—

The room was sparse, with just a bed and a closet for Steve to put his stuff in. Wrapping the white towel around his waist, Steve got ready to go through the halls and find some happy little fag to fuck. All day all he could think of was Dale, and how Dale had told him he didn't want him. Like Dale was some great, well cultured guy. The best thing Dale ever had going for him was Steve, and now he didn't have that. Steve was a good guy, just ask anyone. Hell, ask his roommate, Jay. Jay thought Steve was a great guy. He probably didn't even understand why Dale didn't want Steve. Steve didn't even know why Dale didn't want him. As it was Dale should be happy that a guy like Steve would even want to be around his little pansy ass. Didn't Dale know that it made him look good to hang around Steve? Hanging around Steve probably made him look less like a pansy. Dale never did know what was good for him. Not only that, but Dale didn't know what he was giving up. Soon he would.

Steve tightened the towel around his waist, then felt his hardening shaft. He was ready to go out there now and find some little faggot to fuck. The hallway was dim, but he slowly made his way through. Guys greeted him, most of them old trolls searching for fresh meat. But Steve was looking for just the right guy. That was all he wanted, some pretty little queer with a nice body and mouth. It was easy to find someone who wanted to suck him off, but tonight he was going to be picky.

The showers were up ahead, on the left. He could hear the sound of shower water hitting tile as he approached the entrance. Looking inside, he saw some fat, hairy bald guy rimming some firm assed boy who had his hands up on the chlorine green tiled wall as two other guys sat on a wood bench and looked on. The fags on the bench were probably going to hook up. Nobody else was inside. It didn't matter, Steve had all night. He didn't have to find someone right off the bat. He went over to the bench to the right and took a seat. Sooner or later some little gay boy to his liking would stroll by.

What about that Saturn in front of Dale's condominium? Was that just coincidence? He couldn't have found some stupid fuck to stick it to him already? The idea of Dale sucking some guy's fat cock was unnerving. Steve rubbed his palms on his knees, then looked up. It was a slow night. Hopefully it would get busier. He didn't want to think about Dale. There was no way he had someone. No way. He was going to be sorry he'd passed up the chance to get back with him. Jay had been right when he'd said Dale had made a mistake. He sure had.

Some little fag boy with curly brown hair glanced into the shower, then at Steve and stepped inside. The boy had a tight swimmer's build and an ass that looked firm and round beneath the white terry cloth. He smiled at Steve then walked past him, slowly slipping off the towel and dropping it at Steve's feet. Keeping an eye on the kid's firm ass, Steve picked the towel off the floor without getting up from the bench. "Looks like you dropped something."

"Silly me," the boy said, his voice soft and queeny. "I can be such a klutz sometimes."

"It's fine, especially since you dropped it here." Their eyes met. "You have a great ass."

"So I've been told."

"I have a room," Steve said.

"Really?"

"Yes."

"Then what are we doing here?"

They didn't say a word as they walked to Steve's room, then, once inside, began to kiss. Steve's cock was rock solid from the mere thought of sticking it up that fag's ass. He moved around the guy until his shaft was between the firm mounds of the little fucker's cheeks, then wrapped his arms around him and began to dry hump.

"I want to fuck you," Steve whispered.

"I'd like that."

Of course he would, the little fairy, Steve thought. He pulled back, took his stiff dick in his hand and rubbed the head up and down the fag's crack. "Bend over."

"Put a condom on."

Steve didn't stop rubbing his prick against the guy's ass. "I don't have any."

"They're on the bed," the fag said.

There were two condoms on the bed, along with a couple packets of lubricant. Sure, Steve would use one, but not because the little pansy told him to. No little faggot was going to boss him around. Steve rolled the condom over his prick then resumed his previous position. He didn't wait to slam dunk his prick up the little shit's hole.

"Go slow," the little fairy moaned.

Fuck you, Steve thought as he reached up and planted his right hand on the guy's shoulder. He pulled his shaft back then slammed it back in. The little homo groaned, but didn't protest. Steve tightened his grip on the faggot's shoulder and started fucking him hard. No little queen was going to take control of him. Steve was the one in control. Steve was going to teach this little shit a lesson. He was going to prove once and for all that nobody fucked with him.

Saturday

Michelle wouldn't be back from visiting her parents until Sunday, and now Ian had to go to yet another party with Iris. If she hadn't been so upset that he'd taken his father's side on Thanksgiving he would have told her he didn't want to go and be done with it. But he had to go now just to smooth things over. He hoped Michelle didn't let him down just so he could get Iris off his back. Michelle would be much easier to handle than Iris. At least he wouldn't have to cater to her every party invite and hang out with a bunch of fags talking about interior design, a subject about which he knew and cared nothing. The woman throwing the party tonight wasn't a designer, but one of Iris's clients. Maybe there was a chance of her having a better group of people to talk to. Ian certainly hoped she would as he looked in the mirror and fixed his tie. It was casual, and he was as casual as he could be and still look like a gentleman. Appearances meant more than anything else in the world, or so he'd learned.

The downstairs door opened then closed. It had to be Iris. If only he'd never allowed her to talk him into giving her a key to his house. Maybe his father had been right about Ian allowing her to boss him around. The idea got on his nerves and he had no use for such emotions at the present time. He had a party to go to, which meant he had to appear dapper, charming and likeable.

"Ian, I was thinking that perhaps I should drive since I know where Dolores lives," Iris said as she entered his bedroom.

The hell she would. "And make me look like a kept man," Ian said. "Why don't we take my car. Unless you're too embarrassed to be seen in a Saab." He turned to see Iris looking as beautiful as ever in a burnt orange dress that accented her breasts, waist and wonderful ass.

"Are the pearls too much?" Iris asked as her fingertips drifted over the delicate strand that hung just below her neck.

"Perfect," Ian said, assuming that she didn't care who drove and that was why she hadn't bothered to respond. He checked himself out in the mirror again. He wouldn't bother with a tie clip, he wanted to look as informal as possible.

—

Dale turned into the apartment complex where Bob lived. It was a maze of wood sided boxes with a very seventies look. Didn't Bob make enough money to live in a better place than that? It's not like he had to pay child support. Dale couldn't imagine that Bob thought the complex was anything extravagant. At least he hoped not. It wasn't horrible, though. Just dated. Mid to late 1970s, Dale thought. It reminded him of some tacky swinging singles complex. Bob probably got hit on by every available female living there. Building 5C was coming up on the left. Dale parked next to Bob's Saturn, which happened to be the best car in the lot. Dale shook his head while walking up to Building 5C. Maybe Bob had been in a hurry to find a place?

After being buzzed inside the building, Dale made his way up to the second floor, then down the endless hall until he found Bob's apartment.

"It isn't much," Bob said as he closed the door and gave Dale a kiss.

"It's fine," Dale said, scanning the white walled living room filled with cheap, nondescript furnishings. A Dunkin' Donuts calendar hung on one of the white walls of the small pantry of a kitchen. Bob wore simple beige chinos with a deep blue shirt and tie with just enough color to make him look sharp. At least years of trying to be straight hadn't taken all of Bob's fashion sense away from him, for which Dale was thankful. Dale did not know what he would have done if Bob had shown up in some awful holiday cheer ensemble complete with a smiling Santa tie clip.

Bob slipped his hands inside the flaps of Dale's wool coat and around his waist. "I have to confess that I'm a little nervous."

"Don't be, these people are as boring as everyone else," Dale said before giving Bob a little kiss on the lips. "I worked on my pecs today, can you tell?"

Bob let out a chuckle, then moved his hands up Dale's chest. "You're going to get me horny."

"That's my intention."

"But shouldn't we be going?"

"Nobody arrives on time," Dale said before gently running the tip of his tongue over Bob's lips. "I was hoping to have a little time alone with you before we left."

Bob held Dale tighter as he moved both his hands to his ass. "You're a sex fiend."

"I know," Dale said.

———

Iris glanced at the little smirk on Ian's face when Dolores answered the door in a soft pink dress that would have suited a twenty year old woman. The dress was too low cut, and the hem line too high. The pearl necklace and matching earrings were a nice touch, though. Iris held back the urge to give Ian a kick when she saw him give Dolores the fake smile she knew meant he was silently making fun of her. Didn't he have any manners?

"What a delight this party is becoming," Dolores said as she ushered Iris and Ian inside. "My last party in this old house. I can't wait for the other house to be finished."

"Soon," Iris said.

"Yes. Here, let me take your coats," Dolores said.

After handing Dolores her coat, Iris scanned the crowded room of possible new clients. The room was already somewhat full, and here she'd feared that she and Ian were arriving too early. It didn't seem as if anyone she knew was present.

"I invited Dale Pagnali, I think you know him," Dolores said.

"Is he here?" Iris asked, looking past Dolores's shoulder to scan the crowd of well dressed men and women standing inside and talking.

"Not yet, but I expect him. Kyle told me he was coming," Dolores said. "Most of the people here now are Timothy's friends. Business acquaintances, really. "

"Iris," Andrew called out. Then Iris saw him walking towards them, looking handsome in a simple pair of slacks and an oxford shirt. His tie was a captivating assortment of blues and greens. She shook his hand, then introduced him to Ian.

"I wasn't aware you two knew each other," Dolores said.

Andrew nodded. "She designed the new law offices."

Dolores's eyes grew wide. "Iris, I'm impressed."

"It's nothing, really," Iris said, pleased to have a reason not to look at Andrew. She feared a blush might rise to her cheeks and her legs already felt weak. Thankfully Ian had put his arm around her waist.

"Well now, I'm going to put your coats in the master bedroom. When I come down, I don't want to see the three of you spending any more time together. I want you mingling," Dolores said.

"We mingle very well," Ian said, flashing a smile at Dolores.

Dolores looked Ian up and down, then said, "Yes, I'm sure you do." She walked towards the staircase, then stopped and turned back towards Ian and put out her hand. "Andrew and Iris know the house, but you've never seen it. Let me show it to you. This just might be the last time I get a chance to show it again."

"I would love to see it, " Ian said. He turned and gave Iris a kiss on the cheek, then shook hands with Andrew. "I'll be back."

"The new place is so much better than this," Dolores said, then shooed Andrew and Iris away. "Go and be sociable. I'll take good care of Ian."

"I love that woman," Andrew said as he walked towards the living room with Iris. "I'm Timothy's attorney."

"Her husband?"

"Have you met him?"

"Not yet," Iris said, looking into Andrew's deep brown eyes. She couldn't help but recall how nice his lips had felt pressed against hers. And the feel of him. She stepped back. "I've heard so much about him, though."

"He's a great guy," Andrew said, then moved close to her as if about to tell a secret. "He practically worships Dolores. Do you know how he proposed to her?"

"No."

Andrew turned towards Iris, then, keeping his voice low, said, "He took her out to dinner at Cappricio's, then had a man play the violin at their table while he went down on one knee and proposed. Right there in the middle of the restaurant."

"That's so sweet," Iris said. Behind her there was the crackling of applewood burning in the fireplace, and the soft, sweet smell of it filled the room. She couldn't imagine Ian doing anything as romantic as proposing to her in public.

Andrew waved to a tall, gray haired man in a dark suit jacket and cranberry tie with a small pattern of holly leaves. The man said something to an older couple that Iris guessed to be in their mid forties, then waved back at Andrew and motioned for him to come over. "Come with me, I'll introduce you to Timothy," Andrew said, then brought her over to where Timothy stood.

"Do you know the Van Dorfs?" Timothy said. "Vivian and Ed."

"We've played golf," Ed said, pushing his hand out to Andrew for a shake. "I didn't know you were dating anyone?"

"Oh Ed, don't be so presumptuous," Vivian said, the sparkle of her diamond necklace and matching earrings overtaking her slender face. She turned towards Iris. "He's always been that way."

"That's okay," Iris said.

"We're not dating," Andrew said. "She did the interior design for the law firm."

Timothy's eyes lit up as he turned. "You must be Iris, then. Dolores can't stop talking about you."

Vivian turned towards Iris. "I hear you're doing the most amazing things to that old house Timothy bought."

"Hopefully she'll be just as happy with it once it's done," Iris said, then gave her best smile.

—

"Do you know any of these people?" Bob asked Dale in a hushed voice.

Dale scanned the crowd, noticing a few faces, mostly wives of men with high powered jobs. Christina was closest, holding a wine glass in front of her thin frame. The dress she wore had a low neckline and made her breasts look smaller than they were, but her long wavy blonde hair had a healthy shine from regular hot oil treatments. Dale pointed her out to Bob, along with a few other people whose hair he knew all about. Then he saw Iris standing next to some tall, dark and handsome man who was not Ian. She and the unknown man were talking to a few other people, all of them older. It looked as if they were laughing, then the man was leading Iris away from the small group, towards the bar across the room. She was far from pale. In fact, her face had an amazing glow. He pointed her out to Bob.

"She's the woman who designed your salon," Bob said.

"She's amazing," Dale said. "You should have seen the salon when I first bought it. It looked good, but nothing like now. Everything she designs reeks of class."

Iris waved, then said something to the man she was with and made her way towards him, alone. Dale gave her a kiss, then introduced her to Bob, who shook her hand.

"Where's Ian?" Dale asked.

"He's upstairs with Dolores."

"Do you think he can handle it?" Dale turned towards Bob. "Wait until you meet her."

"She's sweet," Iris said. "At first I thought she hated me, but we've come to understand each other."

"And you trust her alone with Ian? I've seen how she paws Kyle over."

"Doesn't everyone want what they can't have?" Iris winked at Bob before turning back to Dale. "So tell me, who do you know here?"

———

Dolores's house wasn't interesting enough to please Ian, although he pretended to be engrossed in every last detail. Guessing the old bat's age was more interesting to him. It was obvious the bitch had spent a fortune trying to look young, but as far as Ian was concerned it was money poorly spent. Her ass looked like shit, her tits drooped, and her face was so tight that her mouth appeared to be slightly off center. Her way of speaking was also a little dramatic and far too familiar. The worst part was how she kept touching his arm, which gave him the creeps.

"Iris must have told you all about our new home," Dolores said, escorting Ian down the hall and back to the stairs leading to the first floor. "She's doing such a splendid job with it."

"Sometimes I think there's nothing she can't do," Ian said, hating himself for having to give her more credit than she had due.

"You must be very proud of her," Dolores said. "Sometimes I wish she were my own daughter. But of course, she's not. What is her mother like?"

"I've never met her," Ian said, wishing he'd been able to lie. She'd love him all the more if he said great things about Iris's mother. But what if the crazy bitch knew that he'd never met Iris's mother? That would not look good.

"That's too bad. I was hoping you had," Dolores said. "Only an amazing woman could have raised such an extraordinary girl." Dolores stopped at the foot of the stairs and turned towards Ian. "I would love to meet her."

"From what I know they're not that close," Ian said, playing with the old hag. "They hardly ever talk."

Dolores's eyes grew wide with fright. "Really? Please say you're only kidding. Iris seems like such a nice girl. I can't imagine her not talking to her mother."

Ian smiled. "You found me out."

"Oh, you evil man," Dolores said, playfully slapping Ian's upper arm. "For a minute you had me believing you."

———

It was the second time that night that Steve had driven past Dale's condominium and Dale still wasn't home. The Saturn wasn't there either. He was probably hanging out with Kyle and Trent or some other group of fags. He considered waiting for Dale, then thought better of it. That was a bit severe. At least for now.

———

Iris fixed her dress, flushed the toilet, then went to the counter to wash her hands and check her make-up in the oval mirror above the white marble sink. Downstairs the party continued while she'd gone off to find a private bathroom upstairs. It wasn't that she wasn't enjoying herself, it was just that she'd needed some time alone. She didn't think Dolores would mind her using her private bathroom. Dolores would understand her need to get away from things. Andrew had seen her go upstairs and waved, so at least one person had an idea of where she was. She'd practically blushed from being found wandering off. And by Andrew no less.

Well, she was fine where she was. She wouldn't be missed. Ian had been hitting it off well with Timothy and that handsome man who had come with Dale when she'd gone upstairs. Dale certainly knew how to pick them. She'd seen Steve once and had thought he was a looker. She wondered what Dale thought of Andrew, but there was no way for her to ask without looking suspicious. The last thing she needed was for anyone to find out about that one incident, especially since it was not going to happen again. She'd made herself clear.

Stepping out of the bathroom, she scanned the dark interior of the bedroom. The bedroom door was still closed, as she had left it when she'd entered the room. She'd thought nobody would dare go into a room with the door closed, and she'd been right. Not even Andrew would dare to do such a thing, unless he'd been looking for her. But she didn't think he would do that. There was no reason for it.

There was a click, then dim light filtered through the room from the short lamp on the night table across the room and showed Andrew standing next to it. "I had to talk to you alone," he said. "I hope you don't mind."

Iris's hand was still on her chest from the shock of having been found out. "So you followed me?"

Andrew walked up to her and put his hands lightly on her shoulders. "I never do this type of thing."

"Then why are you doing it now?"

Andrew looked into Iris's eyes. "I can't stop thinking about you."

Iris fought the urge to kiss him. "Ian is downstairs."

"Timothy never lets people go once he has their ear," Andrew said. "We're safe for a little while. I've been going through what to say to you the moment I saw you here tonight, but now I have no idea of what to say."

Iris's nipples brushed against the inner fabric of her dress, forming small embossed dents. Then she felt Andrew's free hand on her waist. "I shouldn't be here."

"Tell me that you love him," Andrew said.

"We shouldn't be doing this."

Andrew's hand was warm as it slid around her waist. "Do you love him?"

Iris felt her knees begin to buckle. If he only knew how moist he was making her. She wanted to seduce him, but knew that could not be an option. She looked down, then pushed away from him and sat on the bed. Had Ian ever pleased her the way Andrew had? Iris knew the answer, but she also knew that Ian would allow her to have the career she wanted. Would Andrew love her enough to do that? "This isn't fair."

"For you or for him?" Andrew asked.

"He trusts me," Iris said. "I've never cheated on him before."

Andrew turned and looked at her. "I'm not asking you to cheat on him. I would never ask you to do that."

Iris gripped the edge of the bed as she crossed her legs. Between Andrew's legs she saw his manhood bulging. It was clear what he wanted, but how could she do such a thing? How could she leave Ian for someone she hardly knew. Especially when Ian gave her the freedom she needed. Was sexual fulfilment that important?

"I want you to be fair to yourself," Andrew said.

"I am."

"Are you?"

Iris couldn't bring herself to look up. Ian might not give her sexual gratification, but he did give her what she needed. And hadn't her mother said finding a man who understood her need for a career was the best thing she could do for herself.

"I should go," Andrew said.

Iris looked up at him and said nothing.

"You know how to get in contact with me," Andrew said, then walked out the bedroom door.

Iris watched the door close, then turned off the lamp on the end table. Andrew was seducing her the way other men had tried to seduce her in the past. Men from college. Men Iris's mother would later deem unacceptable. Men who were virile, rugged and sexy. But none of them had lasted. But the moments Iris had spent with them had been sexually fulfilling. It hadn't been until later, when Margot caught wind of the end of the relationship that shame and guilt came into play. She'd never told Margot that she'd become sexually active in college, but Margot seemed to know. "There's more to men than pleasure," Margot had often said. Not once could Iris recall Margot consoling her at the end of a relationship. "Those aren't relationships, they're affairs," Margot had said on the night Robert had broken up with her.

Robert had been in the process of getting his doctorate in English literature. They'd met at a poetry reading in a local coffee shop, walked down dimly lit streets arm in arm afterwards and talked about their ambitions. Then they sat on the dark lawn of the historic John Brown House and looked up at the moon. It was then that he'd bent over and kissed her, then slipped his hand in the front of her blouse and touched her. And when he'd lain on top of her she'd felt his hardness pressing against her thigh. She'd thought a lasting relationship with Robert had been a possibility, and had told Margot about him. A week later Robert had broken up with her, saying that they hadn't connected any way but physically. Without knowing the reason for the breakup, Margot hadn't been surprised. "When will you learn to set your priorities?" Margot had said.

"I have my priorities set," Iris had said. "Why can't I work and have a relationship?"

"Those aren't relationships, they're affairs," Margot had said.

By the time Iris had become a sophomore at Rhode Island School of Design she'd stopped telling Margot about the end of any of her affairs. Still, even across the telephone lines during their monthly conversations, Margot had sensed something was amiss after each man had left Iris.

—

As if the party wasn't bad enough, especially having to get a tour of the entire house from some old bitch who didn't know when to act her age, now Ian had to lie naked next to Iris and not fuck her. Why was she suddenly holding herself back? It wasn't as if she was sick, or they'd fought. There was no reason for it, but they were in bed and her back was to him. On the ride home she'd seemed a bit sullen, almost distant. Ian had asked her about it, but she'd simply brushed it off as having had too much to drink. Since when did Iris have too much to drink? She'd probably only had a total of two glasses of wine. Her faggy friends seemed to have drunk more than that, and he wasn't even paying attention to them. Maybe Dolores had slipped her whatever it was that she'd been on. The thought of that made Ian grin. He knew it wasn't an actual possibility, but it was funny to think about Iris stumbling around, oblivious to the fact that she was high on something. At least if that was the reason he could understand her not wanting to let him get off.

Ian smoothed his hand over Iris's stomach, trying as hard as he could to put on the charm. He kissed her shoulder. "You looked so beautiful tonight," he said. "I couldn't help watching you and thinking how much I want you."

"Not tonight," Iris said as she placed her hand over Ian's.

"Come on," Ian said as he moved his hand lower, so the tips of his fingers were dipping into Iris's bush. "I'll make you feel so good."

"My way," Iris said.

Ian slid the tips of his fingers over the top most opening of Iris's sex. "I don't understand."

"Missionary."

"Iris."

"My way or not at all," she whispered.

"You know I can't get off that way," Ian said, rubbing his stiff dick against the crack of her ass. "That's why I never do it like that."

"But what about me, Ian," Iris said, not bothering to turn

around.

"Missionary?" Ian let out a chuckle. "How dull."

"Anything done a thousand times over becomes dull, but if it's never been done it can't be dull."

Ian tried to put his fingers deeper into her pussy, but Iris turned onto her stomach. He wasn't going to let her win. "Iris, why are you mad at me?" Ian said as he kissed the back of her neck.

"Don't start something you can't complete," Iris said.

Ian slowly rubbed her back. "Haven't I always gotten you off?"

"With your fingers." Iris said, then sat up and dangled her feet over the edge. "I can do that on my own, thank you very much." She stood up and grabbed her panties from the floor.

Ian shot up and watched Iris as she defied him. She was getting dressed. He couldn't believe it. "What are you doing?" he asked.

"What does it look like?"

"You don't get what you want so you up and leave? Don't you think that's a bit childish?"

Iris stomped over to the closet and grabbed her dress from inside, then slipped it on. "How often do I get what I want, Ian?" she asked as she reached behind herself and zipped it up. "I'm not being childish, I'm giving you something to think about."

Ian fought the urge to bolt out of bed and grab her. That would only make Iris feel as if she had him by the balls, which she didn't. Instead, he slipped back under the cover and rested his head on the soft pillow. He heard the bedroom door close. Let the stupid cunt leave, he was going to dump her anyhow. Ian's father had been right, she was good for nothing. This was probably just some stupid game to get him to marry her. His father had always said that was what women did, they played games. He turned onto his side then brought the covers closer to his neck. She would call him, ask for forgiveness, and he wouldn't bother to forgive her. How would she feel then?

How often do I get what I want, Ian? Hadn't he gone to that stupid party for her? He hadn't wanted to go. What did that dumb bitch think she was doing? He gave her everything she needed, so who did she think she was kidding. Trying to make him look bad, that was her plan. Well, it wouldn't work. Ian knew he wasn't a bad guy. Everyone did. Iris's mind games were not going to work on him. He'd show her. He just wouldn't call her, then see how long it takes for her to come running back asking for forgiveness. The thought of hearing Iris's sobbing voice made Ian grin. He'd play with her a little, drag it out. Not call. He wouldn't even return her calls. And when she came back, he'd give it to her and she would take it. Who did she think she was playing with?

Sunday

Jay sat on the sofa, kicked his feet up on the coffee table and was about to finish reading *Vile Bodies* when the front door flew open and Steve stomped in. "Bad night?" Jay asked, resting the open book on his chest.

Steve walked into the kitchen. "I don't want to talk about it. Sometimes I don't know how I even got involved with him." Steve slammed a door closed.

Jay considered coaxing Steve into talking about what was bothering him, but thought better of it. If Steve was slamming doors he was in no mood to talk. Not only that, but Jay had a good idea that it had to have something do with Dale. He hated seeing Steve all torn up and wished Dale would smarten up and see how much pain he was putting Steve through. Jay had never thought Dale could be so terrible. Dale had always seemed so sweet and caring. But that was only what Dale had allowed him to see, sometimes people were different once you got to know them. Jay thought Steve would feel much better if he would talk to him about what was going on.

Steve let out a scream. He needs to be alone, Jay thought as he slipped the small piece of paper he was using as a bookmark into the book. He went into his bedroom to put on his shoes and head out. He could finish reading *Vile Bodies* at the Coffee Exchange or at the park.

—

"I couldn't help myself, I just had to buy two," Norman said as he sat and spread his long legs down the leopard print chaise longue. He picked up the crystal champagne flute filled with Moët Chandon, took a sip, then sighed. "Isn't it decadent to be sitting here on a Sunday afternoon, sipping champagne and lounging on one of the most ravishing pieces of furniture ever created? It just makes me want to cum."

Iris couldn't help but smile as she also sprawled out on a matching chaise. Just being in Norman's habitat was enough to change the sourest of moods, and Iris had needed something to change hers. She still hadn't told Norman what was troubling her, but she knew she would have to. Norman loved it when people gossiped, especially if it was about themselves.

Although it wasn't very cold, Norman had lit a fire. The wood crackled and filled the room with the sweet smell of applewood. "I might just buy a chaise for myself," Iris said. "Dolores is eager to see her new house, especially since the living room is going to have one."

"But you didn't come here to talk about chaise longues, did you?" Norman looked about the room. "If only we had raspberries. Nothing goes better with champagne than raspberries. Plus, I think you have bad news, and it would help you smile."

Iris sipped her champagne, feeling the bubbles against her tongue. "I don't know why you don't find a man and settle down."

"And give up my boys! Oh no. I would rather be shot like Saint Sebastian. Very dramatic, don't you think. Me against a tree, hands tied above my head, chest heaving and stuck with arrows. Let me tell you, he has Camille beat as far as drama is concerned."

"I would rather live, " Iris said.

"Well then, tell me about your living drama. How was Ian's family?"

Iris took a sip of champagne. "Margot would not get along with Ian's mother. Ian's mother is like June Cleaver on acid. All she cares about is serving her man and keeping peace at any cost.

She actually took me aside and said she would teach me how to cook."

"She sounds dreary," Norman said. "What about the father?"

"The man refused to take me seriously," Iris said, feeling herself getting angry. "I wanted to strangle him, not to mention Ian. Ian's sister was more willing to stick up for me than Ian. The poor thing has a brainless ditz for a mother and a Rush Limbaugh wannabe for a father. I wanted to scream! He expects me to give up my job once I marry Ian. The worst of it all was that Ian acted as if he agrees with the guy! Not once did he even attempt to get his father to shut up. Not once! I didn't know what to do."

"So you took it," Norman said.

Iris crossed her arms. "For the most part."

"You should have told the old coot off."

"And be uncomfortable every time I see them?"

"That depends."

"On what?"

Norman raised his champagne flute in the air as if in a toast. "On what you have to tell. Now, go on with your story."

"There isn't much more," Iris said.

"Did you make-up with Ian? Something tells me you didn't."

"It's that obvious?"

"If you had, there would be no reason for your being here," Norman said. "So tell me, why didn't you make-up with him?"

Iris felt her stomach churn. She trusted Norman, but wasn't ready to tell him how she felt about Ian. She didn't even know how she felt about him. And what about Andrew? She knew Norman would understand about her one indiscretion. What was one indiscretion to a man who'd had many? "It's complicated."

"What isn't?" Norman said. "Especially when it comes to love and sex. How did it begin?"

How did it begin? Iris thought about that for a minute, then looked up at Norman. She took a breath. "I cheated on Ian."

"That's wonderful!" Norman said. "With whom?"

"With one of my clients." Iris picked up the champagne flute and felt the cool crystal against her fingers. "I was checking on the progress of the law offices I'm designing when one of them walked in."

"One of the partners," Norman said.

Iris nodded. "Andrew Tyler."

"He's more than a partner, darling. Bravo."

"Well, we were alone, and one thing led to another."

"And he fucked you right there, amongst all the sawdust?"

"Against a wall, actually," Iris said. "There was very little thought to it, it just happened. Chemistry, I guess. It's not going to happen again, though. I won't let it. I can't. But I can't stop thinking about it. It's something I've never done with Ian."

"Maybe you should? Have you talked to him about it?"

Iris paused, then said, "Yes, I have." She knew Norman didn't understand what she meant, but how could she tell him? Especially when it would be fun to see him surprised.

"Then you have to be the one to make the move. Who knows, maybe he'll like it?"

"No, Norman, he won't," Iris said. "Believe me. There is only one thing Ian likes."

"Really?" Norman hunkered down in the chaise. "Is it bondage? You can never be spontaneous with bondage."

"No, it's not." Iris took a long, slow sip from her champagne flute. "It's anal sex. He won't do it any other way."

Normal's eyes grew wide, then he grinned. "There's no such thing as a female prostate, is there?"

"No, there isn't," Iris said. "Nor does he seem to care."

"Missionary is out of the picture," Norman asked.

"He doesn't even want to hear about it," Iris said.

"And you don't love Ian, or am I wrong?"

"I care very much about him."

"That's not the same thing," Norman said with a flick of his wrist. "If you don't love him, then get rid of him. Let me tell you, sucking the same dick year after year gets tiresome, and if you don't love the guy it's pure torture. Why put yourself through all that?"

"Sex isn't everything," Iris said before taking a sip of champagne.

"But it is part of a relationship," Norman said. "You can't

discount it."

"You don't think I'm just confused because of Andrew?"

"I think you're afraid Ian could turn into his father, along with being sexually dysfunctional. For a straight man, that is."

Iris had never thought about Ian becoming his father. Was it a possibility? "I don't want to hurt him," Iris said. "What if I'm wrong?"

"You wouldn't be talking to me if you thought you loved him. Plus, feelings are meant to be hurt, that's why we have them."

Iris looked quizzically at Norman.

"It gives us a reason to cry," Norman said. "Thankfully I had mine surgically extracted."

"How should I do it?" Iris asked, still unable to believe she was planning on breaking up with Ian.

"Do it over the phone, that way if he cries you can hang up."

"Is that how you do it?"

"There's a difference between romance and fucking. Personally, I find fucking much more exciting, and it has fewer strings."

"And how are your boys doing?" Iris asked, pleased to change the topic.

"I'm down to two," Norman said, then continued to tell her about each one in full detail.

———

Bob hadn't wanted Dale to make a big breakfast, he'd told him a bagel would do. But Bob hadn't had any Lox, so Dale had gone out and bought some. Together they'd lounged out in bed drinking coffee and eating bagels. After that they'd fucked again. It seemed as if Bob was insatiable, and Dale was still smiling from the memory on his drive home. Yes, he was dating an insatiable computer nerd. It was about time he'd found someone who wanted him for more than just a meal. And Bob knew how to be sociable, Dale couldn't forget what a smash he'd been with Timothy. Even Kyle and Trent thought Bob had handled himself splendidly. For the first time in a while Dale could honestly say he was happy.

Had he ever felt truly happy with Steve? Perhaps, he thought. He hadn't been miserable, that much he knew. Annoyed, but not miserable. Especially with the way Steve had been consistently late for everything. And having sex with Steve had never been all that fun. Steve wouldn't go out of his way to make sure he got off the way Bob did. Steve had never seemed to be fully into doing it, or even wanting to be near him. Dale thought about the way Bob had touched him last night. Bob's big hand on his upper thigh. The way Bob had wrapped his arms around him as if he wasn't going to let go.

Dale giggled. Bob was perfect for him.

—

Ian hadn't expected a phone call from Iris yet, maybe not even the next day. Mid week would probably be as long as she could hold out, though. He grabbed the remainder of the baguette from the plastic cutting board and ripped off a chunk, tore it in half, then wiped the rest of the tomato sauce off his plate with it. Dinner was nothing special when he ate alone, and he hated eating alone. At least he could be comfortable and eat in his blue plaid boxers and a t-shirt.

Michelle had said she'd call when she got back from visiting her parents, but he wasn't sure if she would call Sunday or Monday. He hoped she would call him today, that way he could make dinner plans with her for Monday, maybe even get her in bed. It was about time she gave in to him, not that he'd pushed to have sex with her yet. The telephone was just an arm's reach away on the dinner table. He sunk his teeth into the bread and tore a chunk away. Monday night with Michelle would be so perfect, so right. He could have her come to his place for a drink and dinner, then slowly make his move. She'd give in to him and he would have his way. Iris could act as high and mighty as she wanted, he wasn't going to let her control him. He hoped she would drop by so he could see her face when he said he didn't want anything to do with her; that she'd dug her own grave and now she could wallow in it.

The telephone rang. Ian waited for the next ring, then the next. One more and the machine would pick up, so he grabbed the phone and put it to his ear. It was Michelle, sounding pleasant and charming.

"And how was your holiday?" Ian asked.

"Oh, it was so good to be home," Michelle said. "I got a chance to catch up with some friends. We went out and had dinner, then went for drinks."

Ian listened to the rest of Michelle's few days at home after the holiday and acted as if he cared. The only good thing that came of the conversation was that his dick got hard and she agreed to meet him for dinner.

—

Iris sat on the sofa wrapped in a thick cotton robe with her legs tucked up under her, staring at the phone in her hand. She'd spent the day talking to Norman and he was right, she had no choice but to break it off with Ian. But was she doing the right thing? Did one slip mean the end of her relationship with Ian? Iris knew her mother would be concerned, especially since she seemed to like Ian. She approved of him. She'd even mentioned the possibility of Iris marrying Ian. To her mother Ian was one of the few men who would understand his wife wanting her own career. Until Thanksgiving Iris had thought the same. Now she was beginning to wonder. She had to keep that in mind when she explained her decision to him. It wasn't the sex alone, it was also the way he wouldn't stick up to his father for her. That had meant a lot. She looked at the phone. But was it enough? She wasn't sure.

Iris tossed the phone on the sofa and watched it bounce a few times before it lay motionless. Norman had a way of always making things sound easy. Not everything was easy, at least not for Iris. She knew Norman didn't go around hurting peoples' feelings with little to no regard, despite the way he put things. He'd even told her not to do anything unless she felt secure with her decision. Norman just liked to make light of things; he'd often told her that people have a way of taking things too seriously. But some things were serious, like ending a relationship. Iris's mother had always told her that women should put careers first and husbands second.

"Once you establish yourself the world will open up to you," her mother had told her ever since she was a little girl, and Iris had always believed her. Women didn't have to be house-wives or secretaries, they could be lawyers or doctors or whatever they wanted. Every time Iris had watched television and seen a man in a high powered job her mother would say, "You could do that, too." Now Iris was grown up and had given her mother the daughter she'd always wanted. The daughter she could tell her friends about. The daughter she could be proud of. Soon she would be the daughter who let the one good man in America fall to the wayside because of one infidelity.

At the Harkins School, where Iris had gone during her teen years, she had been pushed to be the best of her class. Here she had learned the true meaning of competition. The school had the reputation of sending over eighty percent of its students to Ivy League colleges. That was why Iris's mother had insisted she go, and why she'd been proud when Iris had been accepted. None of the boys Iris had dated had been good enough for Iris's mother, despite the fact that they'd been members of some of the best families in Connecticut. The same held true to the boys she'd dated in her years at Rhode Island School of Design. Especially Vino, whose dark eyes had seemed an invitation to sexual fulfillment and whose full lips had longed to be kissed. His olive complexion, long hair and scruff of beard went well with his wrinkled and paint splotched clothes, giving him the bohemian look all the students strove for and few truly achieved. His full name was Robert Vino, but everyone called him Vino, which Iris felt made him seem much more romantic.

Iris's parents had come up for a weekend visit, and to meet the new love in her life. The four of them had gone to dinner, then her father had driven them back to Iris's small off campus apartment. The following day, after breakfast with her parents, Iris pulled her mother aside and asked what she thought.

"You're just a girl to him, Iris," her mother had said.

"But mom, I am a girl," Iris had said.

"No Iris, you're a woman. A smart woman with the world in front of her who will not throw it all away for a man. Especially one who will toss you to the wayside the first chance he gets."

A week later her mother had been proven right. Iris had been single once again. From that day on Iris called her mother by her first name when thinking of her. She couldn't call her Margot to her face, but she could do it in private.

So far Margot liked Ian, or what she knew of him. Iris rolled her eyes and let out a huff. What if she was wrong about Ian? What if she did love him? But Norman had even been able to figure out that she didn't love Ian. And if Iris did break up with Ian, what would Margot say after she told her? Iris could almost hear Margot now, *The one good guy you've ever dated and you had to get rid of him.*

Iris wasn't sure what to do.

—

The room was dark as Steve sat up in bed, the sheets covering his bare legs. He played with his flaccid dick and looked into the night. It was almost midnight and he couldn't sleep. All he could think about was Dale. Dale and that Saturn wagon. Who did that car belong to? If only he'd gotten the license plate number, then he'd be able to go to the registry and find out. Or even better, maybe he would follow the Saturn wagon next time he saw it. He could hang out and wait until the guy stuffing his cock up Dale's ass came out and he could follow him. Steve lay back in bed and brought the covers up close to his chin. He would get to the bottom of this, one way or another.

Monday

Ian slammed down the telephone, then tugged at his tie until it was undone. As if he hadn't had a bad enough day at the office, now this. Who did that little cunt think she was, telling him they were through? He let out a scream to vent his anger. Michelle was coming over and he didn't want to appear angry and have to lie his way out of his bad mood. Everything would go to pot if Michelle found out about that bitch Iris.

"Worthless cunt," Ian muttered as he snatched his tie from the bed and began to slowly undo whatever was left of the knot. Iris had broken up with him, he couldn't believe it. He was the best thing that she had and she was just going to throw it away like that. He laughed. She'd said it wasn't working for her, and that he didn't care about her needs. It was funny how she hadn't bothered to pinpoint any specific needs. Wasn't that what women said when they didn't have any real reasons for their actions. Needs. Fuck her! She'd be back, then he would tell her to slam it up her ass. That made him grimace. Wasn't she already used to having things shoved up her ass? He imagined she must be feeling high and mighty, but that would change once she realized what she had tossed out the window.

He went to the closet and flicked the switch for the turnstile. The vacant spot for that particular tie made it around, so he replaced it. Everything had its place, that was something Iris had to learn. Like so many women, she didn't know where her place was. He kicked off his shoes and placed them neatly in the space they'd occupied that morning when he'd gotten dressed. It was too bad for Iris. She no longer had a place with him. He had Michelle now. She was going to come through. Michelle was so much smarter than Iris anyhow. His dick began to stir in his slacks at the mere thought of sticking it up Michelle's beautiful ass. He gave it a rub through his slacks, then began to unbutton his cotton shirt.

Tonight would be wonderful. After tonight he'd kiss Iris goodbye. He was better off without her. His father hadn't even liked the bitch. His father had seen Iris for the worthless rag she was. But Ian's father had always understood women better than anyone he'd ever known. All his life his father had been right about the girls he'd dated. "You need someone like your mother. Someone who will take care of things around the house so you can concentrate on what's really important," his father had often said. His father had been right. Ian was sick of women who told him what to do. He had to take a stand.

After dropping his shirt on the bed, Ian unbuckled his belt then slipped it out of the hoops and hung it in its place on the back of the closet door, lined up with the other twelve belts he had hanging there. He slipped out of his slacks and looked down at the tent his semi hard dick made in his purple silk boxer shorts. He'd take a shower before Michelle arrived, he had time. He would be nice and clean for her. There would be nothing she wouldn't do for him. Tonight was going to be special. Ian was going to get exactly what he wanted.

—

Gerald sat behind the oak desk at the front of the furniture store and did paper work as Iris and Dolores walked down the parquet path with living room sets on either side. Iris had been going to Gerald's since he'd opened the store three years ago. She'd heard about the shop through Norman, back when Gerald was the new hot boy on his arm. Back then he looked to be about eighteen although he was twenty-three. Gerald blamed it on his Portuguese heritage, although Iris had never heard of Portuguese men being predisposed of youthful appearances. Iris had been looking forward to going to Gerald's with Dolores for no other reason than to have something to take her mind off what she'd done. It had been the first time she'd ever broken-up with anyone and she couldn't shake feeling guilty about it.

Dolores gently rubbed Iris's upper arm as she studied a dreadful Victorian reproduction love seat. The cloth was all wrong, and the stitching around the cushion was poor at best. "What's wrong, dear? You seem distracted."

Dolores had noticed. Iris didn't know how she could let herself be so unprofessional. "I'm so sorry, Dolores. There's so much going on right now. Perhaps I should have rescheduled."

"Nonsense," Dolores said as she sat on the love seat and patted the cushion to her left. "Forget that I'm your client, just for a minute."

Iris took a seat, then felt Dolores's cool hand gently touch the top of hers. "It's fine, Dolores."

"Is it boy trouble?" Dolores asked.

Iris didn't know what to say. Dolores was a client, not a close friend or relative.

"The furniture can wait for another day, dear," Dolores said, looking into Iris's eyes as if searching for a way to help her feel better. "Let's concentrate on you for a minute. Tell me what's bothering you."

Dolores gently stroked Iris's hand as if she were petting a cat, which Iris found to be calming. "I broke up with Ian today," Iris confessed.

"He seemed like such a nice young man," Dolores said. "I'm sorry it didn't work out. There are lots of nice, available men out there."

Iris didn't know why, but she suddenly found herself fighting back the urge to cry. When she was composed, she said, "Maybe I should just concentrate on my career."

"Iris, dear, even career girls need romance." Dolores dropped her black leather Coach pocket book on her lap, then rummaged inside. She pulled out a small metal pillbox with inlaid amber on the top, opened it and handed Iris a small blue tablet. Dipping her hand back into the pocketbook, she pulled out a small piece of facial tissue and used it to wrap up the tablet. "Take this once you get home. It's generic Valium," she said as she handed Iris the tissue. "I think it's called Diazepam." She took a moment to think. "Yes, that's what they call it. All these silly names. What was so awful about Valium, at least you could remember it."

Iris reluctantly took the gift and stuffed it in her clutch before anyone noticed.

"They work like a charm," Dolores said. "When I first started taking them each tablet had a little V carved out of the center. When you turned one upside down it looked like the roof of a house."

Gerald wasn't in sight, so Iris assumed he'd walked away when he'd noticed the two of them talking. "Perhaps we should leave," Iris said.

———

Steve had caught Dale as he was leaving his condominium and decided to follow him. He kept a good distance back, so as not to be noticed, especially since Dale knew what he drove. Dale drove down Blackstone Boulevard, then onto Butler Avenue with its mix of businesses and houses. Up ahead was the plaza with the East Side Marketplace, Brooks Pharmacy and BankRI. With any luck he would go to his little fuck buddy's place. If Dale took a left he would head past The Salvation Army and toward River Road. Dale took a right at the light. Steve followed him up the road, then took a left at the traffic light and went onto Gano Street, past more apartment houses, the flower shop that hired the handicapped on the left, then further, towards the on ramp to the highway.

Once on the Route 195, Steve made sure to stay a few cars behind Dale. The Route 95 split was just up ahead. Dale stayed to the left, onto Route 95 North. It wasn't until Dale took the exit for Route 10 that Steve realized he might be going to visit his little faggy friends Trent and Kyle. He followed him, hoping he wouldn't take the Reservoir Avenue exit. Route 10 was a two lane highway, which meant Steve had to be careful. The last thing he wanted to do was get caught. He slowed down once he was on Route 10. He didn't bother following Dale once he took the

Reservoir Avenue exit.

—

"Come in," Ian said as he opened the front door to Michelle. He knew even without the gleam in Michelle's eye that he looked charming in his casual gray slacks and dark green ribbed pullover. It seemed that Michelle had also taken some time getting herself ready, and he was pleased that she'd chosen to wear a simple dress and pumps. He took her coat and hung it up in the hall closet while she looked around. He gave her a peck on the lips, then said, "I haven't started cooking yet."

"That's fine," Michelle said. "I would love to watch."

"I'm not making anything extravagant, just a simple noodle soup with shiitake mushrooms." Ian walked into the kitchen, where the vegetables had been precut and all the ingredients had been measured and left on the kitchen island. The stove was set in the center of the island, which made it easy to cook and entertain.

Michelle's eyes widened as she looked around the kitchen, taking in the stainless steel stove, white tiled floor and the rack of wine glasses hanging over the island in the middle of the kitchen. "A real chef's kitchen," she said.

"I like to cook, although I hardly get the time these days," Ian said. "I'm too busy. And I'm alone. It's no fun cooking for one." He opened the refrigerator, took out the bottle of Chardonnay from the Alice White Vineyard and held it out to Michelle. "It's Australian, but very good all the same."

"I don't know enough about wine to be fussy," Michelle said as she took a seat on the stool in front of the island. She looked over the small white porcelain bowls filled with chopped onions and assorted herbs and spices as Ian opened the wine. "I feel like I'm on one of those cooking shows."

"Cooking is easier when you have everything pre-measured and chopped," Ian said. "The wine glasses are hanging on the rack above your head. Could you grab two?" He watched Michelle's round ass as she stood on the balls of her feet and grabbed two glasses. Her ass was beautiful, and soon to be his.

"It's so rare to have anyone cook for me," Michelle said. "Other than my mother. My dad tried once, back when my mom wasn't feeling well. It was so bad we had to order out."

Ian turned the bottle to keep it from dripping as he lifted it from the glass he'd filled. "Hopefully we won't have to order out."

"That's not what I meant."

"I know." Ian lifted his wine glass to her. "To good meals."

"To good meals," Michelle said as she clinked glasses with Ian.

Ian winked at her. "And many more to come."

Michelle grinned, obviously pleased to have a man pay such close attention to her. She was just a college girl, unable to understand the world around her. Ian knew he would get his way with her. It almost seemed too easy. He turned to the stove, fired up the gas burner under the wok, then began to cook. First a little oil and garlic, then some onion and shrimp. With a wooden spoon he sauteed the ingredients so they wouldn't burn as he began to cook the noodles in a separate pan.

"Is there anything I can do?" Michelle asked.

"No, just sit there and enjoy your wine. And keep me company, of course." Ian took the white cup with the dried mustard and freshly chopped ginger and tossed them into the wok. "Sometimes all a cook needs is someone to talk to."

———

Iris sat at her desk with the floor plans for the second floor of Dolores's house unrolled in front of her. She hadn't talked with Dolores about knocking down walls on the second floor, nor did she think any major work was needed. She was simply wasting time, and she knew it. What she really needed to do was try to scrounge up more work to begin once Dolores's house was done. The law offices of Tyler, Wescott and Allen were almost complete.

She thought about moving to Boston or New York, where it was easier to survive as an interior designer. As much as she liked Providence, people here didn't spend as much money on their interiors. The majority of the work she did was for businesses, which had never bothered her before. Most of the people in Providence didn't have enough extra money to spend on redecorating their homes. The task of decorating fell on the owners, who didn't always do the best job. Boston and New York had more people willing to pay to have their homes redesigned. She would be able to get more work if she moved. More homes with owners who would fight with her about her ideas, only to change their minds about a certain design once it had been chosen. At least with a business the concept of the store was discussed beforehand, and designs went along with the idea of what the store was trying to become. The goal was much more concrete with a business.

Iris let out a groan as she twirled around in her chair. Across the room was a cork board with a few pictures of interiors that Iris had done and liked along with an old post card of the Providence skyline at dusk. She'd bought the post card her senior year of college. She'd been thinking of moving to New York when she realized how much she would miss the small city where she'd spent the last four years of her life. Looking at the post card of the small city she began to feel silly and sentimental, which was better than guilty. She wondered what Ian was doing as she whiled away the time looking at the walls. Not only that, but how was she going to spend the next twenty minutes before she could leave for Kyle's place.

Iris had run into Dale on her way back to the office, when she'd stopped at The Coffee Exchange for a cup of Chai. Dale had been there, waiting in line and had asked her how she was. She'd told him about how she'd broken up with Ian and was feeling a bit down because of it. "I'm going to Kyle and Trent's for dinner, why don't you join me. I know they won't mind" Dale had said. She'd turned down a few of Dale's offers to get together outside of the salon and had felt slightly obligated to say yes. It wasn't that she didn't like Dale, but that she wasn't sure how much they would have in common outside of the salon. Plus, she wanted to get away and have a few laughs, and although Norman wouldn't mind her dropping in on him, she didn't want to become a nuisance. Since she'd already been to The Coffee Exchange, going back was out of the question. Going to the mall was an option, but she wasn't in the mood to shop. Kyle lived in the next city over from Providence, which was a fifteen minute drive, twenty if she drove slow.

Iris glared at the telephone on the desk, then at the fax machine sitting across the room on it's own table. If only one of them would ring, then she would have something to start. The thought of dropping in on the law offices to check up on progress was appealing. Wasn't that how this had all come about, a simple visit to the law offices? No, she told herself, it just seemed that way. It made things clearer for her. Ian hadn't cared about her needs, and it was a good enough reminder of that. That and meeting Ian's family on Thanksgiving. She felt bad for his sister, Donna. What was it like for her to live in a house that didn't value women? It was no wonder she'd been so willing to start a fight with her father. Donna did have balls. Not even Ian was willing to fight with his father, even if it was in defense of his girlfriend. Thankfully she'd only been his girlfriend. She couldn't imagine what she would have done if he'd proposed to her and she'd accepted. Would she have been so ready to dump him if she'd made that type of commitment to him? She didn't think she would have, not even with Norman's guidance.

Iris stood, then grabbed her pocketbook from the desk. She was not going to sit in her office and brood. She could do that in the car or anywhere else. What she needed to do was pick up something to bring. There was no way she would arrive empty handed. She could waste time at the liquor store, pretending to find the perfect wine.

Iris locked up, dropped herself into the car and drove off to Swan Liquors on Hope Street. She roamed the open store, browsing through the stock. A Chardonnay was always a safe choice if you didn't know what your host preferred, but she wasn't sure which one. There was a Georges DuBoeuf Chardonnay that she'd had before and had enjoyed. Then she ran across a bottle of Elvenglade Pinot Gris. She remembered Ian telling her that a Pinot Gris was the same as a Pinot Grigio, which was what everyone was drinking. At least she'd gotten something out of her relationship with Ian. She knew Dale kept up with that type of thing, so he would be impressed. She brought it up to the counter, paid for it, then went back to her car and drove to Kyle's.

As she drove she decided not to tell Andrew about her break-up until after the new offices were complete, and even then she might not tell him. She could not allow herself to get involved with her clients. That was unprofessional and in bad taste. She also knew what would happen if she did speak with him, especially if they were face to face. Not that sex would be unwelcome. She'd gone without a proper fuck for so long that once she'd gotten one she'd turned into some type of nymphomaniac.

Iris slowly rubbed her legs together as she maneuvered the car down Hope Street, heading towards Wickenden Street. It was the long way to the highway, but she didn't want to be the first to arrive, even if it was a small group. When was the last time she'd been laid? It had been with Andrew. Andrew was the last person she needed to think about. The last thing she should feel is horny, especially after what she'd done to Ian. She hoped Ian wasn't sitting at home alone, although that was probably exactly what he was doing. Isn't that what people who had been dumped generally do? That was what Iris had done all the times she'd been dumped. But she'd always had Norman to go to for support. Norman had always known what to say, and had kept quiet when she'd needed to talk. He'd also always sprung for the wine, and never anything cheap. They'd drunk and talked. Norman had even been able to get her to laugh after the most painful break-ups. Like when Vino had left her for another woman. That had made her feel so inadequate and ugly. At least she hadn't done that to Ian. She hadn't left him for Andrew. Andrew was just a reminder of what wasn't working out in her relationship with Ian.

Iris was on the highway, heading towards Cranston when she began to wonder what her mother would think about her breaking up with Ian. Thankfully she'd never met him. She had spoken to him briefly on the telephone once, but they hadn't talked long enough for Margot to have an opinion of him. All Margot knew was that he'd told her that he liked Iris having a career. Iris was going to bring Ian to meet her parents for Christmas. Margot had even said she was eager to meet him face to face. Now Iris had broken it off with him. What would Margot say? Iris assumed Margot would follow suit and make it look as if Iris had been the one to make the wrong decision. She imagined Margot saying something like, "The one good guy and you can't keep him around," or, "Too bad, I actually liked him." With Margot and the men Iris dated there was no winning, and she knew it.

Iris found Kyle's white ranch, then pulled up in front of the house. She sat still for a minute as her heart began to calm down. Just thinking about Margot's reaction to her news had made her pulse quicken. The Diazepam tablet Dolores had given her was still in her clutch. Maybe she would hold onto it until she spoke with Margot. She might actually need to take it before, during, or after their talk.

Reaching over, she grabbed the wine then made her way up the bricked walkway leading to the front door. Hopefully the interior would not be something horrible. Just because they were gay didn't mean they had taste. Please, nothing tacky, she thought as she rang the bell and waited. Kyle answered the door and asked her to come inside. Iris almost sighed when she looked around. There was a teak bookshelf. The carpet was a thick pile, beige wall to wall.

"What did you bring?" Kyle asked as he took the wine from her and pulled the bottle out of the bag. He studied the label. "Sounds nice. Shall I open it?"

"Feel free," Iris said, taking in the black leather sofa and the teak coffee table that matched the bookshelves and the entertainment center against the wall across from the sofa. What looked like last season's issue of the International Male catalogue was on the coffee table, along with an issue of *The Advocate* magazine. The bookshelf was jam packed with paperback books, all of which looked as if they'd been read more than once.

The door to the left of the bookshelf opened and out walked Dale, who held onto the door as he turned back into the room and said, "I can't help it if I'm a control freak" He turned towards Iris and smiled. "He put too much salt in the sauce."

"I did not. Get out," said a male voice from inside the room Iris assumed to be the kitchen. She also assumed the voice belonged to Kyle's boyfriend, Trent.

Kyle held up the wine bottle. "Do you want some?"

Dale's eyes grew wide as he read the label. "Why don't I pour the wine while you take Iris's coat."

Iris slipped out of her coat, then handed it to Kyle. She began to look forward to an evening of titillating conversation.

—

Passing cars and street lamps lit the night as Jay and Erik walked close down Thayer Street. Just a block away was where the store fronts began to line up one after the other. There were bookstores, record stores, drugstores, restaurants and an endless procession of people. In the center of it all was the Avon Cinema, its old fashion marquee proudly jutting out in triangular formation. Jay knew the layout of Thayer Street as well as any college student living on the East Side.

"I don't know how long before we have to break out the winter coats," Erik said, then slipped his arm around Jay's waist and pulled him in close. Their lips met, mouths opened. Erik's tongue dove into Jay's mouth and Jay gently sucked on it. When their lips parted, Jay was stunned and aroused. Never before had anyone kissed him in a public place.

"I couldn't help myself," Erik said.

Jay held both of Erik's hands. "It's okay," he said. "I'm happy you wanted to kiss me."

"Why wouldn't I want to kiss you," Erik said.

Jay could think of a few reasons, like his age and the fact that he was holding back information. He reached out and held Erik's hand. "What if I was younger?"

"I'll take you as you are, if you don't mind."

But Erik didn't know exactly how old Jay was. Jay didn't think Erik would be happy if he suddenly found out. But he had to find out sooner or later.

"Are you into getting a bite to eat?" Erik asked.

"I'm sort of broke right now."

"On me," Erik said. "We'll get a nice meal, a bottle of wine."

If they ordered wine Jay might get carded. What an awful way for Erik to find out the truth about him. "I'm not really that hungry, how about just grabbing a sandwich at Geoff's?"

"Are you sure?"

"I'm really not hungry," Jay said. "Plus, Geoff's is just down the street." Jay didn't mention that Geoff's didn't serve alcohol.

Erik shrugged. "If that's what you want."

"We can go to a nice restaurant when I'm hungry and can really enjoy it,"

"Well, I'm hungry now, so let's go."

—

The lights were low as Michelle sat next to Ian on the sofa, the gentle sound of Chet Baker's horn playing in the background. He slipped his arm around her shoulder and pulled her in close before kissing her. He'd spent dinner listening to Michelle carry on about the stock market and the falling price of tech stocks and anything related to computers. She never trusted tech stocks and wasn't surprised that they were falling in price. It had seemed too trendy, she'd said. Now it was Ian's turn to get what he wanted and she was going to give it to him. All he had to do was continue playing with her.

Bringing his hand up, he rubbed the tips of his fingers along Michelle's delicate neck, feeling her soft skin. She sighed and nuzzled closer to him. Finally she was quiet. That was a sign to continue, and as Ian continued to rub her neck, he brought his hand up higher, slipping his fingers into her hair, drawing the soft strands over his hand.

"You like that?" Ian whispered.

"Yes," Michelle purred as she rubbed his stomach. "I'm so comfortable." She looked up at him and the two kissed once more, only deeper this time.

Ian slid his hand from her neck to her back, then lower. He had to go slow, time each move perfectly. Their lips parted and he looked into her deep brown eyes. He shifted slightly in his seat so she could notice his arousal. "You're so beautiful."

Michelle smiled shyly as a blush rose to her cheeks.

"I thought that the first time I saw you," Ian said. He rubbed her back, then slowly moved towards her. Their lips met again, her mouth opened to greet his tongue. Then slowly, he laid her down on the sofa and rested his body on top of hers. Michelle's hands rubbed his back and her legs parted as they kissed, their tongues sliding one over the other. Ian caressed her thigh, lifting her leg slightly higher. Once more their lips parted and Ian nuzzled into her neck, gently nibbling her flesh. "I want to make you feel good," he whispered. He slid down her body, gently kissing her small breasts, her stomach, then lower. He lifted her skirt to expose her nylons and the soft pink panties beneath. Placing his hand between her legs he gently rubbed, then applied a little pressure. He would get her worked up so much that she would do anything to have him get her off. Anything. Bending down, he kissed between her legs, then moved his fingers under her skirt, dipping them into the waistband of her nylons and pulling them off. Her legs were so soft as he discarded the nylons on the floor. Michelle let out a soft moan as he kissed her inner thighs and rubbed her calves. He was giving her everything she wanted, needed and craved.

Michelle's pink panties covered her juicy mound. There wasn't a single moist spot on them. If she were Iris her panties would be dripping wet by now. He ran his tongue down the inside of Michelle's thigh, moving closer to her pussy. Massaging both her thighs with his firm touch, he bent down and took in the scent of her sex. He gently kissed and rubbed his face in her crotch, then moved back. There was some moisture evident now.

Ian moved up closer to her, then kissed her cheek and he dipped his right hand into her panties and rubbed his middle finger against the opening of her sex. He gently pressed his finger inside the wet folds and heard Michelle sigh. He looked at her, then gently brushed his lips against hers. "I want to make you feel good."

Michelle smiled.

"Do you want that?" Ian asked.

"Yes," she said, her hot breath rushing against Ian's face.

"That's good." Ian moved his finger inside her sex. She was giving herself to him the way it was meant to be. He was the man. He was the one in control. "I want to be inside you."

Michelle rolled slightly and brushed her lips against his.

She would not feel pleasure unless she did as he pleased. "Do you want that?"

"Yes," Michelle said softly.

Ian felt his cock twitch with excitement. He was going to have her. "I want to be inside you and feel you with my fingers." He found her clit and began to slowly rub it with the tip of his finger. "I want to take you from behind." He kissed her cheek, then her mouth. She was almost panting.

Michelle unzipped Ian's fly, then dipped her hand inside his slacks and wrapped her fingers around his shaft. This was going to work. He could almost feel his prick easing up her ass, slowly fucking her in a way she'd never been fucked before. There was no turning back now, she'd shown that she wanted it, she would look like a horse's ass if he didn't do what he wanted. He had her.

"I want to do something special with you," he said.

"Oh Ian," Michelle said as she gave him a little kiss.

Ian moved his hand from her sex to her round ass. "We can make each other feel so good." Her ass was smooth just like the rest of her. "Your ass would feel so good."

Michelle let out a little giggle. "What are you talking about, Ian?"

Ian caressed her ass. "You know what I mean."

"Don't be shy, Ian," Michelle said.

"I want to have anal sex with you."

There was a pause, then Michelle kissed him. She pulled away and looked into his eyes. "Let's stay how we are."

"I want to be inside you," Ian said as he slid his hand down her ass and pressed his middle finger against her tight hole. "Here."

"I don't do that," she said.

Ian was annoyed, but refused to let it show. "Not even for me? Just this once? I'll go slow."

Michelle took her hand away from his shaft. "No, Ian."

No, Ian. Those words were like a slap in the face. Who the fuck did she think she was? He grabbed hold of her ass and pulled her closer to him as she began to push away. She didn't seem to understand that he was in control. "Come on and let me."

"No."

Another high and mighty little bitch, Ian thought. He held her closer to him as she struggled to get herself loose.

"Let me go," she said. "Come on."

Ian held her tighter, almost laughing at how she wasn't able to handle herself. She was a big fucking bitch until push came to shove. His father had been right, these fucking cunts were all trouble. First that stuck up cunt who'd always thought she had the upper hand, now this one. She was kicking him now, but not hard enough to do any damage. Barely hard enough to feel it. This stupid bitch thought her ass was too good for him. Fuck her. He pushed his finger up her asshole and heard her scream. Let her fucking scream, she'd come to like it. Then he felt her hand slap him hard on the face. The fucking cunt tried to push out of his grip, but he reached up and grabbed her arms as the two of them fell off the sofa and onto the floor, crashing into the edge of the coffee table and pushing it away.

Who did she think she was to slap him? Ian was playing with her and she had to go and act like some stupid bitch. Ian grabbed her as she tried to stand up and run, then knocked her back to the floor. Her fucking skirt was already up over her ass, and his cock was hard as he straddled her legs to hold them still and tried to grab her free left hand. He'd show her who was boss. But he wasn't fast enough and she used her free arm to push herself up slightly, just enough to turn and glare at him as she tried to kick her feet. Then the back of her hand connected with the left side of Ian's face, knocking him off her just enough for her to get free and run to the door.

At the door, clutching her pocketbook, she struggled with the doorknob. He'd locked it with the dead bolt and she was too stupid to realize it. Ian lunged at her. He almost laughed as he pressed his crotch against her ass. He grabbed the back of her neck and pushed her face against the door. But then her elbow jammed into his stomach, sending him back as he gulped air and clutched his stomach. Ian felt a sharp, burning pain as Michelle's heel connected with his nuts. Bending in a fetal position, Ian grabbed his crotch and grunted before falling to the floor.

The front door flew open and Ian watched Michelle run into the night.

—

Michelle sat behind the wheel of her beat up Ford Taurus in

the driveway of Ian's house and tried to compose herself. She was not going to cry, or at least that was what she'd told herself. She'd always hated women who cry at the drop of a hat. She was not going to be one of them. She wiped dampness from her eyes and told herself to stop. She was shivering, but that was from the cold. It wasn't her nerves. Fumbling through her purse, she tried to find her keys. She didn't want to have to go back into that house again, not even for her coat. She could go back later. She pushed her wallet out of the way, flicked the tube of lipstick to the side. Where were her keys? She had to drive out of there before he came back. She couldn't bare looking at him again. Her legs were shaking. Once she got the car started and the heat kicked in she would be fine. Her keys were pushed to the far corner of her pocketbook.

Michelle sniffed, then wiped more wetness from her eyes. All she had to do was put the key in the ignition, but she couldn't get the key to do what she wanted. The front door to Ian's house was closed. What if he came out? What would she say? The key slipped into the ignition and she sighed. She put her foot on the break, feeling the pedal against the sole of her foot. Her shoes were also inside. They were her favorite pair. Going inside wasn't an option. Her shoes could wait. There was a dull pain under her right eye from where her face had connected with the door. She didn't have to look in the mirror to know it was bruised. Looking at it would do no good. She turned the key and heard the engine roar.

There was a tap on her side window and Michelle jumped at the sound. Was it Ian? She didn't want to look, but knew she had to. It wasn't Ian. It was an old woman in a thick white sweater that she pulled around her frail body. The old woman looked startled. Did Michelle look that bad? She unrolled the window and saw that the old woman had walked up to the car, her thin hand reached inside and delicately touching Michelle's cheek. Michelle tried to speak but couldn't control the trembling of her bottom lip.

"Are you alright?" the old woman asked.

Try as she did, Michelle couldn't get herself to say a word. Tears blurred her vision and she couldn't help but gasp for air. It wasn't long after that when she began to sob uncontrollably.

"Why don't you turn off the car and come inside. I live next door," the old woman said. "Is there someone you would like to call?"

Michelle nodded. "The police," she managed to say through trembling lips before turning off the engine.

"We can do that," the old woman said.

Michelle stepped out of the car and stood on shaky legs. The old woman came up to her shoulders, there was no way she'd be able to use her for support. Hopefully she wouldn't have to as she followed her across the lawn and to her house.

"My grandson is a lawyer," the old woman said. "Maybe you should give him a call."

Tuesday

Anita was at the receptionist desk wearing the headset Dale had bought so she could have her hands free while on the telephone. Whenever he saw the little microphone suspended in front of her mouth all he could think of was when he'd seen Madonna's Blonde Ambition tour. Nobody looked better in a corset than Madonna, and her hands-free microphone had been all the talk after the show; that and how great Madonna looked. When Dale had found the same type of microphone as a telephone he had to have one for the salon. Anita had taken well to the new telephone, especially since he'd found one that wouldn't mess up her hair. With the addition of the computer system the salon was beginning to look so high tech. He walked behind the desk and looked over Anita's shoulder. The schedule for the month was up on the screen, along with each stylist's client list ready to come up at the click of the mouse. Tony was getting a decent client base, which pleased both him and Dale. What was good for Tony was good for the salon.

"This makes my life so much easier," Anita said. "I love you for it."

"What about the stylists?"

"They're catching on," Anita said. "Your niece called to say she's dropping in to see you."

"Do we have an open chair?"

"Yes, but she said she wants to talk." Anita moved the cursor to point to the time block in which she'd placed Laura's appointment. "I can't remember the last time she was here for a haircut so I went and booked her."

Dale gave Anita's shoulders a gentle squeeze. "You're perfect."

"I know," Anita said, then spun her chair around. "I know you have a boyfriend, but you have to see Tony's new client. He's cutting his hair now." She lowered her voice for the next bit of gossip. "I think the guy was hard when he walked in. You could see everything in his jeans. Tony was so good about not staring at his client's crotch. The guy is huge."

"Is he from Texas?" Dale asked.

Anita smiled, then said, "I don't know how Tony does it, but he has a lot of hot men in his client base." She moved the cursor over to Tony's address book and clicked to display his client phone list. All but two listed were men. "From what I hear word got around at Mirabar that he's a hairdresser and things started picking up."

"If it brings in clients, I'm not complaining," Dale said. He walked up to the cutting floor, then glanced to his right and noticed Tony was wearing a pair of tight leather pants that showed off the curve of his ass, along with the curves in front. His body shirt was the same shade of black and accented every ripple of muscle as he moved. It was enough to make Dale's cock come alive, so he tried not to look. Instead he studied the well chiseled jaw of the man whose hair Tony was cutting. Such beautiful dark eyes, and an aquiline nose. His lips were full, perfect for sucking cock. Most people getting their hair cut look into the mirror to make sure their hair wasn't being cut too short. Not Tony's client; he was watching Tony's face, perhaps even trying to make eye contact. The best relationships started with lust, even in business.

"Uncle Dale," Laura called out from the stairs, her hair was tied back in a pony tail that swung with her stride. She gave him a big hug. "Did Anita tell you?"

"Yes, what's so important?" Dale asked, assuming it was about some boy. Dale remembered what it was like when he was fifteen. All he could think about back then was boys.

"I guess I don't rate," Kyle said from his area on the left side of the room. Mrs. Christianbaum sat in his chair with her hair partially curled and waited for Kyle to resume his work.

Laura gave Kyle a hug and a kiss on the cheek. "I need to talk to my uncle for a little while."

Kyle grabbed the end of Laura's pony tail and inspected it for split ends. "We need to cut the tips of your hair later."

"Dale, you have siblings?" Tony asked. "I didn't know."

"What, you thought I was hatched?" Dale said, which made Mrs. Christianbaum burst into laughter as Dale brought Laura into the back office.

"Who was that?" Laura asked once the office door was closed.

"Tony. He's a stripper at night," Dale whispered.

Laura's eyes grew wide as she took a seat at Dale's desk. "Really?"

"He said it's only until he builds a client list, but I'm not too sure about that."

"Like Chippendales?"

"A little raunchier."

"Wait 'till I tell Theresa. She'll die. I know she will." Laura burst into giggles. "That is so cool."

Dale sat up straight. He was the cool uncle, he liked that. "So tell me, what did you come here to talk about? I don't think it was about strippers."

"Well, not really." Laura looked at the floor and studied her worn out Nike sneakers. "It's about this guy I'm dating."

Dale tried not to smile. She was probably getting nervous because they'd started kissing and he didn't want to make her feel any more silly than she already did. "What's his name?"

"David," Laura said. "He's so cute. All the girls love him. I mean, you know. He's built like a football player."

"He sounds like a hottie," Dale said, happy to be able to use the latest slang.

Laura rolled her eyes. "Oh my God, Uncle Dale, he is so cute! You should see him. I'm not popular, so I can't believe he's dating me. Not that I'm a geek or anything, don't get me wrong."

"I know you're not a geek."

"Well, that might change. I mean, this is going to sound so dumb to you."

"No it won't," Dale said, then bit his tongue. Laura was coming to him for personal advice. Not only did she like him but she also trusted him.

"I've been seeing David for a while now. Like, two months. He wants to . . . you know. I can't believe I'm talking about this."

"It's cool."

Laura grinned. "Okay. Well, he wants to go all the way."

If it wasn't for the wall holding him up, Dale would have been on the floor.

"We haven't done it. Not yet," Laura said.

Dale was glad to hear that. At least this wasn't going to be like the song Pappa Don't Preach, from Madonna's second album. She was only fifteen years old, which was how old he'd been when he'd started thinking seriously about actually having sex. Did he have any condoms hanging around?

"Uncle Dale?"

"Oh my," Dale said, then let out a nervous chuckle. "I didn't expect that. Guess I'm the nerd now."

"I have nobody else to talk to."

"Come here," Dale said as he opened his arms and hugged her close. Although she was fifteen years old, Dale still thought of her as a baby. Dale knew there was little he could do. If she was going to have sex, it would be with or without his consent. "I'm not going to tell you its wrong, but you *do not* have to do it. You do know that? You do not have to do it."

"I know, but he wants to. And, well, I've never been popular before."

Dale grabbed Laura's shoulders and sat her back down. "Something tells me that this won't make you popular. Not only that, but he probably won't know what he's doing."

"I won't know what I'm doing either," Laura said.

"All the more reason to wait for a guy with a little experience."

"So you don't think I should do it?"

"I think you should do what you think is right and not let yourself feel pressured into anything. I hate to say this, but he might only want you for that one thing."

Laura sighed. "That's what Theresa said. And that I would be a slut if I did."

Dale rolled his eyes. A slut? Such nonsense. He opened the top desk drawer and rummaged through it. He thought he'd once put some condoms in there just in case anything might happen at work. One had to be prepared for such things. He found some, pulled them out and checked the expiration dates. They weren't expired.

Laura's eyes grew wide. "I am so embarrassed."

"Look, if you want my opinion, I think you should wait. But that's not for me to decide, so if you do end up, well, doing it, please use one of these." He handed her three condoms. "I do not want to see you pregnant or with HIV."

"Uncle Dale!"

"You don't know where he's been or what he's done."

Laura quietly weighted the facts, then gave him a hug. "I don't know what to do."

"Nobody ever does," Dale said. "That's why we have Madonna."

"Uncle Dale, I think you're obsessed."

Dale held the ends of her hair in his hand. "And I think you need to have these split ends cut off."

———

Iris didn't know why Andrew wanted to meet with her at his office. He'd said it had nothing to do with the new offices nor was it anything personal between them. Whatever it was, it had better be good. If it was some stupid trick to see her again she would not be impressed. She didn't care how good looking he was or how suavely he came off. Being played for a fool was not her idea of a good time.

She pulled into the parking lot next to the drab brick office building, then went inside. The law offices of Tyler, Wescott and Allen were on the second floor. She'd forgotten how plain the old offices were. No color, just a beige industrial carpet and off white walls. Not even the furniture was interesting, just simple upholstered blocks that didn't even look comfortable to sit on. As she recalled, Andrew's office wasn't much different. It looked like the office of a lawyer who had to run advertisements on television to get clients. She bet Andrew couldn't wait to get into the new place just to be in more pleasant surroundings.

The receptionist told her to go right in, that Mr. Tyler was waiting for her. And so he was, sitting behind his desk with his jacket off. He stood up from the leather high back chair and shook her hand. "I'm glad you could make it," he said, then motioned for her to take a seat in one of the two brown leather chairs in front of his desk.

"What's this all about?" Iris asked, hoping to sound cold and slightly annoyed.

"Iris, this really isn't about us," Andrew said, slowly walking to his desk and leaning against it. "I wish this wasn't happening, but I feel the need to tell you before it hits the press."

This had to be some type of bad joke. What would hit the press that was so important that she had to be braced first. Iris crossed her legs and glared at him.

"It's about Ian."

Iris was stunned. "What about him?"

"He's being charged with attempted rape."

Iris sat and stared at Andrew for a moment. Ian would never do such a thing. She had to have heard wrong. Not Ian. He was a decent man. He'd never even cheated on her, how could he possibly be charged with such a horrible thing?

"My client is pressing charges."

Iris stood. "Your client is wrong!" She walked away from him, to the corner of the dull office where the brass coat hanger stood, Andrew's navy blue coat hanging on it. "We just broke up, Andrew. He'd never even thought of other women. He was a good man." She put the strap of her clutch over her shoulder. "Are you so hard up for money that you'll take anyone who comes in?"

"Iris, I didn't ask you here to argue." Andrew's voice was soft and calm. "I believe my client."

"You'll believe anyone who helps pay your bills."

"I know you don't mean that," Andrew said. "You're upset."

"You call me in here to accuse the man I spent a year and a half with of rape, then wonder why I'm upset? Don't you think I know him well enough to say that he would not rape anyone? He's just not capable of it, Andrew. He wasn't capable of cheating on me, what makes you think he would do that?"

"I didn't want to argue with you," Andrew said.

"Then why did you bring me here? Did you think I wouldn't be upset?"

"Not like this."

"Not like this?" Iris fumed. "Then how upset did you think I would be?"

"This isn't how I expected it to go." Andrew let out a huff, then rubbed his eyes with his thumb and index finger. "There is one thing I would like to know, Iris. I didn't want to bring this up, but I'm afraid this may be the only time I have for it. Did Ian have any particular sexual act that he liked? Any fetishes?"

"What? I can't believe you're asking me this."

"I'm sorry," Andrew said. "It's something I need to know."

"So you act as if you're doing me a favor, but really all you want is information. All you need to know is that you have the wrong man. Ian would not do that. I don't date rapists."

"That's not what I'm saying."

"Then what are you saying?"

Andrew sat back and looked apologetic. He tapped his lips with his index finger.

"Well?" Iris said. "You brought me over here, you might as well ask away."

"It can wait."

"No, it can't. I'm already upset, what more harm can you do?"

Andrew slowly nodded. "Did he like anal sex?"

Iris was silent. How could he have known? What business was it of his what they'd done in private? She glared at Andrew as he stood there trying to be calm and sane. Who was his client? It had to be a woman. Just because Ian liked anal sex didn't mean he was gay. He'd never even noticed men's bodies, but she'd often caught him looking at women when he didn't think she would notice. That had been proof enough that he wasn't gay.

"You don't have to answer that right now, Iris."

"Who is your client?" Iris asked.

"She's a student."

"She."

"Yes, Iris, she."

—

Ian sat in the passenger seat of his father's Toyota Corolla and stared out at the passing scenery. He'd had nobody else to call to bail him out of jail but his father, who looked disgusted each time Ian caught him glancing at him. That stony look of his father's had given him the creeps when he was a kid and still did. It was the same look he'd gotten when Anna Spitz had beat him in the fifth grade spelling bee. Now Ian had to find a way to get out of this mess with as little trouble as possible. At least he was out of jail.

"I can't believe it," Ian's father said, slowly shaking his head. "I hope you don't try anything stupid. You know they won't let you go into work because of this."

"I'll pay you back for the bail money," Ian said as he slid down in his seat and put his hands over his face. There was no way she could win, he hadn't even penetrated her. Attempted rape, that's what he'd been charged with. Something like that couldn't be hard to get out of. All he would need is a good lawyer.

"Rape," his father said.

Ian let out a huff. "I did not rape her."

"That doesn't matter. Not in the world we live in today. They'll call it rape, even if she came onto you then got all shy about it after. Those feminists have it so a guy is wrong no matter what he does." He shook his head then slapped the steering wheel. "I told you she was trouble. All high and mighty. Full of herself, that's what she was. She even got Donna thinking she could have a career of her own some day."

"It wasn't Iris."

The car slowed to a stop, but still Ian didn't want to look up.

"Then who is making these preposterous accusations?"

"Michelle," Ian said. "I was cheating on Iris with Michelle."

Ian's father sighed. "You do know that doesn't help matters."

Ian sank lower in his seat. "I need a good lawyer."

"We'll get you a good lawyer, don't worry about that. What we need to do now is think. Did she know about Iris?"

"No."

"Are you sure?"

"I'm sure," Ian said, knowing his father wasn't going to lighten up on it. All he wanted was a little quiet time to try and forget about everything.

"Then what does she want? Why is she doing this to you?"

"I don't know, dad."

"Okay. I'm staying with you until this all boils over."

Ian was thankful when the car began to move again. His father was going to stay with him, which meant it would be an endless roll of questions until they could find a way for him to get out of this mess. Didn't his father understand that Michelle was just a man hating little cunt? She hated him and that was why she was doing this to him. All Ian had wanted was a little sex, and look what he got for it. He rolled his eyes.

—

It was 6:15 when Iris's telephone began ringing. Expecting the worse, she'd turned the volume on her answering machine to zero. She didn't want to know who was calling. Even with the television off she knew why people were calling, which was the same reason she didn't bother picking up. The local news had covered the story about Ian attempting to rape Andrew's client. She could imagine how the news must have blown the story out of proportion. Making things sound worse than they were was how the news hiked up their ratings. Andrew had said it had been attempted rape, not an actual rape. Had Ian brought a girl home thinking she would sleep with him and have it blow up in his face? Perhaps he'd misinterpreted her actions and had made his move too quick. It had been a while since he'd been single, and he was upset because Iris had broken up with him. But Ian had known how to interpret Iris. He'd been forceful on occasion, but never so much that he wouldn't back down if she'd said no and meant it. But what if he was feeling rejected and hurt? Could he be so angry that he would do such a thing as rape? Iris didn't think so. Not Ian. Not somebody she'd gone out with.

Iris walked over to the bar and poured herself a vodka tonic. She shook the glass and listened to the ice jiggle around. Her house had always been a calm place for her, with subtle earth tones and large, open rooms. It didn't seem soothing to her now. Hanging above the bar was one of her favorite paintings, The Place L Under Construction by Paul Klee, with it's abstract shapes in bright greens, purples and earthen browns. There was an S Shaped line that was the street, then child-like line drawings of houses and lots on either side. Running parallel to that was another S shaped road with no buildings on it. Abstract landscapes, the beauty of color and open space. Iris let out a sigh, then swirled the liquid in her glass. Once again the ice tinkled. She felt as if her world was falling apart.

She still had to call her mother. But not tonight. She couldn't deal with it tonight. She'd go out and rent a movie but she didn't want to risk running into anyone who just might happen to know her. If she did she knew that Ian would be the topic of the conversation, and the last thing she wanted to do was talk about Ian behind his back. People would want to know what she thought, especially after she'd just broken up with him. She couldn't blame them, it was juicy gossip.

She fought the urge to call Ian and get his side of the story. How would he react to her after she'd broken up with him only to call and pry into his life when he was in trouble? She wouldn't look good, that much she knew. But she had to hear it from him, she had to hear him say that he hadn't done it. The idea that he would do something so horrible was unfathomable. He'd never lifted a hand against her. He wasn't a violent man. Had he hidden it? Could he have hidden it the way he'd supposedly hidden his affair with Andrew's client? She couldn't believe he'd cheated on her. The thought that he would do that had never even entered her mind. She took another sip from her drink and wished she'd made it a double. There was nobody for her to drink with so she might as well just drink alone. Behind her the answering machine clicked on yet again.

Although Iris didn't feel like listening to music, it was better than hearing the machine click on and off. Glass in hand, she walked across the room to the bookshelf and scanned her CD collection. In the morning she'd run through the messages as fast as possible just to make sure none of them were actually important.

———

Dale and Bob cuddled on the sofa at Dale's condominium. They'd watched the news, where they'd found out about Ian's arrest, then they'd flipped through the stations hoping to find something of interest on television. There had been nothing, so they'd stayed on the sofa and cuddled. Dale had made two attempts to telephone Iris, but she either hadn't been home or hadn't bothered to answer. Not even for Dale.

"I've got to get going," Bob said, then gave Dale's knee a playful slap. He stood up from where he rested with Dale in his arms.

"Not yet," Dale said. "It's only ten o'clock."

Bob bent down and gave Dale a kiss on the lips. "I have a big day ahead of me. I should get some sleep."

"Why not sleep here?"

Bob smiled. "Like I would get any sleep."

Dale leaned forward and wrapped his arms around Bob's waist, then pressed his face close to his crotch. He felt Bob's dick shift inside his chinos. "It wouldn't hurt to try it once."

"You're so sweet." Bob ran his fingers through Dale's hair. "Don't you want to try to get in touch with Iris again to see if she's all right?"

"I'm sure she's just not answering her phone." Dale looked up at Bob and pouted. "What if my mean ex-boyfriend comes over and tries to rape me? Who will save me?"

"You said he's not like that."

Dale kissed the bulge of stiffening meat between Bob's legs. "It would be nice to have you here for an entire night."

"I don't have a toothbrush."

"You can buy one in the morning."

Bob rubbed his big hands against Dale's head. "You're one sexy man."

Dale looked up at Bob, hopeful that he would stay. "Does that mean yes?"

"Come up here," Bob said, then planted a wet kiss on Dale's lips.

—

Steve sat in his car and watched the light in Dale's condominium go out. The fucking Saturn wagon was still parked outside, only this time in the parking lot. He'd seen the guy come out of his car and ring the bell to Dale's place. He'd looked straight, which was what Dale had liked about Steve. So that little butch asshole thought he could take Dale from him. There was no way Steve was going to stand for that.

How had Dale found this stupid ass so fast? He better not have been dating him while he'd been with Steve. Wouldn't that have been a typical queer bait way to act, cheating on his boyfriend then taking on the thing he'd kept around to plow his faggy ass once they were broken up. Dale had never cared about him, and now it was clear. The one time he'd tried to have a relationship with a guy and he cheats on him, then flaunts it in Steve's face. Dale was probably just trying to get him back by making him jealous. Steve would teach him a lesson, that was for sure. Didn't Dale know who was in control here? It wasn't Dale, it was Steve. There was no way Dale was going to get the best of him. No way.

Steve opened the glove compartment and fingered the jackknife he'd put there earlier in the week. He pulled out the jackknife and rubbed his thumb against the smooth black plastic casing, then got out of the car. First he would teach Dale's new fuck not to mess with him, then he would give Dale a little warning. Street lamps lit the road, but none illuminated the parking lot. The outer edge was semi-lit, but where the Saturn was parked had enough shadow to hide Steve as he ducked down and pulled out the knife. He ran his fingers over the outside wall of the rear passenger side tire, then plunged the knife deep into the rubber. Air hissed out as the tire quickly deflated.

Standing, Steve casually walked to the sidewalk and glanced over once to see the Saturn looking somewhat lopsided. That would show him who was boss.

Wednesday

The door to the salon was already unlocked when Dale got there, the leather laptop computer carrier strapped over his shoulder. There was Anita, sitting at the receptionist desk and reviewing the stylists' appointments for the day. She looked up as the door closed behind him.

"I couldn't believe I was here before you," Anita said. "At first I didn't know what to do, then remembered that you'd given me a key."

"Bob had a flat tire this morning," Dale said. "I offered to call AAA but he said he'd change it. He wouldn't let me help, not that there was anything I could do but watch him acting butch. Did you know there's a special order in taking off those lug nut things?"

Anita nodded. "He can probably get it patched."

"He doesn't think so," Dale said. "It was punctured on the side. Isn't that kind of strange."

Anita raised here eyebrows. "Just a little."

"Me too," Dale said. "I'm taking him out to dinner this week, it's the least I can do."

There was a moment of silence, then Anita said, "I wonder what Tony's going to wear today."

"Who knows," Dale said as he walked up to the stairs, then paused and turned towards Anita. "I just can't wait to see what he wears this summer."

Anita giggled.

As long as the customers came in and Tony wasn't being too revealing, Dale didn't care what he wore. In all his years of owning the salon he'd never had to tell a single one of his stylists how to dress.

He walked into his office, closed the door and took a seat at the desk. He hoped the punks who had slashed Bob's tire didn't return to his neighborhood.

—

A day later, and Iris felt even more frantic. What kind of man was Ian? She hoped it hadn't happened, but wasn't sure. And if so, what could have driven him to do something like that? Had he been so upset about the break-up that he'd gone nuts? She tilted her head under the hot spray of water and rinsed the soap out of her hair. She'd slept horribly and knew she'd have to apply concealer under her eyes to hide the dark circles. Perhaps if she spoke with Andrew's client it would help. But would he allow her to do that? He would have to, that was all there was to it. He'd been the one to tell her, he would have to allow her to speak with this woman to ease her mind. She'd prefer hearing it from Ian, but she knew that would be impossible. Would she be able to trust him anyhow? Had she ever been able to trust him? What kind of fool was she?

Iris finished her shower, then dried herself off. The Valium tablet was on the dresser where she'd put it. Despite what Dolores had said, drugs were not the answer. Andrew's business card was also on the dresser. After wrapping a towel around herself, she sat on the bed then dialed his office. The receptionist put her through.

"What can I do for you, Iris?" Andrew said.

Iris tried to stay calm. "I need to speak to your client."

"I'll talk to her about it and get back to you."

"She has to talk to me, Andrew." Iris bit her lower lip to stop herself from crying, but it was no use.

"I'm not sure if it would be such a good idea, Iris," Andrew said. "You dated Ian, there might be a conflict of interest."

"You had no problem telling me about the case before."

"I wanted to tell you before you learned about it on the news.

I care about you."

Iris began to pace. "And I thought you'd done it for information. How silly of me."

"That's not what it was about, Iris."

"Then let me talk to her," Iris said, her voice growing louder with the last word. She paused to take a deep breath. "Please, Andrew. I need to talk to her. It's the only way that I'll know the truth."

Andrew was silent, obviously contemplating his choices. "I'll talk to her, explain your situation and see what she says. The decision will be hers."

"Thank you," Iris said, then pulled the phone away from her ear and turned it off.

—

There was a loud knock on Steve's bedroom door, waking him from sleep. Then Jay's annoying voice. "Steve, you're going to be late for class."

Which class? Steve hadn't gone to class in so long that he'd forgotten what his schedule was. "Oh shit!" he said, hoping to fool Jay into thinking he cared.

"I take it you're awake, so I'm off."

"Sure, thanks again." Steve waited until he heard the front door close before pulling the covers over his head. Jay was getting annoying, butting into his life like this. What did he care if Steve went to class on time or not? If Steve didn't feel like going to class, he didn't have to. He was smart enough to catch up once he got Dale back. The tricky part was getting rid of that little fuck who was poisoning Dale against Steve. Steve imagined the guy telling Dale about how rotten ex-boyfriends are, and how there had to be something wrong with Steve because he didn't use him like some kind of sex freak.

Steve wasn't like the others. His relationships didn't revolve around sex, they were something more. He had to let Dale understand that. Once Dale understood, then he would go back with Steve. Dale would see how good Steve was for him and not want to continue living some perverted life where he was only used for sex. Steve could take Dale away from that faggot life and show him what he could really have.

Hopefully puncturing that freak's tire was enough to keep him away from Dale, but what if it wasn't? He would have to take more drastic measures. Steve punched the mattress. He couldn't just sit around and let that stupid fuck walk all over him. Steve's father had always told him to stand firm and let justice prevail. But sometimes you have to push to get what you want, Steve thought.

He threw the covers off, then glared at the ceiling. He needed a plan, something that would force that creep away from Dale. First he would have to see Dale again, make sure he didn't forget about him. He needed to be fresh in Dale's mind, a memory of how good their life together had been. He also had to get a look at that asshole who was fucking Dale. Get a real good look at the guy so Steve would know just who his enemy was.

Steve crossed his arms and grabbed the sides of his chest. He'd also need pictures so he could really target the guy. Find out where he lived, what he did, where he hung out. Dale knew Steve's car, so he'd have to get a rental. How would he explain the rental to Jay? He didn't have to, he could park it down the street. Nobody would notice. As long as Jay didn't see him drive it he would be fine.

—

The round table was just small enough to accommodate two cups of coffee and the slice of cheese cake, which Jay and Alma were sharing. Jay plunged his plastic fork into the creamy slice, then left it there to lift his coffee cup. Feeling it was too hot, he put the cup back down.

"Just tell him the truth, darling," Alma said as she lifted the coffee cup to her lips and blew steam off the top before taking a sip. "You make so much out of little things."

"You weren't there the first night, at the club," Jay said. "He doesn't like twinks. He made a big thing out of it. He even mentioned it last week, and earlier this week. I can't tell him."

"Perhaps he was just making conversation. Do you think?" Alma grabbed Jay's discarded fork and broke off a piece of cake for herself. "I think he was."

"But what if he dumps me?"

"Then he's an asshole. But I do not think so, I like him." She raised her eyebrows. "And you?"

Jay studied the wall across from him, at the ads of people looking for roommates, plays about to open at the local theaters and the comings and goings of local bands. Above his head pots and pans loomed, seemingly ready to fall on his head and knock him unconscious. Nobody sitting around them in the tightly packed coffee house seemed to care about their conversation.

"Well?" Alma said.

"You're not in the middle of this, it's easy for you to say anything." Jay slumped down in his seat. "This never happens to me."

Alma raised the plastic fork as if conducting an orchestra. "Life is all about risk. You can trust nothing and only hope for the best."

"No offense, Alma, but that doesn't help." Jay grabbed the fork from her and pushed it into the cheese cake. He held a small piece of cake at the end of the fork and let it dangle in front of his mouth. "You have men and women falling at your feet, so it's easy to say those things. It doesn't matter to you. There's always someone else waiting."

"Please eat that piece of cheese cake, darling, the hunger is making you delusional."

Jay gulped down the piece of cheese cake, "It is true. You always have a date or two waiting."

"And I go out, darling. I talk to strangers. I take risks." Alma paused. "Perhaps some day it will all get me killed. But I think I'm a good judge of character. I've only met one psychopath."

"Only one?" Jay knew better than to believe her.

"Please darling, let me be. Only one." Alma reached out and held Jay's hands. "And it has not stopped me. Jay, I think Erik likes you for you. Take a chance and tell him the truth. If I'm wrong, then there will be others."

"There will be?"

"There are always others," Alma said, leaning back in her seat.

"Maybe," Jay said. Steve came quickly to mind. What if Erik

did stay with him, then dumped him a month or two later with no explanation? How would he feel then? If Dale could do it to Steve then it could happen to anyone. He tossed the fork on the table and let out a sigh. He was beginning to think dating wasn't worth the emotional turmoil.

"Stop thinking so much about it," Alma said.

"I'm thinking about Steve."

Alma rolled her eyes. "Where has he been?   People are starting to wonder."

"What are you talking about?"

"He has been acting odd, don't you think?"

"His boyfriend dumped him, give him a break."

"No need to get defensive, darling."

"I'm not being defensive. It's just that I would be upset if that happened to me."

"Upset enough to stop going to class?"

Jay was silent.

"He hasn't been showing up to classes," Alma said. "At least I haven't seen him in Western Civilization."

"Really?"

"He wasn't there today."

"He told me he was going to class," Jay said. "Are you sure he wasn't there?"

"Well, darling, I didn't see him."

Maybe Steve was more depressed than Jay had thought? Did Steve need to talk to a counselor about it? It probably wouldn't hurt, but how would Jay bring it up in conversation? "How many classes has he missed?"

"Not many. A few people have noticed and were curious about him. I'm sure it's nothing."

"I hope so," Jay said.

———

Steve waited outside the Dale Pagnali Salon in the rented dark blue Dodge Neon. The interior didn't seem as open as the VW Jetta, but the car did serve a purpose. Dale would never suspect him of driving another car.

Steve had already seen Kyle and a few of the women who

worked there leave, now he was just waiting for Dale. As usual, Dale's Lexus was parked out front waiting for him. Dale stepped out clutching a leather briefcase. He put it down briefly to lock the door, then went to his car. Steve crouched down and slipped into a pair of cheap plastic glasses that tinted when it got bright. He had to make sure not to get too close to Dale's car, and he wanted to make sure he was not recognized if he did.

Keeping two car lengths behind, Steve followed Dale's car around corners, past houses and apartment buildings, back onto Wickenden Street with its many shops and restaurants. At the light just before the on ramp to the elevated highway, Dale kept to the right. He looked into the windows of the framing shop that gave a ten percent discount to fags and dykes. The light changed and Dale went onto the highway. Once on the highway, Steve made sure there was always a car between them.

—

Slipping into highway traffic, Dale turned up the volume to Madonna's new CD and tapped his fingers against the steering wheel to the beat. Madonna was brilliant, there was no doubting it. He didn't know if the highway was the quickest way to get to Bob's place, but it was worth a try. He'd go a new way the next time he went to Bob's, and another after that until he found a route that he liked. He didn't mind driving, and if it took him longer than expected, he always had Madonna with him, so what did it matter.

He was pleased that Bob had accepted his invitation to dinner, even if it meant that Dale had to stay at his bachelor pad. He'd felt horrible that some delinquent had slashed Bob's tire. It was the only way to make it up to him. Maybe once they'd been together for a year or so he would have Bob move into his condominium. Or perhaps they would buy a house together? Somewhere in the country, with a white fence and big yard. Maybe in Bristol or Barrington. What about Newport? No, Newport was too far from the salon and driving over that damn bridge in winter would be a bitch. If they got a place in Bristol they would be next to Colt State Park. Plus Bristol was more interesting, with its colonial houses and the famous Fourth of July parade that people from all over flocked to see.

Colt State Park was on the bike path. He and Bob could get some bikes and ride the path. Maybe they could get some kites, too. People always flew beautiful kites at Colt State Park. They could buy a colorful box kite, or maybe even one of those stunt kites. And if they lived in the country they could get a dog to bring with them while they flew their kite. A German Shepard with a pink dog collar. They could name the dog Butch, and he could sit next to them while they ate a lunch of bread, cheese, wine and assorted grapes and strawberries. They could tie the kite string up on a post in the ground and watch it fly while they ate and played with Butch. It would be a perfect way to spend a perfect day with Bob.

—

Steve followed Dale onto the School Street exit off 95 North. From there Dale drove through the back roads of Pawtucket, past beat up apartment houses, liquor stores, an Irish pub. They were heading toward Newport Avenue. Dale had to be going to that guy's apartment. Steve made sure to keep a good distance now. He followed Dale into an apartment complex, past one wood sided building after another, each with its own parking lot. He couldn't believe Dale would date anyone who lived in a place like this. Dale turned into one of the parking lots, then Steve spotted the Saturn wagon! He noted the number on the building, then kept driving so Dale wouldn't take notice of him. Once past the building, he pulled into a lot and parked at the far end, out of sight. There was a note pad and pen on the passenger's seat. He jotted down a few notes. That was enough for now. He'd come back later, when everyone was asleep.

—

Iris sat in front of her desk staring blankly at page after page of furniture. Not a single item was recognizable. Thankfully Dolores was understanding and wasn't in a hurry to get moved into the new house. Iris wasn't sure how well she would hold up if she was under a lot of pressure. Still, she needed to get more work for when she finished with Dolores and Andrew. If only she had the drive to go out and hunt for work, but the truth was that she didn't.

She'd broken up with Ian and now he was all she could think about. Had she done the wrong thing? The telephone rang and she answered it. It was Andrew. Iris twirled around in her chair and looked down at the hardwood floor.

"She'll talk to you," Andrew said. "Can you come by my office at noon tomorrow?"

Iris sighed. "Yes, I can make it." She was going to find out the truth. Finally.

"I'm worried about you," Andrew said.

"Don't be. I'll be fine once I talk to her," Iris said. "She has to be wrong."

"And if she's not?"

Then did I know Ian at all, Iris thought.

"I hate this," Andrew said. "I hate knowing you're upset."

Iris swallowed back tears. "I have to go. I'll see you tomorrow." She hung up the telephone. Tomorrow she would find out the truth. The idea made her stomach knot. What would this woman have to say that would convince her?

There was a gentle tap on the office door before it opened. Dolores stepped inside, the heels of her shoes making a hard noise against the floor. She looked around, then at Iris. "Such a smart office, Iris," she said. "I hope you don't mind my dropping in on you like this."

"I'm still looking for furniture to show you, but come in," Iris said

"That's not what I came here for," Dolores said as she placed her brown leather pocketbook on the edge of the desk.

Iris did not feel like talking about Ian, but that was what Dolores had come to do. She looked up and tried not to let her annoyance show, Dolores was a client, after all.

"Timothy is having dinner with the boys tonight, clients mostly, so I thought it would be fun to take you out to dinner," Dolores said.

"That's nice of you, but I really am not up to it," Iris said.

"Nonsense, dear, we can talk about anything you want. Timothy is all up in arms over the Presidential elections and the mess in Florida. I don't know what I'll do if Bush gets into office.

Timothy despises the man."

It was obvious that Dolores knew what had happened to Ian, but was not about to discuss it. Iris's own mother would never have taken that path with her, she would have confronted her immediately. Margot would let her disappointment be known.

"Everyone thinks plastic surgery is a breeze," Dolores said. "It isn't. At first, after they've cut you open and done all their ghastly procedures, you come out looking worse than when you went in. After my first procedure I cried. But once the healing began and the pain went away I felt new and beautiful again and was able to go out and be seen. I acted like nothing had happened and so did everyone else."

Iris looked up at crazy Dolores, who at the moment seemed to be the smartest person she knew. "Okay," Iris said. "Let's go."

"Do you like Al Forno, dear? It will be my treat."

"Dolores, really, you don't have to do that."

"I want to do something nice for you."

Iris's eyes began to water and she knew tears were soon come. It was silly, but there was nothing she could do about it. This crazy old woman knew her better than her own mother. Iris stood and gave Dolores a hug.

"It's all right," Dolores said as she brushed her hand over Iris's hair. "Would you like a Diazepam?"

"No thanks," Iris said as she pulled away from Dolores. "I'll be fine without it."

Dolores patted her pocketbook. "They're here if you change your mind. Now, why don't you go and fix yourself up. I'll be here, looking around. I find all this fascinating."

Thursday

Dale was still riding high from the kiss Bob had given him before sending him out the door. Dale wanted to be at the salon early to get some paperwork done and show Anita how to keep track of the stock on the computer. Bob was good with computers and seemed to take an interest in the salon, not to mention Dale's body. The stairs let out a hollow, metallic bong as he bounced down them. He loved how Bob's big hands roamed his body, smoothed over his ass and delved into the crack. Just remembering the sex they'd had stirred up Dale's lust. Bob was so wonderful that Dale didn't even mind drinking out of a mug with the logo of some football team on it. It probably made him look butch just drinking from it anyhow. Dale could use a little butchness in his life.

Stepping outside, Dale took in a breath of cool, fresh air. Why couldn't he have met Bob earlier? There were their cars, parked next to each other. Dale had backed up into the parking spot the previous night to show Bob how good he was at being butch. Bob had said he'd been impressed, as well he should have been. Then they'd gone into Bob's apartment and ended the perfect night with some of the most amazing sex Dale had had in a while. Dale was about to walk between the two cars when he noticed something on the side of the Saturn. He looked closer. It was white spray paint.

He sucked in a sharp breath as he read the single word that had been sprayed over the driver's side door: faggot.

Dale ran back into the apartment building, rang Bob's apartment, then was buzzed in. He couldn't believe this was happening. What would Bob think, and how would he react? Dale stormed down the hall. Bob met him at the door, pulling a white t-shirt over his head. "What's wrong?"

"It's your car," Dale said.

"Not another flat?"

"Worse."

"What?"

"Spray paint."

Bob rolled his eyes. "Great! Let me get dressed."

Dale waited in the living room while Bob dressed, then the two of them went back out to Bob's car. Bob glared at the word painted on the side of his car, then shook his head. He rubbed his thumb against the word. "It's dry," he said.

"I'm sorry," Dale said, hesitant to say any more.

Bob's eyes didn't leave the white marking. "I'll have to call the police."

"You don't have to," Dale said. "We can get it painted."

"This is vandalism," Bob said as he pointed at the word. "It has to be reported."

"Do you want me to stay?"

"No, go to work," Bob said as he pulled Dale in close and gave him a hug. "I'll take care of this."

Dale slipped his arms into Bob's coat and hugged him back. "You know what," Dale said.

"What?"

"I think I'm falling in love with you."

"Well now, that's the best thing I've heard all day."

———

Steve slowed as he drove around the block one more time. He spotted Dale and his faggot boyfriend near the cars. Steve's mouth dropped open and he almost gagged when he saw the two of them hug. What were they thinking, anyone could see them. That guy Dale was with was probably proud to be a pansy. Steve was shocked he didn't have any stupid pink triangles or rainbow stickers on his car. This was too much. He'd have to try harder next time. That little fag was going to pay.

—

Iris was back in Andrew's office, this time not alone with him. Michelle was there, tall, thin, with small breasts under a thick lavender sweater. Long auburn hair fell to her shoulders in soft curls that shone under the overhead lighting. Iris sat in the chair to the right of Michelle's, then turned towards Andrew and asked if they could be alone.

"Is that okay with you?" Andrew asked Michelle.

"That would be fine," Michelle said, her eyes lowered as if she were ashamed. Once Andrew was out of the room she looked up at Iris. "I didn't know he had a girlfriend."

"It's over between us," Iris said, though she felt awkward at disclosing even that small bit of information. "How long have you known him?"

"About a week and a half. We met at the College Hill Bookstore." Michelle looked past Iris, then at the floor. She swallowed. "Is that what you want to know."

"No," Iris said, not wanting to ask about what had happened between her and Ian but knowing she had to. It was the only way to know for sure. "How did it happen?"

"You need to know that," Michelle said, her voice soft and low.

Iris couldn't bring herself to look up at her as Michelle told her how she'd gone to Ian's for dinner, then sat with him on the sofa. "I didn't think anything of it, really," Michelle said. "Guys have put their hands on my knee before, and I'm not going to say that I didn't like it. He's handsome and smart, and comes off real sweet." Michelle looked down at her feet and sniffled. "I thought he was it, that perhaps things would work out. I had told all my friends about him. How nice he was and how he likes to cook, and knows all about wine and good food. It was the last thing I expected." She began to cry, and Iris searched her pocket book for a tissue, but was too late. Michelle had pulled one out of the box on Andrew's desk. Iris thought about her first time with Ian, and how she'd also been surprised by his fetish. But she hadn't said no, although she'd thought it odd.

"He had this nice music," Michelle said. "Some type of horn. It was jazz, and this guy was singing. He had this raspy voice, almost like he'd smoked one too many cigarettes."

Chet Baker, Iris thought.

"And we sat there, listening to the music. I thought, This is so romantic." Michelle let out a nervous breath, almost like a forced laugh, then continued with her story. "He started out slow. You know how guys can be when they're trying to be smooth about it. Then we started kissing. Slow at first, with his hands feeling me. Making me feel good, which made me think he cared about making me feel good. And I wasn't afraid, you know. At that point I was fine with it. He was making me feel special, and I liked that."

"Who wouldn't," Iris said, keeping her voice calm. Ian had been that way with her. He'd made her feel so good while she gave into him. It had felt good at first, but later it had seemed more like a compromise.

"Then he did more. He put his hands between my legs and told me that he wanted to make me feel good. I thought he was going to concentrate on me, you know. He'd already started. But then he said he wanted to do something special."

He'd told Iris the same. He'd told her that he wanted to do something special, and that it wouldn't hurt; that he would go slow and make sure she enjoyed it. Iris had said yes, but what would have happened if she'd said no?

Michelle looked up. Her eyes were bloodshot and wet with tears. "I can't believe I'm telling you this."

"It's okay," Iris said, feeling her hands begin to shake. "You don't have to tell me any more."

"Did he do that to you?" Michelle asked.

Iris didn't know what to say, and was thankful when Michelle blew her nose and told her that she didn't have to answer. "Why else would you be here?" Michelle said.

"No," Iris said, "he didn't rape me."

"But he would have."

"I don't know," Iris said, but deep down a part of her said yes.

If Ian had done that to Michelle, he would have done it to her. The thought chilled her. How well had she known Ian, if at all?

—

Jay sat behind the counter as people walked through the racks of video boxes looking for something to watch. He had some reading to do for his literature class, but didn't feel like reading. Two guys were cruising each other in the classics aisle, both of them pretty hot in a perfect kind of way. They had the right kind of loose fitting cargo pants and tight shirts. The one on the left, checking out the blond's ass was taller, with dark skin and a navy pea coat. The other had a fleece lined jacket that looked a little worn, but could have been bought that way. The brunette started talking to the blond, probably making small talk about some movie on the rack. Jay knew he'd never be bold enough to approach a total stranger like that. He didn't care if he was in a very gay place on the East Side of Providence. He could see Erik doing it, though. Erik was so self-assured and handsome.

Jay watched the boys talking and tried to forget about Erik. Instead he thought about Steve and how his car had been parked in the driveway all day but he'd never come home. Jay had hoped he would, especially since he'd wanted to talk to him about Erik. Steve always took his car with him, unless he was going somewhere close. Maybe he'd made friends with someone close by and was visiting? It didn't seem likely, but one never knew. Whatever it was, he wasn't home when Jay had wanted to talk to him about Erik. No big deal, though.

Alma had said Jay was being trivial, but he wasn't too sure about that. It was rare enough to find a guy who wanted him as is and now that he'd found one he wasn't all that keen on losing him over his age. Still, he'd told Alma that he'd tell Erik that he was an undergraduate and not going for his masters degree.

The door opened and in walked Erik, a smile plastered on his face as he stepped up to the counter, his old work boots making a dull sound. "What are you up to after work?" he asked.

"Nothing," Jay said, remembering how Alma had told him to come clean to Erik about his age. Hopefully Erik had only dropped in to say hello, the last thing Jay wanted to do was ruin everything.

"I was hoping to see you, maybe even spend the night with you at my place for a change."

"I have school in the morning."

"I can take you to school."

There was no way Jay could say no, not that he didn't want to spend the night with Erik. Jay nodded, then said, "We can do that."

"Is something wrong?" Erik asked, staring suspiciously at Jay.

"I have a lot on my mind."

"Care to talk about it?"

"Not really," Jay said, hoping Erik would drop the subject.

"Steve still acting weird?"

According to Alma he was, but Jay hadn't seen him much to be able to tell for himself. Jay shrugged. "I still think he needs time."

Erik slowly nodded. "I see. And what do you need?"

Jay planted his hands on the counter to keep them from covering his mouth. He hadn't expected Erik to put him against a wall. What he needed was someone like Erik, but Erik didn't want someone like him. "We need to talk."

Erik raised his eyebrows, took a step back, then crossed his arms. "I was hoping you would say that you needed me."

"I do," Jay blurted out.

"Why don't we talk about this later tonight," Erik said.

"Tonight?"

"I can come back when you get off work."

Jay rubbed his sweaty palms on his pants. "I get off at nine."

Erik looked at his watch and nodded. "I'll be back in a couple of hours."

Jay watched as Erik left the video store. The two men who had been cruising each other rented a film and went off together. An older woman came in and rented the most recent version of *Emma*. For the remainder of the evening Jay counted the hours until closing, then closed out the register and locked up the store. Outside, Erik was waiting in his car. Jay climbed into the passenger seat and said hello, bending over to give Erik a gentle kiss on the lips. The kiss wasn't returned.

Erik didn't bother to set the car in motion, but turned towards

Jay instead. "Are we suddenly okay?"

"I don't know," Jay said, unable to face Erik. Now he had no choice but to say something, but first he wanted to stall and get as much time as possible. "Let's talk about this at your place." Erik's voice held no emotion. "Are you sure?"

"Just go," Jay said, then looked forward. With the radio off and no music coming from the speakers the interior of the car felt claustrophobic. Erik looked out at the road without saying a word. Jay felt sad and guilty, as if nothing was going as he'd wanted. He was going to end up where he would have been if he'd told Erik the truth about himself. Once again he would be single and alone with a lifetime supply of K-Y Lubricant and cum towels. Looking outside it seemed that the night was much darker than usual.

Finally they pulled into the driveway of Erik's ranch in Barrington.

"You're not going into the garage?" Jay asked.

Erik crossed his arms, then tilted his head back as he turned towards Jay. "First I want to know what all this is about."

Jay braced himself for the worst. "You know how you don't like twinks."

"I don't like them, so what," Erik said, then turned towards the white garage door.

"Well, you're dating one."

"What?" Erik turned towards Jay in disbelief.

"I'm not even twenty-one."

Erik slowly shook his head. He tapped his palm against the steering wheel. "I don't believe this," he said half under his breath as he turned the key in the ignition.

Jay sat back in his seat. It was over, he'd had the perfect man and now it was done. He looked down at his hands. Single again. Then he heard the garage door crank open. He quickly turned towards Erik, who still looked unamused. "What's going on?"

Erik kept the car in park. "That's what this was all about," Erik said. "I thought you were going to break up with me. That's what I thought. But no, its something stupid about your age. You know, Jay, I don't like twinks because they act like idiots. They play games and are too young to know what they want. You don't act like that. You have your shit together. I admit that I would have been more leery if I had known your age the first time we'd met, but I know you now." He cupped Jay's face in his hands and gave him a kiss. "For the first time in my life I've met someone I want to be around."

"I'm sorry," Jay said.

"Let's go inside."

Friday

The tablet of Diazepam sat on top of Iris's bureau waiting to be taken. Iris felt her hands shake. She still could not believe Ian had raped that poor woman. Not raped, attempted rape. It was the same, Iris knew, but it sounded slightly better. Grabbing the tissue, Iris unwrapped the tablet and held it in front of herself. The tablet was scored down the center, which made Iris feel slightly better. If she was going to take it, perhaps she should cut it in half. Anything Dolores was able to take and operate in her world had to be stronger than anything Iris could handle. Half a tablet had to be the normal dosage for anyone who just needed to relax.

But how would she cut it? She hadn't slept well the previous night, and doubted if sleep would come easy this night. But first she had to get herself through the day. Thankfully she didn't have to see any new clients. All she had planned was to see Andrew's new office space and talk to Dolores about furniture. Dolores had gone to Gerald's store to take another look at the furniture he had. Gerald wanted to talk to her about some of Dolores's choices, too. Iris wondered what Dolores had done to make Gerald call her. Never before had he done such a thing. She flipped open her laptop computer, booted it up, then searched through the address book for Gerald's number. She dialed, then waited for an answer. Just then, as the phone rang, the idea that Gerald could be calling to find out more about Ian came to mind. There was a pick-up before she could hang up. It was Gerald.

"You wanted to talk to me about Dolores's choices?" she asked, hoping he wouldn't want to discuss anything else.

"I would like you to come in and take a look at them," Gerald said. "It's not that they're gaudy or anything, I'm just not sure what you intend to do with her house. I tried to ask, but she kept going on about movie stars and a chaise longue."

Iris smiled for the first time since finding out about what Ian had done. "We found a wonderful place in Boston that had one we liked. I hope you don't mind."

"I'm not stocking any chaise longues anyhow. Should I?"

"It's a personal item, Gerald. She's bent on having one, so we're decorating an entire room around it. Perhaps if you're nice to her she'll invite you to her house warming. It's an amazing space. The living room is very open and modern, but with a touch of style that one never sees in modern houses. The windows are those huge type you only see in Merchant Ivory films. You can open them up and walk out onto the stone patio if you want."

"It sounds inviting," Gerald said.

"I hear she's going to invite Norman Rezza to the house warming. He just redecorated his study. You should see it. Two chaise longues. It's decadent."

"Two chaise longues? He must have known I didn't have any in stock. Or were they bought on impulse? We all know how he can be."

Iris grinned. She knew that soon Gerald would be stocking a few styles of chaise longues if she didn't say anything. Playing with him was fun, and it took her mind away from Ian and Michelle. But still, she couldn't make him think he should stock up on an item that wouldn't sell. "He happened to run across them at a little shop in Boston. And yes, it was purely an impulsive buy. I'm sure he'll visit with you if he decides to do more than move things around and paint the walls."

"Do you think he'll refurnish?" Gerald asked. Iris was sure

dollar signs were dancing around his head. Norman never did anything in a small way.

"I'm not sure," Iris said. "But what about Dolores's choices?"

"When can you drop in?"

"How does two o'clock sound?"

"I'll expect you then," Gerald said before hanging up.

Iris sighed as she threw the telephone on top of the bed. Gerald hadn't asked about Ian, but someone was bound to. Hiding wasn't something she'd ever wanted to do, so there was no use in starting now. Maybe she'd give Norman a call later on and tell him about how Gerald had been all concerned about chaise longues. Norman would get a kick out of it. And if she felt like talking, he would be the perfect person to talk to.

—

"Don't you look happy today," Kyle said to Dale as he pulled strands of Mrs. Dutchfield's hair through the cap so he could apply the color.

"I couldn't be happier," Dale said. He held onto the strap of the leather laptop computer case as he made his way to the office. Once in the office, he closed the door, put down the laptop, then took a seat at his desk. He couldn't imagine anything getting better than it was now. Even with the troubles Bob had had, their relationship seemed to get stronger. It was as if the two of them were indestructible. And Bob was such a good eater. It was a pleasure to feed him. Bob always ate everything on his plate, and complimented him. And now that they'd cooked together it seemed as if their relationship had gone to new heights.

Dale twirled in his chair and recalled the previous night. He and Bob made tortellini stuffed with Gorgonzola cheese. They'd talked and drunk Merlot as they'd folded pasta rounds over the cheese until they were shaped like little tiaras. Never before had he had a boyfriend who wanted to cook with him and now he wondered why he'd never realized that culinary enthusiasm was an essential part of the man of his dreams.

What a beautiful evening it had been. So peaceful, just the two of them. They'd even made extra tortellini for tonight. He would make a vodka sauce and fry up some Tilapia covered in turmeric, then coat it with flour. He'd light candles, put on soft music, use his best crystal wine glasses. If things went right, Bob would never want to leave. At least Dale hoped Bob wouldn't want to leave. But he wouldn't push it. Not when things were going as well as they were.

—

Iris laughed as she stepped into her house and dropped onto the living room sofa. Dolores had done a wonderful job choosing furniture, and it seemed as if Gerald hadn't known if she was crazy or just some rich, ditzy woman. Iris had assured him that Dolores was just herself. "Once you get to know her, you'll understand," Iris had said. In some ways she was surprised Gerald hadn't already met Dolores. He did sell furniture to women in her circles.

Iris was pleased that Dolores had understood what it was they were doing with her new home. Every piece of furniture she'd picked out was in simple, soft tones and fabrics that didn't cause any one piece to stand out. And although the chaise longue was in the same, unobtrusive tones, it would still be the one object people would notice. Iris couldn't help but grin as she imagined Dolores reclined on the chaise with a crystal champagne flute in one hand and her pillbox in the other. She remembered a cool spring night she'd spent with Norman, back when they'd been in college. Vino had broken up with her, Margot had been horrible when Iris had told her about it, and Norman had said she'd needed something to take her mind off it all. So she and Norman had snuck into Swan Point Cemetery. It hadn't been hard, just a quick walk through the wooded area that led to the rear of the cemetery, then a climb over the squat stone wall that surrounded the outer perimeter and they were there. What had made it difficult was sneaking inside while holding two crystal champagne flutes. Norman had brought along a bottle of Tattinger champagne and had insisted he carry it.

They'd found a gravestone with a life size angel standing barefoot on a tall, rectangular stone. The angel had her hands held out as she looked down at them, her wings outstretched. Iris and Norman had taken a seat on the cool grass beneath the elaborate gravestone. In the dark sky, the moon had shone a bright golden yellow and its light gave the surrounding graves an enchanting feel.

Iris had heard stories of Satan worshipers sacrificing small animals in Swan Point Cemetery at night and hoped they wouldn't run into any. When she'd mentioned her concern to Norman, he'd simply told her that the Satan worshipers would have to drink from the bottle. "People like that are notorious for breaking good crystal," he'd said. He'd held the mouth of the champagne bottle out and let the cork shoot into the night.

"You know," Norman had said as he poured the champagne, "I don't think Margot means you any harm. She just wants you to be what she never was."

Iris had held up her champagne flute and watched the bubbles rise to the surface. "I need her to be supportive, which she never is," Iris had said.

"In her own way, she is." Norman had said, then took a sip of champagne. "You just don't see it because she's your mother."

"Let's not talk about her."

"It's your night," Norman had said. "So tell me, how big is Vino's dick?"

Iris smiled from the memory of that night with Norman, then gave Dolores a call to further discuss her furniture choices.

———

The salon was closed when Steve parked the Dodge Neon across the street. He'd already driven around the block twice looking for Dale's car, but couldn't find it. He had to be there, though. Dale never missed a day of work for anything. Then he saw Dale's car pull up to the curb, but Dale wasn't driving. The driver's side door opened and out came a tall guy in a pair of loose slacks and a plaid shirt. He walked up to the store and stepped inside. Steve waited, then saw Dale and the guy walk out of the store holding hands. That was him. That was the guy who had ruined his relationship with Dale. Dale paused at the passenger side door, then opened it and climbed inside. Dale was going to let that homo drive his car. Steve slouched as the tall guy walked around the car then ducked inside.

Steve couldn't believe how fast that faggot had taken his place. It was obvious that the guy had poisoned Dale against him. He watched as the Lexus drove off. It was that butt-fucker's fault that

Dale didn't want to get back together with him. Steve had to take more action to get the guy away from Dale before things got worse.

Twenty-four hours, Steve thought. That was all it took before he would have a gun in his possession. On the seat next to him was his copy of the paperwork he'd filled out for the permit, along with a few brochures for shooting ranges. The old guy behind the counter had looked like somebody's father, and Steve had always done well convincing parents that he was a sweet kid. He'd introduced himself to Steve as Tom, then talked about safety and personal protection. He'd shown Steve the Lutz M197 handgun. There were two versions of the gun, the M197 and the Commander. Both versions had the same matte blue finish that looked black to Steve, but the Commander was a flat gun with a shorter barrel that resembled something a soldier would carry. The plain M197 had a slightly longer, sleeker barrel that was rounded on the top and bottom, and had a certain simplicity that Steve liked.

Tom had picked up the M197. "You like this one, I can tell," Tom had said. "This is the one I have at home. I keep it in a safe set in the floor near the bed. You point this at some little punk looking to rob you blind and they know you mean business."

"Robbers," Steve whispered as he gripped the steering wheel.

Tom had also been pleased that a young guy like Steve would want to protect himself. He let Steve hold a few of the guns while giving him advice on the best choice of hand gun.

Steve smiled as he leaned back in his seat. Robbers. That was what that queer was, a robber. He'd stolen Dale from him and Steve would get Dale back.

—

"I'm glad you're still here," Andrew said as he walked into Iris's office.

Iris glanced back down at the floor plan for Dolores's house and pretended to be making a decision about something. "Is it important? I'm very busy."

Andrew stood in front of Iris's desk and rubbed his fingertips along the surface. "I think it is."

"Andrew, please, I'm having a hard time with all of this." Iris looked at Andrew's tie of deep purples and greens, then up to his well defined jaw, his full lips, until she finally met his eyes. "This is a bad time to ask for my help, if that's what you're here for. How can I testify one way or the other when I feel as if I didn't even know Ian?"

"Testify?" Andrew walked around the desk until he was standing in front of Iris. "That's not what I'm here for."

Iris bit her lower lip. All day her emotions had been out of control and she wished she'd taken that half tablet of Diazepam with her. She felt Andrew's hand on her left shoulder, the warmth and strength of his touch. She looked into his deep brown eyes and felt as if he might be telling the truth. But how could she know?

"Maybe you should take some time off," Andrew said.

"I can't," Iris said, feeling as if she could cry. She swallowed. "There's too much going on right now."

"Like what?"

"Dolores's house, your offices," Iris said. "Plus I need to get more work for when those projects are complete."

"It's okay if you hold back my new office, and I'm sure Dolores will understand if her project gets put back a little. I talked to her today." Andrew slid his fingers through Iris's hair, gently rubbing her scalp. "We're all concerned about you."

Iris didn't know what to believe. All she knew was that she was about to cry. She looked up at Andrew and forced a grin as tears began to wet her cheeks.

"It's okay," Andrew said, pulling her close to him.

Iris wrapped her arms around Andrew's waist and felt his firm stomach against her cheek. As she gently sobbed, she took in the soft scent of Andrew's body and felt his fingers gently combing through her hair. Perhaps he wasn't lying and really had come to see how she was doing? Maybe she could trust him? She looked up at him knowing her mascara was smeared and her eyes were bloodshot.

"You're so beautiful," Andrew said.

Iris shook her head. "No, I'm not."

"You just don't feel it right now, but you are."

Without thinking, Iris stood up and gently brushed her lips against Andrew's. Andrew put his arms around her and returned her kiss, only deeper, and Iris felt herself give in.

—

Bob wiped up the creamy pink vodka sauce with his bread and popped it into his mouth. He was such a good eater, Dale thought. He reached for his wine glass and smiled at Bob. The candle flickered, sending a gentle yellow glow across the table. "You're an incredible cook," Bob said and saluted Dale with his raised glass. "Here's to you."

"You helped with the tortellini," Dale said. "You should take some of the credit."

"It's the sauce that makes it."

"With a good meal everything works together," Dale said. The telephone rang. Dale let his eyes rest on Bob. "Please, don't let it be bad news."

"Why don't you get it and I'll clean up," Bob said, grabbing his plate. He stood and held his hand out for Dale's plate.

"You don't have to," Dale said.

"Just get the phone."

Dale went into the living room and picked up the telephone from the coffee table. It was Laura, sounding distraught. "I can't believe it, uncle Dale," she said. "He dumped me just because I wouldn't do it with him." Sarah's muffled yelling was in the background, then Laura yelled out, "I'm on the phone!"

"Is everything okay over there?" Dale asked.

"It's just Mom," Laura said. "She thinks I'm being a baby."

Dale let that last comment pass. He sat on the sofa and put his feet up on the coffee table. "Do you think you did the right thing?"

"I don't know. Uncle Dale, he's so cute!" Springs squeaked in the background. "He didn't even try to understand my side of it."

"Is that the kind of guy you want to be with?"

Laura sighed. "Why did he have to be like that? I mean, is it that important?"

"It's only part of a relationship," Dale said, choosing his words carefully. He knew Laura wanted to be treated like an adult, even if she wasn't. "But it's a part you can't rush into."

"I want my first time to be special."

"Then don't rush it," Dale said, remembering that night during his sophomore year of high school, wrestling on the living room floor with Joey Spandelli while Joey's parents were out for the night. Dale had felt Joey's hardon pressed against his thigh as he'd lain pinned to the floor. Their eyes had met, then Joey had bent down and gently kissed him.

"I can't believe I dated the cutest boy in school and now I'm single," Laura said.

"Why don't we go to the movies tomorrow?" Dale said. "After that, we can have ice cream."

"Really?"

"Sure. I can pick you up at five, we can go for dinner, then the movie, then ice cream."

"But it's Saturday night," Laura said. "Don't you have a date?"

"Bob won't mind."

"Bring him."

"Are you sure?"

"I want to meet your boyfriend," Laura said. "I bet he's fun."

Dale considered her proposition. It probably wouldn't be a bad idea, and Bob could say no if he really didn't want to go. "He may already have plans, but I'll ask anyhow."

"I'm feeling better already."

"Great, I'll see you tomorrow," Dale said before hanging up. He walked back into the kitchen to find that Bob had already rinsed all the pots and pans and put them in the dishwasher.

"Who was that?" Bob asked. He wrapped his hands around Dale's waist, then gave him a kiss.

"My niece," Dale said. "She wants to know if you want go out with us for dinner and a movie. Ice cream after that."

Bob's eyes widened. "Ice cream. I love ice cream."

"You're being silly."

"That's because I'm happy," Bob said.

Dale gave Bob a hug, then rested his head on Bob's chest. "I'm happy, too."

—

Steve was restless as he lay in bed. He couldn't sleep. All he could think about was the gun.

Saturday

"I need to go," Jay said. He lay on top of Erik, their warm, naked bodies frosted together by a layer of spunk. Jay sat up and felt their bodies separate. "It's almost like glue."

"I told you to wipe up, but you didn't listen," Erik said playfully as he rubbed Jay's sides. "Why don't we take a shower."

"We?"

"I want to get you full of suds." Erik raised his eyebrows and gave Jay a perverse grin. "Maybe we can have another go at it?"

Jay let out a laugh. "You're insatiable!"

"I know," Erik said. He grabbed Jay and threw him onto the bed. The springs let out a groan as Erik dropped on top of him and gripped Jay's wrists, pinning him against the mattress. "Now I've got you, and now I'm going to kiss you."

Jay playfully kicked his legs. "But I haven't brushed my teeth."

"The monster doesn't care." Erik chomped his teeth a few times. "It wants your beautiful body."

"The monster is blind as a bat," Jay said.

Erik slid his hips down, causing Jay's dick to flop semi-hard against his thigh. "Perhaps it will eat your belly?"

"Your victim needs to shower and get his ass into a library before he flunks out."

"Oh, like that's going to happen," Erik said in his best monster voice. He got off Jay, lifted his arms in the air and said, "You're free!"

Jay put his feet on the cold, hardwood floor. "I'm hoping Steve will be home. I haven't seen him in a few days."

"I assume he's usually in a better mood," Erik said.

Jay shook his head as he made his way into the bathroom. "That isn't him. He's upset about Dale breaking up with him, I told you. I just wish he would talk to me about it instead of holding it in."

Jay was standing in front of the toilet holding his dick when Erik slipped his hands around his waist. "You're sweet," Erik said.

"I'm trying to pee."

"Can I hold it?"

Jay laughed. "That won't help."

———

Steve ran his fingers over the handle of the Lutz M197 as it rested on the passenger seat of the Dodge Neon. It was a beautiful gun, and reminded him of the detective shows he'd watched as a kid. He lifted it, feeling the weight in his hand. It was beautiful. Personal protection, the thought made him smile. Not only was he protecting what was his, but he was getting it back. Dale was his, he thought as he placed the gun back down on the passenger's seat.

He started up the Dodge Neon and drove off. First he would drive past the salon and see if Dale's car was anywhere in sight. If it wasn't there, then he would go past Dale's condominium. Maybe he'd get another look at Dale's little fuck buddy. Steve extended his right arm towards the passenger side window and pointed his hand out like a gun. "Bang," he said as he cocked his hand back to simulate recoil.

———

"Why can't you just spend one Saturday out of the salon?" Bob said as he poured coffee into Dale's mug.

Dale cut into his pancakes, then speared a piece with his fork and dragged it through the thick maple syrup. "I'm going in late as it is just so I can stay in bed with you a little longer."

Bob poured maple syrup over his pancakes. "I can't get enough of you."

"And I thought it was only for my cooking."

Bob smiled at Dale. While they ate, they discussed which movie Dale thought Laura would want to see. Dale wasn't sure, but he thought it might be some romantic comedy. Neither Dale nor Bob knew of any new releases, so they didn't bother trying to second guess her choice. Bob said he'd walk up to Wayland Square and pick up a newspaper. Dale told him to drop him off at the salon and take the car. It was going to be a cold day, and he wouldn't want him to freeze to death.

After they had finished eating and Bob had loaded the dish washer, the two of them put on their coats and went out the front door. "I want to take her to Z Bar," Dale said as they walked out of the building and took a left into the parking lot. "Have you ever been?"

"I've heard of it," Bob said, taking the outside end closest to the sidewalk. He noticed a blue Dodge Neon approaching, the passenger side window open. Bob buttoned up his thick hunting coat. "I'm glad you're letting me use your car."

"So am I," Dale said, then heard gun shots ring out. Bob pushed into Dale, then there was the screeching of tires, a dog barking, a child screaming. Bob was on the ground clutching his right arm. Blood poured out from beneath Bob's hand, trickling onto the black tar and forming a puddle. Dale covered his mouth with his hands as he fell to his knees and bent over Bob. Looking up, he saw a woman in dark glasses and her hair tied up in a bun talking on a cell phone.

"It's okay," Bob said softly.

"I called 911," a woman with a French accent said. Dale looked up to see it was the woman who had been talking on the cell phone. She pulled off her London Fog coat, then took off her purple cashmere sweater. Beneath the sweater was a white cotton t-shirt. She took that off, too. Thankfully she had on a white lace bra. "Here, darlings, let me help." She bent down, quickly folded the t-shirt and pressed it against Bob's arm. She turned towards Dale and said, "Could you put my coat on me. I'm chilly."

Dale wiped tears from his cheeks as he snatched the woman's coat from the ground and draped it over her shoulders.

"It was the Neon," a male voice said in the distance.

"I'm so glad you're here," Dale said to the woman who had helped Bob. "I don't even know you."

"I'm Alma," the woman said. "The ambulance should be here soon."

Bob lifted his head, then winced. Blood had soaked through the white cotton shirt and Dale wondered how long it would take before the ambulance arrived. A few minutes later there were sirens in the distance. It had to be the ambulance, Dale thought. He looked down at Bob and tried not to cry. The sirens sounded closer now.

"I'll be fine," Bob said through clenched teeth.

Dale bent down and held Bob's hand. "I know."

The ambulance arrived on the scene, making a quick stop in front of Bob, Alma and Dale. "He was shot," Alma said to one of the men in the white top and navy blue slacks standing over them.

The man bent down and took hold of the t-shirt pressed against Bob's arm. "We've got it from here," he said.

Alma and Dale stepped back as two of the Emergency Medical Technicians strapped Bob onto a Gurney and wheeled him into the van.

"I don't know how to thank you," Dale said to Alma as she slipped her arms through the sleeves of her coat.

"You just have, darling," Alma said. "Now go with him."

Without hesitation, Dale jumped into the ambulance, then went into the back of the van. He sat down in the cramped area next to Bob and held his hand as they rode to the hospital.

—

Steve felt the gun recoil, then saw Bob quickly grab his arm. People had already begun to turn, so he gunned the engine and screeched around the corner. He hoped he'd gotten that faggot good. He wouldn't go near Dale. Not now, not ever. The gun was on the passenger seat where he'd dropped it before taking off.

Steve had wanted to be free to move when he aimed the gun, so he hadn't bothered putting on his safety belt. A cool breeze drifted through the open passenger side window before he closed it using the console on the door. Now he felt so elated that he hadn't even thought of putting it on. He'd carried out his mission.

He glanced in the rear view mirror. Nobody seemed to be chasing him. Perhaps they knew it was all for a good cause. He knew it was foolish to think that, but the thought put a smile on his face. He took a right and drove towards Wayland Square. He passed the two rows of store fronts and stopped at the light at the main intersection. The East Side Framery was on his right, a few pottery vases were on pedestals in the window. A green Saab was in front of him. Steve turned on the radio and ignored the commercial playing.

There were sirens in the background. He looked up at the light. It was still red. He looked back again and saw a cop car with its lights heading towards him. The light was red. The cop car was now a few feet away. The light turned green. The Saab went, then Steve pushed down on the accelerator and took a sharp right hand turn and went down Wayland Avenue. The sirens were still audible. Louder this time. He looked in the rear view again. The cops were chasing him. A yellow VW Bug was two blocks ahead. He laid on the horn and pushed down on the gas. The car lurched forward, towards the VW Bug. Steve swerved around the car, then took a sharp right down a side street. The cops followed. Steve kept his eyes open for obstacles. Luckily most people were busy at work. Blackstone Boulevard wasn't far. He could cross it and lose them in the side streets near River Road. He knew that area well.

Steve was less than a block away from Blackstone Boulevard when he looked in the rear view mirror and saw not one, but two cop cars chasing him. He was in trouble now. He pushed down harder on the accelerator and shot onto Blackstone Boulevard, took a sharp right and felt the driver's side wheels lift slightly off the ground, then land. A blue Toyota was in front of him, going at a steady thirty miles per hour. Steve leaned on the horn but the car wouldn't get out of the way. He swerved around it. The police were still following close behind. The end of Blackstone Boulevard was near. If Steve took a wide left he could flip around the center of the boulevard and head down the side street that forked off the boulevard. He didn't bother to look in the rear view mirror. He knew from the screaming sirens that the cops were still behind him. He had to concentrate. He turned the wheel, watching as a red car pulled out of his way, then blasted down the side road. It was perfect.

He took a sharp right. The tires screeched once more. He turned every other corner hoping to lose the cops, but still the sirens hadn't stopped calling to him. The far end of River Road was up ahead. Steve could see the turret of the stone house shaped like a mini castle where the road curved off to the right and went downhill. He drove towards the castle, then down the hill. The water was coming up on his left, along with parked cars. There were people standing around, talking. Heads turned as he sped past them. He looked in his rear view mirror. The cops were still there. A right hand turn was up ahead. He could take that one or the next. He gunned the engine even faster. He jerked the wheel to the right, taking the corner at break-neck speed. The driver's side tires lifted off the ground, then went back down. At the next block he jerked the wheel to take another sharp right. Steve gasped as he gripped the steering wheel, feeling the driver's side of the car rise as it turned onto its side. The passenger side window shattered as Steve was thrown out of his seat. He quicky extended his right arm to cushion the fall, but it was no use. Upon impact his arm broke, then his head slammed onto the cold pavement and broken glass.

Sunday

There was a police officer at the doorway to Steve's hospital room on the Intensive Care Unit, just as the nurse at the front desk had told him. Jay nodded to the officer, then went into the room. The nurse had also said that Steve was in stable condition, and that he had been sedated and was sleeping, which he was. White bandages capped his head, and there were a few minor cuts on his face. Just under his left eye were stitches. Jay had seen the Dodge Neon parked on the side of road but had never thought anything of it, just as he'd thought nothing of Steve's mood. He'd thought Steve had been upset about Dale, which wasn't really off the mark. But this? He'd never thought Steve would be capable of such a thing. Nor had Steve's father, who had called frantically asking why his son had done it once he'd heard about it on the news. As if Jay would have any answers for him. He wondered how long it would be before the news got wind of the break-up between Dale and Steve and started calling it a love triangle. There was no way they would be able to keep that away from the press.

"He looks so sweet, you would never know," Dale said from behind Jay. Dale wiped some tears from his eyes. "It doesn't make any sense."

Jay gave Dale a hug, holding him close for a little while to let him cry. When Dale pulled away, Jay asked, "How's Bob?"

"He's good. Very little damage," Dale said before he began to cry once more. "I have to get out of here."

"I'll go with you," Jay said as he placed his hand on Dale's back and followed him out. "His parents are coming up later tonight."

"That's good," Dale said. The two of them walked towards the elevators at the end of the hall. "They don't know he's gay."

"I know. I spoke to them on the phone. His mother talked to me more than his father. She wanted to know if I knew. I wasn't sure if she wanted to know if I knew he'd been stalking you or if he was gay. I told her that I wasn't aware of him stalking, but knew he was gay. She got kind of quiet after that. You can tell she doesn't really understand any of it."

"She must be upset."

"To say the least." Jay slid his hands into the pockets of his khakis and slowed his pace. "Why did you break up with him?"

Dale stopped walking and stared at Jay.

"No, I'm not blaming you," Jay said.

Dale nodded. "I know. It's just that I didn't break up with him, he broke up with me."

Jay stood still. Steve had broken up with Dale? Steve had clearly told him that it was Dale who had broken up with him. All this time he'd assumed Steve had been heartbroken, now this. It took Jay a minute before he was able to speak again. "Why?"

"I don't really know. I guess it just wasn't working for him," Dale said, his voice soft. "At one point he did want me back, though. It was too late then, so maybe that was when he cracked."

"Perhaps," Jay said, trying to sift through the truth to find some reason why Steve had lied to him.

"I don't think I ever knew him," Dale said, then sniffled. "At one time I thought I did, but now I wonder."

The elevator door opened. Jay put his arm around Dale. The two of them walked inside and pressed the button for the first floor.

"Last night I woke up and Bob wasn't in bed," Dale said. "I was frantic, looking around. Finally I called his name and he came into the room with his arm in that sling. He'd gone to the bathroom. I was asleep, and he'd gone to the bathroom."

The elevator door opened on the second floor and a group of people walked inside. Jay kept his arm around Dale for comfort, despite the disapproving look from the fat bald guy who stood to their left. "Maybe you should take time away from the salon," Jay said.

"I am," Dale said. "Anita's taking care of things for me. She's such a doll."

The elevator doors opened on the first floor. "How did you get here?" Dale asked.

"Bus."

"Want a ride home?" Dale asked. "I have the new Madonna CD."

———

Dolores walked up to the old, dark wood mantle in the study and ran her hand over the smooth surface. "We don't have to touch the upstairs, do we?" she asked. "Timothy wants us to keep it the way it is."

Iris looked around the room, at the faded eggshell walls. She hated eggshell and could see the room in a deeper color. "I was thinking of having the walls painted. Something to give the room character."

"That's fine, dear," Dolores said. "I assumed we would do that." She walked up to Iris and gently placed her hand on Iris's left arm. "You're holding up well."

A blush rose to Iris's face as she remembered the previous night, lying naked in Andrew's arms before falling asleep. After they'd had sex she'd simply laid there while Andrew held her. In the morning she'd turned and he was there. She'd reached out and held onto him, rested her head on his chest, inhaling his scent.

"Andrew must have spoken to you," Dolores said with a wink. "He mentioned wanting to see you. He's a good man and a fine lawyer."

"I hope so," Iris said.

"Trust me, dear. You deserve the best."

Iris looked at Dolores, at her smooth skin and lips that seemed slightly off center. She fought the urge to reach out and hug

Dolores as if she were her mother. "It's good to know you're on my side," Iris said.

"And why wouldn't I be, dear?"

"Let's look at the rest of the second floor," Iris said. "How do you feel about wall covering in the hall?"

—

Jay was relaxing on the sofa with a beer, his bare feet kicked up on the coffee table. It was a moment of silence, to do nothing but contemplate the passing events. He'd told Erik that he needed a night alone, which Erik understood. The apartment felt so empty without Steve. There had been times when Jay had done nothing but stand in the doorway to Steve's bedroom and look in. The police had gone through every inch of Steve's room, rifled through every drawer in his bureau, searched his closet and even went through his books. All they'd found was the receipt for the gun he'd used to shoot Bob.

Jay put his beer down and hugged himself. Jay had always loved Steve, but never enough to ruin their friendship. Not only that, but he doubted his feelings would ever be returned in kind. He just wasn't what Steve wanted for a boyfriend.

He couldn't imagine what would drive someone to buy a gun and shoot another person. People acted violent out of greed and desperation. Violence is not an act of love. Jay had always thought he'd known Steve, now everything Jay had thought about him was in question.

The doorbell rang. Jay answered the door to find Steve's mother looking at him with red, puffy eyes. Her hands were clasped together in front of herself. Jay told her to come in, then took her wool coat. The delicate gold chain with the small cross he'd seen her wear last time they'd met was still around her neck. Her dress was a dark gray, which matched her shoes. If she had worn black Jay would have assumed she'd come from a funeral. She apologized for arriving unannounced as she scanned the interior of the living room.

"Did you come for some of Steve's things?" Jay asked.

"No. I came to talk, I guess. Marcus won't come. Steve's own father." She began to cry, but stopped herself.

Jay brought Steve's mother to the sofa, where she sat at the edge with her hands on her lap.

"I don't mean to pry, Mrs. –"

"Lilly," she said softly. "Call me Lilly. And you're not prying. I came for answers. I was up all night praying, asking for forgiveness. Needing some kind of answer. Marcus called me to bed, but I wouldn't come. He's very upset."

"Does he know you're here?"

"I left him a note."

Jay paused to take in Lilly's mood and wonder about her true intentions. Nothing seemed real anymore. "Do you want to call him?"

"No. No, but thank you. The note will be enough." Lilly reached out and gently placed her hand on top of Jay's. "I can't turn away from Steven. He's my son. My flesh and blood. Even though I don't understand him." She choked back tears.

"I saw him today. He's going to be fine."

"God willing. Thank you so much for visiting him."

"Let me know if there's anything I can do."

"There isn't," Lilly said.

They sat in silence for a moment, not looking at each other. Then Lilly turned towards Jay. "My mother passed on when Steve was one year old. It was a heart attack, and I believed that God had taken her. She was sixty-one, which to me is still young. As upset and angry as I was, it was my faith that got me through it. My faith has carried me through a lot of troubles."

"It will get you through this," Jay said.

"I hope so."

"It will."

Lilly slowly nodded, looking straight ahead at nothing. "I left my Bible at home. It doesn't seem to have any answers for me. For now at least. There will be, though. There has to be. God loves us all." Lilly's chin wrinkled as her eyes began to water. "God loves my son."

Lilly burst into tears as Jay stood. "Let me get you a tissue," he said, then went into the bathroom and took the box of facial tissues from the top of the toilet. He handed Lilly the box and watched as she took one and dabbed at her eyes before blowing her nose.

"Can I get you anything else?" Jay asked.

"I'm fine." Lilly stood. "I'm staying at The Westin hotel. Can you have Dale call me if he feels up to it. I need to apologize to him for my son."

"You don't have to do that."

"Yes, I do. Not just for him, but for me."

Epilogue
January 6, 2001

J ay walked through the apartment one more time. There was the sofa he'd picked out with Steve, and the pictures of Madonna they'd hung on the wall. It had been four days since Steve's funeral and still he couldn't get past the image of Steve's mother the day she'd told him he was dead. She'd stood in the doorway of the apartment, her face void of emotion. "He's dead," she'd said in a voice with no inflection. Jay had ushered Lilly into the apartment, then sat her on the sofa. Erik had been working late, so Jay had been alone with her. Lilly had talked about Steve's childhood, how she'd held him close when he was a baby and how she wished they'd never sent him off to boarding school. "Maybe we would have become closer," she'd said. "If we'd never sent him away he might have told me." If only, Jay thought as he slowly shook his head.

Erik slipped his hands around Jay's waist, then gently rubbed his belly. "How's my little twink?"

"Steve's father never went to the funeral," Jay said softly. "He never said good-bye to his son."

"His mother did."

Jay tilted his head back and rested it on Erik's shoulder. He wondered what would happen to Lilly. Hopefully she would keep in touch, but he had no way of telling if she would. Erik had mentioned Jay moving in with him, but Jay wasn't sure if that was such a good idea. He was leaning towards getting another roommate. His father had said that he would pay Steve's portion of the rent until he found someone to move in, then asked how everything was going with Erik.

"What are you thinking about?" Erik asked.

"How lucky I am to have supportive parents, and about Lilly."

"I was hoping you were thinking about moving in with me."

"I'm staying here for now," Jay said. "Maybe next year."

Erik rubbed his cheek against Jay's. "That's fine."

—

Dale slipped into his sport jacket and straightened his tie as he waited for Bob to step out of the bedroom. For Dolores's party he'd bought them matching gray suits with different ties so they wouldn't look too cute. He felt lucky to have found a guy like Bob. Although they'd been spending every night together either at Bob's place or Dale's, Bob had understood when Dale had wanted to spend the night of Steve's funeral alone. All Dale had done was drink a glass of Merlot and sit alone in his living room, feeling sad and betrayed. He hadn't even bothered playing any music, not even Madonna. Although he would have liked to have cried that night, he hadn't had it in him.

"What do you think?" Bob asked.

Dale turned to look at that handsome hunk of a computer nerd. Even in a suit he looked butch. Dale walked up to Bob and straightened his tie. The knot was perfect. "If you weren't mine already I would make a play for you."

Bob gave Dale a peck on the cheek, then said, "We should go."

Dale pulled his keys out of his pocket and handed them to Bob.

"The Saturn isn't classy enough for Dolores's party," Bob said playfully.

"I like it when you drive my car," Dale said, which was true. For some reason having Bob drive his car made him feel even more connected to him.

Dale almost gasped as they parked on the street in front of Dolores and Timothy's house, the one Iris had redecorated. It was a large Georgian house with tall windows and a yard surrounded by a stone wall. A matching walkway of flat stones set into the ground led to the green double doors. They rang and were greeted by a handsome man with dark brown hair wearing a black suit with a white shirt. The man escorted them inside, to the main room, then left them alone. The room was so simple and open, with soft, natural colors and highly polished hard wood floors. Sheers covered the tall windows that lined the far wall, almost glowing from the outside light. Soft classical music played on a cello echoed throughout the house.

Dale gripped Bob's hand as they walked into the living room, where the guests were milling about with drinks and hors d'oeuvres. Never before had Dale seen such long windows, and the chaise longue just sitting there in front of the fireplace! Madonna probably had one in her house, Dale thought. Kyle and Trent weren't in sight. Iris was there, though. Her hair was down, hanging past the shoulders of her simple black evening gown. A string of pearls accented the scoop neckline of the dress.

"Maybe some day we can have our own place," Bob whispered.

Dale gently caressed Bob's lower back. "I would like that."

———

Iris saw Dale and Bob standing in the doorway in matching suits with different ties. Dale's tie was full of bright greens and purples bursting all over while Bob's was an ecru background with soft blue diamonds that seemed to bleed slightly into the background. Andrew was across the room talking to Timothy, probably discussing how upset they both were about Bush getting into office. They both thought that Gore had won Florida and that something sneaky had gone on with the Florida polls, although not everyone agreed with their opinion. Iris also agreed with them, but she was sick of talking about it.

Dolores had young men in white shirts with black slacks serving glasses of wine from silver trays. Norman would have had the boys in something sexually provocative. She took a glass of white wine from one of the young men then walked through the crowded room, nodding hello to people she knew as they did the same. She wound her way to the rear of the house, into the kitchen. The center isle was loaded with hors d'oeuvres and servers kept walking in and out without taking notice of her. She didn't feel like being there, even though it was as much her celebration as it was Dolores's. Iris had finished the project and got to hear people speak well of the final product as they saw it for the first time. Something every interior designer likes to get the chance to hear. But she couldn't enjoy herself. She kept thinking about Ian and how it seemed obvious that he would go to jail for assault. There was enough evidence and an elderly witness.

"First offense, he'll get a slap on the wrist," Andrew had said the other day after Iris had asked what he thought would happen to Ian.

What Andrew hadn't said and Iris knew was that Ian would have a reputation that would make finding work a bit difficult. People would always see him as trouble, as a rapist. It wouldn't matter that he hadn't been convicted of rape, everyone already thought of him as one.

Although Iris believed he'd tried to rape Michelle, she couldn't help but feel a tinge of sadness for him. She wasn't sure why, but she did.

"Iris, what are you doing here?" Dolores asked as she sauntered towards her. Dolores's deep purple dress was tight, low cut and made for a woman twenty years younger. She was thankful that Dolores's dress had long sleeves to hide the sagging skin on her arms.

"I needed to get away," Iris said.

"Parties make me nervous, too. Especially my own." Dolores rubbed Iris's back. "I took this little tablet called Lorazepam. I've never taken Lorazepam before. It helped. Would you like one, dear?"

Iris shook her head. "I don't think it would help. I have a lot on my mind."

"Does it have to do with your mother meeting Andrew?"

"How did you know about that?"

"Andrew told me, dear. He said the two of you are driving up next weekend. I think it's a good idea."

Iris thought it was a good idea, too. For the first time in her life she wasn't afraid of anything her mother might say. From now on Iris was going to find men she approved of, not her mother. Hadn't that been why she'd stayed with Ian, because she'd thought her mother would approve of him?

"A lawyer," Margot had said after Iris had told her what Andrew did for work. Margot hadn't sounded loath to meet him, or even said a single negative thing about him. In fact, she'd sounded eager to meet him. But Iris still couldn't shake the thought of the old Margot; the Margot who never approved of any of the men in her life; the Margot who had always said Iris's career came first. But Andrew felt the same way about Iris's career, he'd even said as much to other people.

"Don't worry so much, your mother will like him," Dolores said.

"Do you really think so?"

"Yes dear, he's perfect for you." Dolores winked, then her mouth curled into a grin. "Between us girls, I think he's sexy."

Iris put her arm around Dolores's waist and pulled her close. "I think he's sexy, too."

About the author

Kenneth Harrison is also the author of two collections of short stories and a novel, *Bad Behavior*. His short stories have also been included in the anthologies *Butch Boys* and *Grave Passions*. He lives a quiet life in Providence, RI. For a full list of his publishing credits visit him on the web at http://www.KennethHarrison.com